Christopher Fowler is the director of a film promotion company and lives in London. He is the author of the novels *Roofworld*, *Rune*, *Red Bride*, *Darkest Day*, *Spanky* and *Psychoville* and of the short story collections *City Jitters*, *The Bureau of Lost Souls* and *Sharper Knives*.

Also by Christopher Fowler

Flesh Wounds

Christopher Fowler

Illustrations by
Richard Parker

WARNER BOOKS

A *Warner* Book

First published in Great Britain by Warner Books 1995
Reprinted 1996

Copyright © Christopher Fowler 1995
Illustrations copyright © Richard Parker 1995

The moral right of the author has been asserted.

A CIP catalogue record for this book
is available from the British Library.

ISBN 0 7515 1431 4

Typeset by Solidus (Bristol) Limited
Printed and bound in Great Britain by
Clays Ltd, St Ives plc

Warner Books
A Division of
Little, Brown and Company (UK)
Brettenham House
Lancaster Place
London WC2E 7EN

Dedication

For my brother Steven

Contents

Flesh Wounds

'You've Got To Love
Something Enough To Kill It'

Martin Scorsese said that, and he should know. Here's an old joke: An elderly couple visit their lawyer.

'What can I do for you?' asks the lawyer.

'We want a divorce,' says the eighty-year-old wife, indicating her decrepit husband. 'We've been married for fifty years and we hate each other's guts.'

'Forgive me for asking,' enquires the incredulous lawyer, 'but why did you leave this so late?'

'Well,' says the wife, 'we wanted to wait until the children were dead.'

The joke has some relevance; trust me.

This collection of short stories uses the horror/fantasy genre to look at the ways in which we hurt ourselves and each other. We know it's flesh that wounds, not guns and knives. They merely provide the *how*. We provide the *why*. People not only do spectacularly cruel things to each other, their victims willingly allow it to happen. Couples in awful, disastrous marriages stay together for years for all the wrong reasons. Some people end up in entirely unsuitable jobs and never figure out why they're miserable. Others destroy their children without even realising what they've done.

What *is* it with us?

Why should a perfectly normal person with a single character flaw fall in love with the one partner most likely to exploit it? Which perverse muse is responsible for drawing together victim and bully, virgin and philanderer?

Well, sometimes we choose to punish ourselves and sometimes life handles the assignment for us, the difference being that life's casual cruelties have a terrible random anonymity – the illnesses, the accidents, the acts of violence, all unforeseen. Whereas living together is sometimes like watching a car crash in slow motion; you know something's going wrong but there's nothing you can do to stop it.

Our curse, of course, is to be convinced of our rightness in the face of all reason. Who needs ghosts and demons? *We're* the enemy and we know it, and the knowledge still doesn't stop us.

This kind of doublethink extends beyond the family into the public arena. We know when a government is corrupt, when an advertiser is selling rubbish, when someone is lying for gain – and we go along with it, although we *do* make satirical jibes on late-night comedy shows.

If this ability to destroy each other unwittingly is counted as a yardstick of the new horror, we suddenly find ourselves with a new set of heroes; chroniclers of modern fears would have to include Franz Kafka (bureaucracy, authority), Martin Amis (greed, venality), Aldous Huxley (authoritarianism), Joe Orton (sexual terror), Evelyn Waugh (moral turpitude), H H Monroe (human cruelty), Alan Ayckbourn (disintegration of family), John Collier (retreat from reality), Jonathan Carroll (the end of dreams), Joyce Carol Oates (love's betrayals) and hundreds of other authors not especially linked to the genre, all of whom have spent time cataloguing the cruel ironies of modern life.

A DIFFERENT LIGHT
151 W 19 STREET
NEW YORK   NY 10011

TE: 12/21/96
RN: 352353220722   TER#: 0001

S-A-L-E-S D-R-A-F-T

EF: 0030   BCH: 018
D TYPE: AX
R TYPE: PR
NV#: 4621
MOUNT: $19.38

CT: 378717997743003   EXP: 0598
: 112829

I AGREE TO PAY ABOVE TOTAL AMOUNT
ACCORDING TO CARD ISSUER AGREEMENT
(MERCHANT AGREEMENT IF CREDIT VOUCHER)

_____
COPY-MERCHANT BOTTOM COPY-CUSTOMER

This is an age filled with paradox, a time when the great outdoors is less frightening than the inner city. A time when we use jeeps and mountain boots to get through the urban jungle. A time when even pocket faxes, call-switching, mobile phones and Internet news groups can't help us to communicate with each other on anything other than a superficial level.

Conceptual artist Heath Bunting has a habit of picking through skips in the City of London and noticed people throwing equipment away not because it was broken but because it was no longer wanted. He'd often find a whole computer in a skip – minus its plug. People cut the plugs off because they know how to reuse them. Technology has run ahead of humanity.

There's a saying that America went from barbarism to decadence without passing through civilisation. Well, we can't afford to be too superior, because it looks like our time to be civilised is well and truly over. Wholesale genocide goes unheeded and unpunished while a televised court case about a celebrity murder tops the ratings. Pop culture is supposed to exist alongside real culture, not replace it.

You think this isn't the decline and fall? Check out the regression in the streets, the territorial markings, the speed tribes and grungies, the eyebrow rings and stomach staples, the restlessness, the aimlessness, the sheer lack of interest in anything real. If it's true that the bench mark of a nation's civilisation is the respect it accords its elders, we're in deep trouble.

I know this seems pessimistic, so I must rely on you, gentle reader, to provide some fresh-faced optimism that will redress the balance. Meanwhile, accept these tales of people facing unusual dilemmas. Some of the characters inhabit present-day cities. Others exist in the landscapes of my imagination. All, no matter how bizarre the stories they relate, have reasons to be fearful in this, the closing chapter of the planet's most incredible century.

Christopher Fowler
Soho, summer 1995

The Laundry Imp

I've always been a sucker for urban legends, but most of them seem to be variations on perhaps no more than half a dozen themes. In an effort to tread a less-worn path, I set myself the task of creating a new legend that didn't rely on the involvement of hitchhikers or murderous baby-sitters. I hadn't intended to evolve a connection between monsters and personal hygiene ...

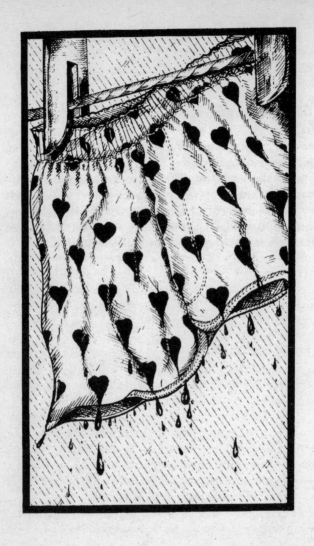

‹THAT WASN'T the way I heard it,' said Charlene, folding her arms across her heavy chest. 'Whoever told you that was lying.' Her wonderbra sailed past the window twice, then vanished from sight.

'You know how these stories get exaggerated.' Lauren readjusted the crotch of her jeans and stared back at her rotating knickers, hypnotised. 'I mean, it's obviously not true or anything. It couldn't be. Someone would have heard the screams, or seen the blood leaking out.'

'Well, it was late at night. There wasn't anyone around to save her.'

The two girls sat back on their grey plastic bendichairs and watched as the huge grey steel washing machines thudded and hummed and shook.

A freezing wind moaned fitfully under the glass entrance door, to be dissipated in the tropical steam heat of the laundromat.

'This place gives me the creeps,' Charlene complained. 'The lights are too bright and the air smells funny.'

'That's from the soap. My sister Beverly got a panty rash from the powder they put in the dispensers. She accused her boyfriend of sleeping around, and by the time she'd found out the real cause of the problem he'd admitted he was seeing someone else, so . . .' She allowed the thought to vaporise and replaced it. 'So she died, then, this girl?'

'I'm not sure whether she did or not. But if she did, it wasn't in the way you'd think. I didn't know her personally, but then you never do, do you? It's always a friend of a friend. Hard to ever know what's really true.'

This much is true.

It was a bitter, desolate winter night. Vernie wouldn't have bothered venturing out to the laundromat, but earlier that day she had spilled a strawberry milk shake down the front of her dress and the stain had stayed even after she had hand washed it. Gary always left his dirty washing in a white plastic bag beneath the sink, so she added the dress to it and set off, knowing that he would never get around to taking his turn with the laundry.

The Albion Laundrette was set in a parade of semi-derelict shops in a high street that nobody used any more. Respectable townsfolk headed for the vast shopping mall at the edge of town, a spotless climate-controlled dome filled with clowns and children and the scent of hot bread. There they could buy Belgian chocolates and novelty greetings cards. Here there was just a sauna, a restaurant of vaguely Arabic origin, a minicab company, a takeaway kebab counter, a porno book store, a closed-down electrical repair shop and a smeary-windowed room filled with fat Greek men playing cards.

On this night, the laundrette was the only illuminated store front in the parade. It stood behind a blizzard of litter, a large rectangular room lit by buzzing fluorescent strip lights. It contained twelve large washing machines, two heavy loaders and six tumble dryers. There were black and white rubberised tiles on the floor, twelve grey plastic chairs, two powder dispensers and a folding bench on which sat a pile of soft, dog-eared women's magazines. A cubbyhole at the rear was reserved for the manageress, who came by at nine in the morning, noon and eleven o'clock at night to lock up.

Vernie pulled the fake-fur collar of the cheap coat around her throat and set the plastic bag at her feet. At first she thought the place was closed, but the door was just stuck. Inside, the sticky warm air smelled of exaggerated cleanliness. The room was empty, but one of the huge front-loading tumble dryers was on. Presumably someone would be returning soon for their laundry. It wasn't a good idea to leave your clothes unattended in this neighbourhood; they were likely to disappear.

Vernie selected a machine and dumped her bag on the top. This was the most depressing place she could imagine spending the evening in. Especially when she knew that her friends were having fun somewhere else. But she couldn't go with them to the club tonight because she had no money, and because Darryl was going to be there with his new girlfriend, the one he'd been seeing while he was going out with her. Instead she was left in the flat with Gary and his boyfriend, feeling like a gooseberry while they sat on the sofa feeding each other scoops of chocolate-chocolate chip Häagen-Dazs.

As she carelessly loaded the machine she nearly started crying. She could not understand why life had to be so unfair. Everywhere she looked other people had jobs and lovers and something to look forward to. Nobody ever asked how she was. They were all too wrapped up in their own lives. She slammed the lid of the machine and dropped in the correct change. Pipes hissed somewhere in the wall as the drum began to fill.

Why should it be me who ends up spending the evening alone in the laundromat, she wondered, *wasting another page in the book of life, dropping another stitch in the tapestry of existence?* It didn't help that she was too damned smart for most of the guys around here. They wanted someone pretty by their side, someone to hold their beer while they took their pool shot, someone who didn't spoil it all by talking too much.

She folded the empty bag neatly and placed it on the table, then checked through the rumpled magazines, but nothing excited her interest. The room was slightly cooler now, and she realised that the tumble dryer had stopped. The metal ticked and tapped as it contracted. The owner of the clothes hadn't returned to collect them. What if he was attractive and single, as lonely and alone as her? Love could flourish in the most mundane places. Hadn't her mother always told her that?

She checked the dusty clock above the machines. Her laundry was still on its first cycle. The room was growing cold. She tugged the hem of her old brown sweater over the waistband of her jeans. What if the owner of the clothes in the dryer *was* cute? She'd dressed in her sloppiest outfit. Perhaps he'd think she was being fashionable in a grungy waif kind of way. What if it wasn't a man? There was one way of finding out. She could remove the clothes from the dryer and fold them for him. It would give them a conversation opener when he finally returned.

'How kind of you! You shouldn't have gone to so much trouble!'

'Oh, it was no trouble. It gave me something to do.'

'I don't understand what a pretty girl like you is doing in here.'

'Well, one needs a rest from partying occasionally.'

'I know what you mean. Why don't I give you a hand with your laundry, then we can go and get a cup of coffee?'

'*That would be lovely. I don't know your –*'

The crash of something falling heavily against the glass doors snapped her from her reverie. A grey-bearded drunk had fallen against the step and was trying to get up without releasing his grip on the litre bottle of cider he carried.

'Fuckin' hell's teeth!' he shouted, rolling uselessly onto his side and thumping the reverberating door. Vernie backed away to the dryers, making sure that he couldn't catch sight of her. She counted to twenty beneath her breath and looked in through the dimpled window at the dried clothes, trying to ascertain the sex of their wearer. When she looked back up, the drunk had moved on and the street outside was once more empty.

She pulled open the dryer door and emptied the warm clothes into one of the red plastic baskets stacked below. The wash definitely belonged to a man. Faded jeans, denim work shirts and underpants, quite sexy ones. She pulled the full basket aside and began sorting the socks into pairs. It felt strange, touching the warm clothes of a total stranger, as if she was breaking some private taboo.

Something rattled in the dryer behind her. Or rather it made a scrabbling noise, as if a lizard was clinging to the roof of the perforated steel drum. She immediately thought that a rat had somehow jumped through the open door, for the warmth perhaps, but it scarcely seemed possible. The interior of the dryer was still scorching hot. She approached the drum and pulled back the door. Perhaps he had lost a cufflink or a bracelet in there and it had become entangled in the holes of the curving steel roof. Enveloped in the searing dry heat, she put in her right hand, extended her fingers and felt about.

Nothing.

She moved her arm further into the drum. Something rattled again, skittering toward her bare skin and clamping down on it. She screamed, jolting upright, cracking her head hard on the top rim of the machine. For a moment her vision clouded and she lost her balance, falling back against the plastic chairs. She briefly sensed something peering out at her from the drum, something dark and spiky with glittering black eyes. Then it was gone.

The air seemed warm and hazy, filled with choking motes of dust. Perhaps the blow to her head had left her with a concussion. Vernie glanced at her arm fearfully, expecting to find a bite wound, but there was nothing, not even a scratch. Her head throbbed, though. She looked at the gaping dryer drum, then across at the glass entrance door with the wind moaning beneath it. Perhaps she had imagined the whole thing. Somebody had been horribly murdered in one of these desolate places recently, a friend had told her all about it. Alarmed, she sat on a corner of the folding table and allowed her breathing to return to normal. And as she sat listening to the flopping and sopping of her laundry in the far washer, she remembered the story that Mrs Delphine had once told her, when she was just a tiny little girl.

Mrs Delphine was from Venezuela but had spent most of her life in Trinidad. She was a heavy, downcast woman who grudgingly visited Vernie's mother once a week to 'help out' as she called it; a matter of pride prevented her from thinking of herself as a cleaning lady. Every Wednesday afternoon after school, Vernie would sit and watch Mrs Delphine as she ironed and folded the household sheets, and would listen as she grumbled about the English weather before fondly recalling her life in an unimaginable tropical paradise.

One day Mrs Delphine held up a corner of a cotton vest in her plump right hand and tutted. 'Dear oh dearie me,' she said sadly.

'What's the matter?' asked Vernie, struggling to see. The centre of the vest was torn to shreds, as if it had been repeatedly slashed with a razor.

'Somebody's brought in the Laundry Imp,' she replied, bundling up the vest and taking it to the bin.

'What do you mean?' asked Vernie. 'What's the Laundry Imp?'

'I shouldn't be telling you, it will only give you nightmares.'

But Vernie could see that it wouldn't take much for the woman to speak. Her mother wouldn't be back for a while yet, and Mrs Delphine loved to recount scraps of lore from her homeland, particularly if they were of an unsavoury, doom-laden nature.

'See, the Laundry Imp is the fiercest little creature you can get in your house. It has a nastier mind than a mongoose and sharper teeth than a weasel, because it's born of lazy dirt.'

She upturned the laundry basket and began looking cautiously through the remainder of the unwashed clothes.

'At first it's very small, see, so small that you can hardly see it, like a shiny black flea. It grows in the clothes that folks have worn too long and worked too little in.' She looked off through the windows of the laundry room, at some middle-distant point of the garden. 'It feeds from the secretions of the rich and the idle, and it moves from one pile of dirty laundry to another to keep from being cleaned. As it moves through the clothes sucking in all the stains and the smells, the imp grows until it is the size of two knotted hands' – she entwined her strong brown fingers in demonstration – 'and it looks like a cross between a lizard and a monkey, with shiny black scales like pointed toenails, and a soft, bare underbelly, and tiny needle teeth, and beady little eyes and long sharp claws. It moves very fast and jerks its head like a bird because it's watching all the time.' She approached the unnerved girl, who had gingerly raised her feet from the floor. 'And because it has grown in the lazy waste of warm, slow bodies, it is very, very poisonous.'

'But what does it want?' Vernie asked, sitting back on the table and surreptitiously checking underneath it.

'It's searching for the scent of the poor,' Mrs Delphine murmured beneath her breath. 'It's a mean-spirited creature of supernatural origins, born from a curse once placed upon a cruelly idle man.'

'Tell me.'

'I'll be getting in trouble . . .'

'Please!'

'Very well.' She moved the iron to one side of her workbench and sat for a minute.

'In Venezuela there was once a nobleman named Count Arturo Lombardini who was very rich but also very mean and lazy. He was searching for a wife, but no woman would stay with him because he never washed, and although his clothes were imported from France with finely embroidered *dentils* and epaulettes and silken panels, the count wore them until they fell from his back because he was too mean to wear them out by washing them. He proudly boasted that he had not washed his hair in sixteen years, but he went to great pains to pomade and arrange the sleek black tangle so that a row of greasy curls ringed his forehead. Such a look he felt no woman could resist.

'Every morning a gypsy girl passed beneath Count Lombardini's bedroom window, hawking warm bread from her basket. The nobleman was in love from his first sight of her and had his servants fetch her to him. But when she was ushered into his chambers (a suite of rooms he rarely left), the terrible smell of his body overpowered her and she fled from his residence, dropping her basket of fresh bread.

'The next day, the count instructed his men to lie in wait for the gypsy girl, and they kidnapped her as she passed the palace doors. In a fever of anticipation, Lombardini sprayed himself with eucalyptus water, but this only produced a more emetic effect on little Sapphire, for that was the girl's name. Her parents had perished at sea long before, and she had been raised by an aged uncle who had taught her that daily acts of cleanliness were something even the poorest could perform to bring themselves closer to God.

'Incensed by the girl's obvious repulsion, the count bound her hands with rope and tied a silken bandana across her mouth. Then, with the help of a corrupt family priest, he arranged a simple wedding ceremony, so that even though it was against her will she would be betrothed to him, and he would be legally entitled to enjoy his conjugal rights.' Vernie did not need to know the meaning of that word in order to appreciate the unpleasantness it conveyed.

'That hot night he bore her to the stifling bridal chamber, and she was horrified to see that when he tried to undress himself the shirt he was wearing was so matted with sweat he could barely remove it from the stickety flesh of his back.' At this point, Mrs Delphine exercised rare restraint in her decision to gloss over the more grotesque details of the wedding night.

'Thankfully,' she added, 'no moon rose in the sky to illuminate the scene, but after the unspeakable terrors of those endless darkened hours the gypsy girl became crazed with grief for her lost decency and decided to take her own life.

'At daybreak, while the count was still asleep, Sapphire ran to the filigreed bedroom balcony and leapt from it, only to be trampled by the count's own thoroughbred horses, which the ostlers were riding below in the street. But before she finally expired, she cried out to the heavens and placed a strange curse upon the count.

'Lombardini was sorry to lose his new wife but thought only of himself in the matter. Raising his sweat-stiff wedding shirt from the bed, he donned it once more and considered how he might secure another bride. The next evening, when he tried to remove the shirt before retiring, he found something growing in the silk – a tiny black imp that hopped from the chemise onto his back before he could stop it. The little mite burrowed into the skin between his shoulderblades, just at the point no man can ever reach to scratch. And it got plumper and heavier with every passing hour.

'Lombardini soon found that he could not sit back in a chair, or lie in a bed, for fear of squashing the imp. You see, every time it was squeezed it screamed and chattered and dug its claws deep into his flesh, almost until it could touch his spine. It crushed his nerves and twisted his muscles and burned his skin, but no one else could see the imp, so they simply thought the nobleman mad. He remained in his private chambers even more than before. All his meals were brought to him and were left outside the door. He cut the backs from his chairs so that he could sit after a fashion, and hacked a large hole in the headboard of his bed so that he could doze without disturbing the imp, but nothing would dislodge the hellish creature, which screamed and hissed as it grew wise to Lombardini's ways and chattered all night to prevent him from sleeping.

'Soon the count was a shadow of his old self, a wasted, yellowing skeleton with dark-rimmed eyes set in a gaunt, haunted face. His hair fell out in slimy clumps and he developed a stoop from the constant cramping of his back. He stalked the rooms at night, whimpering and whining for the pain to end, but was granted no relief. Often the servants stood at the door listening to his half-mad moanings.

'One night he drew a poker from the blazing fire in which it had lain and repeatedly slapped the glowing orange shaft across his back, searing his flesh, trying to dislodge the imp. But it was too quick for him and uprooted itself, scuttling around to his chest, where it tightened its grip more than ever before.

'When the servants finally broke down the doors and found the count with his codfish eyes turned over in their sockets, they saw that his spine had been scratched and frayed until it had severed, as if a hundred cats had reached inside and clawed away in a crimson frenzy.

'But the imp lived on in the nobleman's old clothes. It bred through the palace, multiplying in the rumpled sheets and the piles of rancid laundry left by other idlers, spoiled relatives of the count who lived lives of waste. Then the imps headed out into the streets for tastier, riper fare.'

'So the gypsy girl's curse backfired,' said Vernie. 'She had her revenge, but the imps went on to hurt poor people, and she herself had been poor.'

'Curses always find a way of backfiring,' said Mrs

Delphine, returning to her work with a sigh. 'These days the wealthy wash and perfume themselves, and the imps spring from unhygienic clothes to spend their lives searching for the acrid scent of poverty. They move from one warm place to another, and when an imp finds the clothes of a working man, or a working woman, it draws its strength and burrows in, building its nest, slashing a bed for itself. And if it is disturbed it will burrow through a person, scratching and scrabbling through an ear or through the mouth or through the bellybutton, until it comes out of the other side . . .' She spat on her iron and slapped it onto a shirt. 'So many wicked, dirty things around us, and not even being a good Catholic can save you.'

Two days later, Mrs Delphine was dismissed for filling the child's head with frightening stories. 'What could she have been thinking of,' Vernie's mother asked her husband that night, 'telling the girl such nightmarish things? Isn't the world filled with horrors enough without imagining more?' She felt that Mrs Delphine was insulting the household by implying that her husband, of whom she clearly disapproved, had brought in the Laundry Imp.

But for Mrs Delphine such creatures were real, just as they were for Vernie, who had seen the damaged vest and had spent the rest of her childhood screaming unless she was given clean clothes to wear.

Vernie raised her right leg and gave the dryer door a hard kick with the heel of her shoe. It slammed shut, but she had kicked too hard for the magnetic lock to catch, and it bounced back open. A sharp squeal reverberated within the drum, then there was silence.

Vernie had taken a step class earlier in the same shirt she was wearing now. She had meant to add it to the wash before leaving the flat but had forgotten. What if the imp could smell her and even now was searching for a way to cleave itself to her sharply scented skin?

She realised with a start that her own laundry had completed its cycle and now required emptying. Even if the imp proved to be more substantial than a product of her childhood imagination, she was determined not to be bullied into leaving the laundrette without her washing. Closing the door more carefully this time, she dug out some coins and switched the dryer on. Surely the heat, magnified by the emptiness of the rotating drum, would prove too much for the creature? She walked to the front of the room and stared at the lid of her own silent machine. Gingerly, she raised the metal flap and lowered her arm inside, scooping out the warm, damp clothes.

There was a noise behind the washer, the sound of tiny scaled feet running along a pipe. It was using the water system behind the machines to cross the laundrette. She slammed the lid down hard and backed away. Suppose it could get into any of the tubs in this fashion? She looked at the clothes she had extracted so far, carefully unfolding a T-shirt and holding it up. To her horror she found herself holding a mirror to her childhood terrors. The shirt was tattered beyond repair, scored with a hundred tiny slashes.

The clatter of the lid made her raise her eyes, and she found herself staring at the Laundry Imp itself.

It was the size of a small cat but stood on curving hind legs. Its thin ebony claws formed sharp little hooks. It was worrying one between its teeth now, an eerily human gesture, watching her with quick, furtive movements. Its lips were pulled back about its tiny black snout, so that it seemed to be grinning at her.

The glass front door twanged open and closed behind her. She couldn't bring herself to move. She was sure that if her concentration broke for just a second, the imp would set itself upon her.

'Are you okay?' The question took her by surprise and she jumped, involuntarily turning. The owner of the other wash load was everything she had hoped for, but now the thought of a romantic liaison was the farthest thing from her mind.

'Uh, yes, I'm – fine.' She turned back, but the imp had vanished from its place on top of the washing machine. She glanced to the floor. Perhaps it had dropped back behind the appliances.

'I think they may have mice in here,' said the man, watching her. 'I heard something moving about earlier.'

'Yes – I heard it, too.'

'Hey, thanks for taking my stuff out. Christ, it's hot in here, like the jungle or something.' He walked to his basket of clothes and slipped his leather jacket from his shoulders, dropping it onto the folding bench. His white T-shirt was sweat stained at the armpits. As he began shovelling his laundry into a large blue plastic bag, he looked back at her, concerned. 'Are you sure you're alright?'

'I thought I saw – something – but –' Forcing herself into action, she grabbed a handful of clothes and imitated him, shoving them wet into her bag. *Don't think about what's there*, she told herself, *don't try to rationalise*.

'Shouldn't you dry those first?'

'No, I just need to get outside for some fresh air.' She realised that she was speaking more sharply than she had intended and wanted to explain to the nice young man, who seemed so concerned, but as she looked back she saw the dryer doors all opening in unison, and not one but five of the Laundry Imps appeared, drawn by the acrid tang of his sweat. More were disentangling themselves from the overhead pipes like unfolding tarantulas. And then they were dropping through the grey air, and before she could cry out they were landing on his surprised face, leaping to his shoulders where they swarmed about, nuzzling their teeth into his shirt, burrowing beneath his arms, biting chunks of shocking red flesh from his neck. No longer content to simply live as parasites, the newly urban creatures had adopted the aggressive nature of the city streets and were seeking out prey – but not her, not her.

As they buried themselves in his body, churning aside gobs of fat and splinters of bone, her rescuer fell to his knees with a wet crack, and Vernie began to shake uncontrollably. Then, forcing her frozen muscles into action, she fell toward the door and tore it wide open.

The icy gale that hit her almost drove her back. She had left her jacket at the far end of the room. She would have to leave without it. Looking over her shoulder, she saw that the feral creatures were protecting themselves from the blast of freezing air by ducking behind the collapsed corpse of the young man.

Finally finding the voice to scream, she left the laundromat and ran – and ran and ran – on through the deserted, alien streets.

'What happened to her?' asked Lauren as she eyed her undulating lingerie with new suspicion.

'That's the awful thing,' said Charlene, digging the gum from her mouth and fixing it to the underside of her seat with a practised gesture. 'Guess what I heard she finally died of?'

'What?'

'Pneumonia.' She stretched the second syllable so that it sounded even more deathly. 'When she got home, she took off all her clothes and started examining them for black specks, the seed lice of the Laundry Imps. She ripped all of her clothes to shreds looking for their eggs. Went through her entire wardrobe, tearing everything up and burning it in the garden. She couldn't bear to keep any clothes on her skin after that.'

'I don't get it,' said Lauren slowly. 'Why not?'

'Don't you see? The imps didn't kill her because she knew about them. They sensed that they could use her as a breeding ground. They probably laid their eggs in her dirty laundry while she was at the soap dispenser, right here in this laundrette. She wouldn't allow them the chance to grow on her, so she stopped wearing clothes and kept all the windows open, and it was a very cold winter. The poor thing literally froze to death.'

Charlene's machine stopped suddenly. She folded her magazine shut and rose. She looked around. They were the last remaining customers of the evening. Out in the dark night, the wind was rising. Something clattered sharply against the glass of her machine.

'Wait a minute,' said Lauren. 'I thought you said you didn't know if this girl lived or died.'

'Well,' said Charlene, reaching for the dryer door, 'nothing's ever certain, is it? My granddad has wartime stories that would make your hair perm itself. You hear about these things, stuff that's been going on since before you were born, and you're still never quite sure. Before you can really believe, you have to take a look for yourself.'

Her fingers grasped the aluminium handle and she jerked the broad porthole open.

Hated

You have to be in a pretty bad mood to write a story like this, and I was. For those who pass through life unloved, awareness of the fact is tantamount to annihilation. Stripped of our illusions, we would exist in a vacuum of pure, unending terror. I *was* going to make this tale even darker, but then I cheered up.

THE FIRST inkling Michael Everett Townsend had that something was wrong was when his wife slapped him hard around the face.

She had never slapped his face before. Michael hadn't been expecting the blow. He was carrying a glass of milk, and it shot out of his hand, spattering them both. The glass was cheap and just bounced on the rug, but he jumped back in shock and stepped on it, cracking the thing into shards, one of which pierced his bare foot. Gasping in pain, he dropped down on the edge of the bed just as the blood began to pour freely from his wounded sole. Instead of the sympathy he expected to receive, however, his wife gave a scream of rage and a mighty shove, and tipped him onto the floor. Then she began looking for a knife.

Michael's wife really loved him.

But then, everyone did. Michael was the most popular man in the entire apartment building. The superintendent gave him preferential treatment because unlike the other tenants he never complained about the heating, which was always too hot or nonexistent. Betty, Michael's next-door neighbour, adored him because he had once scared a drugged-up burglar from the hallway at two in the morning, because he professed an admiration for the people of North Yorkshire where she had grown up, and because he had shown her how to replace the washers in her bathroom taps. Mitzi and Karen, the two blonde

Australian flight attendants on the floor below, liked him because he was cute and a gentleman, because he paid them the respect they were denied in the air and because they were attuned to potential romantic material, married or otherwise.

But it wasn't just the apartment building. The staff at work loved Michael and showed it, which was unusual, because in London-based companies very few people are willing to reveal their personal loyalties in any direction. The Asian couple who ran the deli at the corner doted on him, because he always asked after their handicapped son, and managed to pronounce the boy's name correctly. And dozens of other people whose lives crossed Michael's felt a little bit richer for knowing him. He was a popular guy. And if he was honest with himself, he knew it.

Michael had been aware of his popularity since the age of five, winning over creepy aunts and tobacco-stained uncles with an easy smile. An only child in a quiet middle-class family, he had grown up in sun-dappled suburbia, lavished with love. His parents still worshipped him, calling once a week to catch up with his latest exploits. He had been a golden child who remained golden in adulthood.

Golden. That was the perfect word.

Blond haired, blue eyed, broad shouldered, thirty-two, and married to an intelligent, talented, attractive woman. When Michael spoke others listened, nodding sagely as they considered his point. They wanted to call him by a nickname that would imply intimate friendship, Micky or Mike. What they liked about him was hard for them to define; perhaps they enjoyed basking in the reflection of his success. Perhaps he made them feel more confident in their own abilities.

The truth was simpler than that. Michael was at ease in his world. Even his most casual conversations made sound sense. In a life that was filled with uncertainties he was a totally reliable factor, a bedrock, a touchstone. And others sensed it. Everyone knew that they were in the presence of a winner.

Until the night of the accident, that is.

It really wasn't Michael's fault. The rain was beating so heavily that the windscreen wipers couldn't clear it on the fastest setting. It was a little after 11 pm, and he was driving slowly and carefully back from the office, where he had been working late. He was thinking about Marla curled up in bed, waiting to hear his key in the lock. He had just coasted the Mercedes through the water chute that a few hours ago had been the road leading to Muswell Hill Broadway when a bicycle materialised from the downpour. On it sat a heavy-set figure in a yellow slicker – but not for long. The figure slammed into the bonnet of the car, then rolled off heavily and fell to the ground. Michael stamped his boot down on the brake, caused the car to fishtail up against the kerb in a spray of dirty water.

He jumped out of the vehicle and ran to the prostrate figure.

'Jeesus *focking* Christ!' The cyclist was in his late forties, possibly South American, very pissed off. Michael tried to help him to his feet but was shoved away. 'Don' touch me, man, just don't *focking* touch me!' He turned back to his bicycle and pulled it upright. The thing had no lights, no brakes, nothing. And the guy sounded drunk or stoned. Michael was feeling less guilty by the second.

'Look, I'm really sorry I hit you, but you just appeared

in front of me. It's lucky I wasn't going any faster.'

'Yeah, right – lucky me.' The handlebars of the bike were twisted, and it didn't look like they could be straightened out without a spanner. He hurled the bicycle onto the verge in disgust.

'I can give you a ride,' offered Michael. The driver door of the Mercedes was still open. The leather upholstery was getting wet.

'I don' want no *focking* ride in a rich man's car, asshole!' shouted the cyclist, pushing him away.

'Look, I'm trying to be civilised about this,' said Michael, who was always civilised. 'You had no lights on, you came straight through a stop sign without even slowing down, what on earth was I supposed to do?'

'I could sue your ass off is what *I* could do.' The cyclist stared angrily as he gingerly felt his neck and shoulder. 'I don' know that nothin' is broken here.'

'You've probably pulled a muscle,' said Michael, trying to be helpful.

'What, are you a doctor?' The reply was aggressive, the glare relentless.

It was a no-win situation. Time to get away from this crazy person and go back to the car, dry off the seats and head for home. Michael started to back away.

'I've offered you a lift, but if you're going to be –'

'Don' put yoursel' out. I live right over there.' The cyclist pointed across the block. 'Just give me your address. Write it down so I can contact you.'

Michael hesitated. He didn't like the idea of giving his address to a stranger. 'Why would you need to call me?' he asked.

'Jee*sus*, why do you think? It turns out I got a dislocated shoulder or something, I gonna get a claim in on you, make you pay to get it fixed. You just better pray they don' find nothin' wrong with me, man.'

Reluctantly, Michael pulled a business card from his wallet and passed it across. Moments later he was heading back to the car and checking his watch. The whole business had lasted less than a couple of minutes. Behind the wheel once more, he watched the yellow slicker drift away into the rain mist and thought about the accident.

It was unusual for him to be placed in any kind of confrontational situation and not come out a winner. His likeability could defuse the most volatile of personalities. As he turned the key in the ignition, he wondered if there would be any repercussions. Suppose this chap had actually broken something and didn't know it yet? How did he stand, insurance-wise? He was thinking of himself, but hell, it had been the other party's fault. Michael was nice but no saint. His comfortable life made few allowances for upsets, and breaks in the smooth running of his routine irritated the hell out of him.

'Darling, you're all wet. What have you been doing?' Marla reached up and hugged him, her bed-warm breasts goose-pimpling against his damp jacket.

'There was a bit of an accident. I hit a cyclist. Had to get out of the car.' He gently disentangled himself and began removing his clothes.

She pulled the sheet around her. 'How awful. What happened?'

'He wasn't looking where he was going. I could have killed him. Luckily, he didn't seem hurt, but –'

The telephone rang. Marla shared his look of surprise. Their friends all knew that they had a seven-year-old son in the next room and never called the house late. Michael pulled the instrument toward him by the cord and raised the receiver. A wail of bizarre music squealed from the earpiece.

'Hello, who is this?'

'This the guy you *hit* tonight, brother.'

'How did you get my ho –'

'My shoulder's dislocated. Bad news for you. Real bad karma.'

The guy couldn't have seen a doctor already, even if he'd gone straight to casualty.

'Are you sure? I mean, how –'

'Sure I'm sure, you think you're dealing with a fockin' idiot? Patty, she says it's all bust up. Which means I can't work. An' you have to pay me compensation. S'gon be a *lot* of money, man.'

'Now wait a minute . . .' Maybe this was some kind of scam, a professional con trick.

Marla was tapping his arm, mouthing 'Who is it?'

He slipped his hand over the mouthpiece. 'The chap I hit tonight.'

'You still there? You gonna pay me to get fixed up or what?'

'Look, if you think you have a case for extracting money from me, I think you're wrong.' Michael's famous niceness was starting to slip. Who the hell did this guy think he was, finding his home number and calling so late at night? 'But if you really have damaged yourself, it's your own fault for riding without lights and not watching the traffic.'

'You don' know who you're dealing with,' came the reply. 'You just made the biggest mistake of your life.'

'Are you threatening me?'

'I'm just saying that people like you need to be taught a fockin' lesson, treating guys like me as if we don' exist.'

Michael stared at the receiver. This was bullshit. He was in the right, the other party was in the wrong. The law was on his side. And he cared, he had a social conscience. But the thought struck him, what if the accident had somehow been his fault after all?

'You still there? Tell me, Mr Townsend, what's your biggest fear? That your child get sick? That your wife get up and leave you?'

A chill prickled at Michael's neck. He didn't like this crazy man using his name, talking about his family. And how did he know he was even married? Was it that obvious, just by looking at the car?

'No, you scared o' something else even more, but you don't even know it. I see through people like you. Don't take much to break a man like you.' There was contempt in the voice, as if the caller was reading his mind.

'Now listen,' Michael snapped, 'you have no right to threaten me, not when you endangered my life as well as your own. I could get the police –'

The voice on the line cut in. 'When you come to find me – an' you will – it won' be with no damn police.'

Suddenly the line went dead. Michael shrugged and replaced the handset.

'Well, what did he say?'

'Oh, he was just – abusive,' he replied distractedly, watching the rain spangle over the street lights.

'Do you have his number?'

'Hmm?'

'His number, do you have it in case there's a problem?'

Michael realised that he didn't even know the name of the man he'd hit.

He rose early, leaving his wife curled beneath the duvet.

Surprisingly, even little Sean had slept on in the adjoining bedroom. Michael showered and donned a shirt, grabbed a piece of toast and poured himself a glass of milk. Then he climbed the stairs and gently woke his wife.

And she slapped his face.

The glass broke. The milk splashed. He stepped back and cut his foot, but the pain had already given way to hurt. Puzzled, he ran his fingers across his reddening cheek.

'What the hell – what are you looking for?'

She was frantically searching beneath the mattress, then pulled up short in confusion.

'You – shouldn't creep up on me like that.' Marla slunk back beneath the covers, sleep-pressed hair folding over her eyes. She turned her back to him, embarrassed by the vivid dream that had leaked over into reality. Picking the glass from his foot, he watched a drop of crimson blood disperse in an alabaster puddle of milk like a spreading virus.

An Elastoplast took care of the wound. He rattled the glass fragments into a box which he sealed and placed in the pedal bin beneath the sink, then listened as his son thumped downstairs.

'Sean? You want Crunchy-Crunch?' He cocked his head. No answer. Odd. The boy could always be drawn by mention of his favourite breakfast cereal. 'Seanie?'

He looked around to find the boy glaring distrustfully at him through the bannisters. 'Sean, what's the matter? Come down and pour your milk on.'

The child shook his head slowly and solemnly, mumbling something to himself. He pulled his stripy sweatshirt over his chin and locked his arms around his knees. He stared through the bars, but he wouldn't descend any further.

'Come and have your breakfast, Sean. We can take some up to Mummy.' Another muffled reply.

Michael set the dustpan aside and took a step toward his son. 'I can't hear what you're saying.'

'*You're not my daddy*,' the boy screamed suddenly, scrambling back up the stairs to the safety of his bedroom.

Michael checked himself in the rear-view mirror. The same pleasant, confident face looked back, although the smile was a little less certain than usual. He drove through the avenue of sodden embankment trees heading into the city and wondered about the behaviour of his family. He didn't wonder for long; the three of them had managed to maintain a problem-free existence until now, cushioned perhaps by Marla's inherited wealth and his own easy-going attitude. If they got under each other's feet in town there was always the cottage in Norfolk, a convenient ivy-covered bolt hole that provided healing seclusion. But the memory of the slap lingered as clearly as if the hand print had remained on his face.

Michael parked the car in the underground garage and took the lift to the seventh floor where he worked for Aberfitch McKiernny, a law firm dealing primarily with property disputes. The receptionist glanced up as he passed but failed to grant him her usual morning smile. The switchboard operators glared sullenly in his wake. Even the postboy seemed to be ignoring him. Why was everyone in such a bad mood today?

Michelle was already waiting by his door. She was the most efficient secretary he had ever employed. Power dressed in tight black raw cotton, her pale hair knotted carefully at her neck, she impatiently tapped a pair of IBM disks against the palm of her hand while she waited for him to remove his coat.

'You were supposed to take these home with you last night,' she explained, passing them over.

'I didn't get around to them. The Trowerbridge case took up all my time. I'll try to run them later this morning.'

She reached over and took the disks back. 'I don't think that will do any good. Your "opinion" was needed yesterday. No one will want it today.'

She stressed the words strangely, as if she no longer held much respect for him. Michael seated himself behind his desk and studied her. What was going on here? Michelle had always been his biggest fan, his greatest supporter. It was obvious to everyone that she was more than a little in love with him, and he played on the knowledge mercilessly. But today her tone had changed. There was a testiness in her voice, as if she had seen inside him and no longer desired what she saw.

'Michelle, are you okay?'

She folded her arms across her chest, pure frost. 'Fine. Why?'

'I don't know, you sound so –'

'You'd better get into Leo's office. He's been calling for you. He sounds pretty angry about something.'

Leo Tarrant, fifty-seven, the calm centre of the firm, was at peace because he knew he was retiring in a year, and no longer let anything in the world worry him. But this morning he wasn't like that. His usually slick grey mane was ruffled about his head. His face was sclerotic and mottled with suppressed rage. He tipped back his chair and flicked rhythmically at the sides of a gold cigarette case, reminder of his past habit, now a talisman of his strengthened heart.

'You've let me down badly with this Trowerbridge business,' he admitted. 'I thought I'd get an early result by placing it in your hands. Instead it now looks as if they'll have to go to court after all.'

Michael shifted uncomfortably in his seat. He simply couldn't comprehend Leo's attitude. Trowerbridge Developments had been sued by one of its tenants for failing to maintain a property. The company, aware that it had little chance of winning the case, had requested the negotiation of an out-of-court settlement by its longstanding legal representatives. Michael had done everything within his power to ensure that this would happen. After all, the clients were friends of his. They saw each other socially. Their kids even played together.

'I don't know what you're talking about, Leo,' Michael confessed. 'I completed my end of the deal in plenty of time to prevent the planned court action from going ahead.'

'That's exactly the opposite of what I've heard,' said his boss, clicking away at the clasp of the cigarette box. 'According to the client's own progress report you've been holding back the negotiations and leaning so far in favour of the tenants that there's precious little time left for Trowerbridge to cut himself a deal. Neither he nor his son can see any way of making a satisfactory settlement. And there's something else.'

Michael was dumbfounded. He couldn't have worked any harder for these people. If this was their way of showing gratitude . . .

'Have you ever received any financial inducements from the Trowerbridge family? Negative-equity absorbers, anything like that?'

The old man was accusing him of taking a bribe? He

could scarcely believe his ears.

'No, of course not,' he spluttered furiously. 'I'm amazed that you could even consider –'

'Calm down, I'm not saying you did. It's something that the corporation suggested I look into. Think back over your relationship with Trowerbridge during the past few months, would you? You'd better make damned sure that there's nothing in your recent dealings with them that could damage your standing with this firm. Now let's go over these complaints in detail.' He produced a slim red file and carefully unfolded it.

For the next hour and a half Michael was interrogated about his handling of the impending lawsuit. Although he left Leo's office more or less vindicated, he knew from the look on the old man's face that something irretrievable had been lost; a level of trust had been removed. The layer of good faith that had always existed between himself and his superiors had been torn away like the stripes from a dishonoured soldier's tunic. It wasn't just a matter of rebuilding Leo's confidence in him. He wanted to know why his abilities had been so quickly doubted. Clearly the Trowerbridge family, father and son, had lied, and Leo had believed them. But why should they do that? What had they to gain beyond an undesired delay to the lawsuit? It made no sense.

He considered the problem for the rest of the morning, during which time his secretary proved barely capable of common civility. She appeared briefly throughout the day to dump dockets on his desk, and at one point when he glanced up at her looked as if she was about to file a harassment suit against him. Michael felt the ground shifting fast beneath him. As he was leaving the building that evening, the doorman grumpily revealed that his parking space had been switched to a smaller, more awkward stall further away from the main doors.

Marla already sounded bored with the topic of conversation. They had washed up the dinner things together. Now she had turned back to the sink and was wiping down surfaces unnecessarily; the cleaning lady was due first thing tomorrow. Eventually aware that he had asked her a question, she sighed and faced him. 'I just don't know, Michael. These things happen. There's no point in getting paranoid. Nobody's out to get you.'

'Well, it certainly feels like they are,' he complained, digging a bottle of Scotch from the cupboard and pouring himself a generous measure.

His wife made a face; disbelief, dissatisfaction, he couldn't read which. 'You know,' she said slowly, 'maybe you're just experiencing the real world for a change.'

'What the hell is that supposed to mean?'

She gestured vaguely about her. 'You know what you're like. You've always had this kind of – aura of perfection surrounding you. People go out of their way to make things easy for you. Perhaps they're not doing it this once, and you've simply noticed for the first time.'

He drained the glass and set it down on the kitchen table. 'Marla, that's ridiculous and you know it.'

'Is it? You glide through life in a golden haze expecting people to move out of your way just because you're you.' She fell silent for a moment, then turned back to the sink. 'It was something I noticed about you the day we met. A quality very few men ever possess. It's something you normally only find in very pretty girls, and then just for a couple of years. Doors automatically open. No one has ever found me special like that, only you. The rest of us trail in your wake. Well, maybe it's our turn in the sun for a while.'

It seemed to Michael that he was being presented with a day of revelations, that he was somehow seeing himself clearly for the first time, from above, perhaps, or from a distance.

He rose and moved to his wife's side, gently placing his hands upon her hips. 'I can't understand why you've never talked to me about this before,' he said softly, 'why you couldn't have been more honest with me.'

'What's the point when you're not prepared to be honest about yourself?' she asked, coolly removing his hands. 'If you want complete candour, then I'll tell you. I really don't think I can bear you touching me any more.'

The room fell silent and remained so. Sean would not come down to kiss him goodnight and hid behind his mother's skirt until she took him up to bed.

He didn't think the situation could get any worse, but it did.

Marla would not talk about her refusal to allow his touch. At night she kept to the far side of the bed and took to sleeping in a T-shirt and pants. In the mornings she was up and dressed before him. She had usually washed and fed her son by the time he arose, so that the pair of them presented his sleepy form with a smart united front. Although she refused to be drawn on the subject of their halted sex life, she conceded that no one else was stealing her affection from him. It was simply something that had finally, and perhaps inevitably, occurred. Frozen out of his own home, he increased his hours in the office.

But there the situation was just as bad. The Trower-bridge case had been lost and everyone now regarded him with suspicion, as if he'd been caught stealing office supplies and let off with a warning. Sometimes members of staff insulted him just out of earshot. At the very least, they ignored him. Michael became aware that parties and dinners were being arranged behind his back and that he had become the butt of cheap, stupid jokes. Much of the time no one seemed to notice him at all. If he joined a group at the coffee machine and struck up a conversation, they would glance over his shoulder, noting something or someone that interested them more. If he tried to make a social arrangement they cried off with transparently feeble excuses, not even bothering to convince him of their unavailability.

Petty grievances, of a kind that had never occurred before, began to accumulate. He was given the dullest briefs to work on. Someone left a bottle of Listerine on his desk in response to an office perception that he suffered from halitosis. Even the parking attendant had the temerity to suggest that he attend more carefully to his personal hygiene.

At last, at the end of his tether, he asked his secretary to enter his office and to close the door behind her.

'I want you to be honest with me, Michelle,' he said carefully, seating himself and bidding her do the same. 'I find everyone's attitude towards me has changed drastically in the last two weeks, and I'm at a loss to understand why.'

'You want the honest truth?' asked Michelle, pointedly examining her cuticles.

'Please,' pleaded Michael, ready to absorb her reply and analyse it at length.

'Well, it's the way you treat people, like they're satellites around your planet. I used to find it exciting, very masculine. I rather fancied you, all that rugged decisiveness. Others did too. Now I wonder how I could have been so blind.' She shifted uncomfortably. 'Can I go now?'

'Certainly not!' He snorted, wondered, shook his head in bewilderment. 'Explain what you mean. What do the others say about me?'

Michelle stared up at the ceiling and blew the air from her cheeks. 'Oh, you know, the usual ... that you're self-centred, boring, pushy, less clever than you think you are. You're just not a very likeable man any more.'

'And you can sit there and say this to my face?' he asked.

'I've already applied for a transfer,' she answered, rising.

Michael realised then that if he went out and bought a dog it would probably run off, just to be away from him. Seated on a wet bench in the bedraggled little park beneath the office, watching as the pigeons strutted toward his shoes and then veered away, he became seized with the idea that someone had placed a curse on him. Not your usual get-boils-and-die curse, but something subtler. There was only one wild card to consider, one suspect, and that was Mr Whatever-his-name-was on the bike, the Latin chap he'd knocked over. The more Michael considered it, the clearer it became that his troubles had truly begun after that angry night-time phone call. He remembered the voice on the line: 'What's your biggest fear? ... Don't take much to break a man like you ... When you come to find me – an' you will ...' It all began to make sense. Could there be a rational explanation for what was happening to him? Was the guy some kind of shaman in touch with the supernatural, a malevolent hypnotist, or just someone with the power of suggestion? Wasn't that how voodoo worked? He was determined to take positive action.

It was dark by the time he finally got out of the office. Nosing the car back toward the intersection where the accident had occurred, he remembered the cyclist's response to his offer of a lift. 'I just live over there.'

'*Over there*' proved to be a prefabricated two-storey block of council flats. With no other way of locating his tormentor, he began ringing doorbells and facing irate residents, most of whom were in the middle of eating dinner. One of them even swore and spat at him, but by now he was used to that kind of behaviour. Trudging along the cracked, flooded balconies like a demented rent collector, he suddenly recalled a name mentioned in the phone call – Patty. Hadn't she checked out the cyclist's damaged shoulder? At least it was something specific, a person he could ask to see.

After being abused in four more doorways, he was nearing the end of the first floor with only a few apartments remaining when a young Asian man with dragons tattooed on his arms pointed to the flat at the end of the corridor.

'She's married to a Mexican guy who plays weird music all night,' he complained.

Leaning against the garbage chute was the bicycle that he had hit, now repaired.

'That's the one,' said Michael, thanking him and setting off. He stood before the door and read the printed card wedged next to the broken bell.

'You're back sooner than I expected,' said Ramon del Tierro, faith healer, opening the door at his knock and ushering him in. 'I didn't think you'd come to me for at least another week.'

The hallway was in darkness. Mariachi music was playing in one of the bedrooms. The flat was slightly perfumed, as though someone had been burning incense earlier. Ramon was slighter and smaller than he remembered, pallid and unhealthy looking. His left eye was milky, blinded. He led the way to a small, smartly decorated lounge and waved him to a seat. Michael didn't want to sit. He no longer considered the situation absurd. He just wanted an answer, and an end to the hatred.

'You did this to me, didn't you?' The tightness in his voice made him realise how much anger he was holding back.

'Did what? Tell me what I did.' Ramon shrugged, faking puzzlement.

'You made me – made everyone detest me.'

'Hey, how could I do that? You soun' like a crazy man. You want to know how my shoulder is? Thank you for askin', it's gonna be okay.' He turned away. 'I'm gonna make some coffee. You wan' some?'

'I want you to tell me *what you did*, damn it!' Michael shouted, grabbing a scrawny arm.

Ramon glared fiercely and remained silent until he released his grip. Then he softly spoke.

'I have a gift, Mr Townsend. A crazy, pointless gift. If it had been second sight or somethin' I might have made some money from it, but no. When I come into contact with strangers I can see what makes them happy or sad. Sometimes I can sense what they fear or who they love. It depends on who I touch. Sometimes I don't feel nothin' at all. But I felt it with you. An' I made you see how life can be when you don't have the one thing you value most. In your case, it's your popularity. I took away your charm. You're no longer a likeable guy. I just didn't think it would screw you up as bad as this. I guess you must love yourself a whole lot more than you love anyone else.'

Michael ran a hand across his face, suddenly tired. 'Why did you pick on me for this particular – experiment?'

'Because I can, and because you deserved it. Now, what you gonna do about that? Go cryin' to the police, tell them nobody likes you?'

Fury was rising within Michael, bubbling to the surface in a malignant mist. 'What – do you want – from me?'

'I don' want nothing from you, Mr Townsend. You got nothin' I want.'

'You sabotaged my job.'

Ramon shook his head. 'No sir, I did not. Anythin' that's happening to you is happening 'cause people just don't like you no more.'

'Then you can make it end.'

The healer considered this for a moment, scratching at his chin with a thumbnail. 'I guess I could, but I don't want to. See, it's better for you to relearn yourself from scratch. Won't be easy the way you are now, but just makin' the effort would turn you into a better person.'

Michael knew that if he moved too close he would lash out at Ramon. His temper was slow to rise but formidable to witness. Now he clenched his fists and advanced on the little Mexican. 'You get this fucking thing off me straight away, you filthy little spic, or I will beat you unconscious and burn this shit hole down with you in it, do you understand?'

'Now you're showin' your true colours, Mr Townsend.' Ramon took a step back, wary but not nervous. 'A soul like yours takes an awful lot of fixin'. Tell me what it is you want.'

'I want you to make everyone love me again,' he said, suddenly embarrassed by the realisation of his needs.

'That I can do.'

'How soon?'

'In a few seconds, with just a touch. But you won't like it. Consider the other way, I beg you. Relearn. Begin again with the personality you have now. It will be more difficult, but the rewards will be much greater.'

'I can't do that. I need this to happen tonight.'

'Then it will have to be the hard way. Come closer to me.'

Michael walked into Ramon's outstretched arms. Before he had time to realise what was happening, he felt the thin-bladed knife that Ramon had pulled from his pocket bite between the ribs traversing his heart. The fiery razor edge sliced through the beating muscle, piercing a ventricle and ending his life in a single crimson moment.

So many people turned up at St Peter's Church that they ran out of parking spaces and had to leave their cars on the grass verges lining the road. The funeral service boasted eulogies from the senior partners of Aberfitch McKiernny, from friends and relatives, from his colleagues and from his adoring wife. Everyone who went to the burial of Michael Everett Townsend volubly agreed; the man being laid to rest here was truly loved by everyone.

Night After Night Of The Living Dead

The great thing about children is that they talk rubbish with more conviction than politicians. Lies, fantasies and half-truths are glued into a kind of surreal pudding that defies you to disbelieve your ears. I should know; at the age of the boy in this story I used to tell the kind of whoppers that could make your eyes fall out. Every adult still believes one hopelessly illogical, morbid thing from their childhood, like if you eat a sandwich you can't go paddling for two hours or you'll get cramps and drown. What do you still believe?

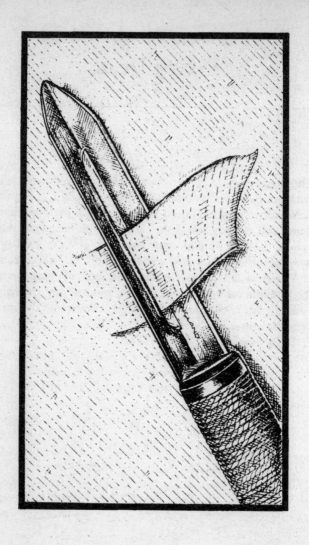

THE BEST thing about the dead is you can't get pregnant from sitting on a chair they've just been sitting on like you can with live people. When live people warm up the seat (especially the toilet seat – that's where AIDS really comes from) and you sit on it after them and it's still warm, the heat activates the hormones in your body and fertilises the egg, and nine months later you have a baby. But the dead don't leave warm seats because their body temperature is about the same as winter tap water.

The worst thing about the dead is they don't sleep, so if you go downstairs for a glass of water in the middle of the night you're liable to find my grandpa sitting at the kitchen table staring off into the dark, and frankly this gives me the creeps. We have the Night Of The Living Dead to thank for all this. The most interesting thing about that occasion (apart from the fact that it happened in the middle of the afternoon) is that such a cataclysmic event didn't seem to bother many people at the time. Personally speaking I find that weird because I was only eleven when it happened and it fucked me up considerably, I can tell you.

You probably know all about it – I mean you'd have to have been living in a monastery on the Orkney Islands for the last three years to avoid knowing – but I'll tell you anyway, because a) it will give like a personal perspective on the whole thing and b) I'm doing this as my mid-term English essay.

For a start, it was nothing like the movie, which was made many years before. If you saw that particular classic (I wasn't supposed to watch it, but a kid in our street lent me the cassette – he'd relabelled it with a *Winnie the Pooh* sticker), you'll remember how the dead came out of the ground and stumped about in waist-high mist with their arms stretched out like sleepwalkers. This was not exactly accurate. Think about it; when they bury someone the coffin is sealed and put in a hole that's packed with earth and tamped down, so we're talking about several hundred pounds of wet dirt to push up, assuming that you can get the lid of the box open in the first place – which you wouldn't be able to do because there's not enough depth in most coffins to give your arms the necessary leverage. The simple fact is, nobody came out of the ground. When the dead came back to life it was only the ones in the morgues and hospitals that reawoke, and if any others were lying around above ground for any reason, they would have risen too.

They didn't walk with their arms raised either; their hands hung limply at their sides and they didn't really move about much, although they did fall over a lot. But the main difference from the film is that they didn't kill people and try to eat their brains. If you think it through logically, how could they? They were dead, and that means brain dead, and wanting to eat someone else's brains suggests conscious thought, which they don't have. Eating a brain isn't going to restore your own. That's like saying if you eat part of a cow you'll grow four stomachs. Also, if you wanted to eat someone's brains you'd have to get their head open, which I shouldn't think is as easy as it looks on the screen. It's like the vampire thing in movies. You know, the biting part, when Dracula makes two holes in someone's neck and sucks the blood out. Excuse me, but did someone just cancel the laws of physics or something? When you open a tin of condensed milk you have to make a hole on either side of the can to allow the milk to escape. So a vampire would have to make sure that his mouth only went over one of the holes, otherwise he wouldn't be able to suck any blood out – unless he could *really* suck hard, in which case the person he was sucking would sort of dent inwards like a punctured football.

So. No coming out of the ground, no eating brains. That's the trouble with the living dead, they're nothing like their movie counterparts. In fact, they're really boring. These days some of them can do rudimentary root-memory things like read the *Sun* or hum songs from *Cats*, but you can't train them any more than you can train really stupid insects or our biology teacher's dog. You can point up in the air and they'll follow your finger but then they'll stay like that for hours, like chickens expecting rain. And it's because they're dead, end of story. I mean, dead is it, *finito*; after you're dead you don't understand the punch lines to jokes or remember to set the video, it's all over, baby.

What was really weird, though, was the reaction of the adults. They didn't think about the basic absurdity of the situation. They didn't wonder how the whole thing could be physically possible. They weren't interested in the mechanics of the dead returning to life. They just completely freaked, screaming the place down every time they saw one, and stopped us from going near them or even looking. You'd expect this from my mother, who has a nuclear meltdown when I so much as bring a dead sparrow into the house, but not from Ted, our revolting old next-door neighbour who lost an eye in the war and talks about stringing up darkies to our West Indian milkman.

I don't specifically remember much about the night it happened except that it was a Wednesday, it was raining hard and I was late home from school. I'd been caught unravelling the elastic inside a golf ball during social studies and had been made to stay behind for detention. I remember walking home and seeing one of the dead shuffling ahead, a man of about fifty. My first sighting. It was a weird experience, as though I'd been waiting all of my admittedly short life to see something like this, and now that I had it made sense of everything else.

The figure before me was drifting more than walking, his feet barely rising from the ground. As far as I could see in the fading light, he was dressed in normal street clothes, although they were dirty and one jacket sleeve was torn, as though he'd been in a fight. His head was lowered a little but he was staring forward and seemed to know where he was going. As I drew abreast of him I caught an overpowering stench of chemicals, formaldehyde I supposed, as though he had just heaved himself up from the mortuary slab. His face was grey and speckled, the texture of my Dad's IBM slipcase, but his eyes were the real giveaway. They had this fixed dry look, like doll's eyes, I guess because there was no fluid to lubricate them, and they were stuck in one position. They looked like a pair of jammed roll-on deodorant balls. I kept pace with him as I passed, and it was then that I realised I wasn't really scared.

When someone is dangerous they give off warning signals, and if you're receptive to the signals you back away. But this guy was just dead and there weren't any signals good or bad, and I instinctively knew that the worst thing that could happen was he could fall over and land on top of me. The street was pretty empty, and the few people who passed us didn't seem to see anything wrong. I guess in the rain-hazed dimness there was nothing unusual to see beyond the fact that the old man didn't have a raincoat on and was getting pretty soaked. Finally I arrived at my turning, and the dead bloke just shuffled onwards into the gloom. I watched him go for a while, then headed home.

I missed the early evening TV news but asked my mother if there had been anything about the dead coming back to life and she made a face and said of course not. I remembered noticing that her eyes were puffy and red, as if she'd been crying about something and was trying not to let me see. Later, on the portable in my room, the footage appeared. There, right in front of me, live on some crappy Sky channel, the anchorwoman was awkwardly reading a report that several cadavers from a hospital morgue in Leeds had been found walking along the corridors of the building. She said that similar phenomena were being reported all over the world, although I don't think she believed a word of it. Then some ecosystems guy who looked like he'd just got out of bed kept patting down his hair and saying it was all to do with the ozone layer, and I thought *As if*. I mean, you don't have to be a rocket scientist to figure out that there's no link between the depletion of the ozone layer and the reanimation of dead tissue. That's like saying Nintendo games give you rabies or something. Get a grip.

I retuned the TV to CNN because they repeat the same stories over and over when they're not quoting Iowa wheat prices, and there it was, actual footage of ZOM-BIES lumbering along roads and bumping into walls and generally looking thick. I rang my friend Joey 'Boner' Mahoney to tell him to turn on the TV but his dog stepmother answered and told me it was too late to talk to him.

The next day I attempted to discuss what was happening with my friends at school, but no one was that interested except Simon Waters. Unfortunately Simon believes that crop circles are made by Venusians, not by a couple of sad guys with a piece of rope and a plank, and is desperate to believe in any scenario that's more interesting than his own miserable existence, which consists of getting lousy marks at school and going home to a father who is having an affair with a foot specialist. That was when I began my Deadwatch, which is a notebook marked out so that I can record each dead sighting as it happens.

With each passing day there were more and more sightings as the walking dead took to the streets. Soon I was recording as many as ten or fifteen on a single Saturday morning (the women are particularly fond of milling around the trolley collection point outside Sainsbury's), and I stopped bothering with the book because there were too many to keep up with. To begin with, most of these ambulatory cadavers were in pretty good condition. I mean their jaws and ears weren't hanging off or anything, but once in a while you'd see one in a really bad state. There was a guy on the bus in a hospital gown, and the stitches down the front of his chest had burst open so that his intestines were hanging out and rolling from side to side as the bus turned corners. There was no blood and his guts were blue-grey, like piles of old school sausages. That was pretty gross. But in the early days most of the corpses seemed to stay in one piece.

You see, it wasn't just a Night Of The Living Dead, as we had thought at first. It was Night After Night. The effects of whatever had revived them were sticking around, so the authorities had to come up with some kind of legislation to cope with the problem. They simply arranged for bodies to be buried at a new standard depth and for mortuary doors to be kept locked. There was talk of freezing and vacuum packing for a while, but I guess it seemed too disrespectful, bowing out like a pork chop. Still, an awful lot of Deadies seemed to be walking around, more every day, so either someone was letting them out (which I'd seen a Right-To-Life group doing on the news) or they were finding ways to escape prior to burial.

The government couldn't settle on a reason for what was happening, and still haven't come up with a satisfactory cause to this day. They set up an independent enquiry to investigate what was going on, i.e., cut open some corpses and had a poke around, but found nothing conclusive. The corpses were just inert organisms that wouldn't lie still. They had no heartbeats and coagulated blood and hardened veins and leathery skin and dry staring eyes. At first the scientists thought it was radiation in the atmosphere, then Rogue Viral DNA, but I knew they really didn't have a clue when everyone started to blame the French.

Anyway, none of this really touched my family or our lives. We continued to see the dead sitting in bus shelters looking neither happy nor sad (looking like they were waiting for a bus really). We saw them in gents' outfitters staring vaguely at the shelves. We saw them standing shell-shocked outside cinemas and pizza parlours (they weren't allowed near food but they seemed to enjoy being in queues). We saw them watching football through the windows of TV rental stores, their foreheads pressed against the glass. We saw them sunbathing in park deckchairs with newspapers over their faces, and the only way you could tell they were dead was because it was raining.

I guess this was about a month after the actual NOTLD, and now that everyone could see the dead weren't going to hurt anybody, all kinds of trouble started. For one thing, no matter how harmless they were, the dead tended to creep people out. It was only natural; the way they looked and smelled was depressing to say the least. The police wanted special powers to round them up because they were always falling onto railway lines and wandering into busy traffic, but all kinds of groups began protesting, arguing that because the dead were walking around they still had souls and therefore had human rights.

Then doctors began worrying that the bodies would decompose and put everyone at risk from germs, but the corpses didn't really rot. Because the newly dead leaked so much they slowly got drier and more leathery, and this was helped by the fact that it was winter and a lot of them had taken to sitting in libraries where the central heating caused an arid atmosphere.

They got damaged and tatty from constantly bumping into things, and some of them lost fingers and clumps of hair, which made them even creepier looking. (Oddly enough, they managed to keep a natural sense of propriety. If one of them tore his trousers he would tug the hole around so that people on the tube wouldn't have to sit facing his willy.) While television shows and newspaper articles preached respect for the dead, teenage gangs began going out and tampering with the bodies, cutting bits off or dressing them in inappropriate clothes to make them look silly. My friend Joey once saw an old man in the high street wearing a glitter wig and a ballet tutu. Sometimes if you were out with a bunch of friends and saw one shuffling along ahead of you, you'd run up and pull his trousers down, then all run away laughing. Also, some unscrupulous entrepreneurs hung advertising on them, but most people disapproved of this.

The dead weren't supposed to travel on the tubes because they never bought tickets, but one or two always managed to get through the barriers, only to spend the entire day trying to open the drawers on the platform's chocolate machines. They never made much noise, I think their vocal chords sort of dried out over time, but God, the older ones started to look awful. The problem was, even if they fell into the river and floated about for a few days being run over by motorboats, they would eventually drift to the shore, only to climb out and begin aimlessly walking around again. Hospital crews collected the most disgusting ones and took them away somewhere.

Around this time I remember seeing an old woman fall off a Routemaster bus and get dragged around the block on her face. I followed her just to see what would happen if her coat strap managed to disentangle itself from the pole. When the poor old love finally hauled herself to her feet (nobody was willing to help her – the dead are kind of ignored now, like the homeless) the remaining part of her face fell off like torched wallpaper, leaving her with tarmac-scraped bone and an expression of annoyed sur- prise. It was not a pleasant sight.

A few weeks after this, one wet Saturday afternoon, my grandpa died. He had lived in the house with us for years even though my mother had never liked him, and at first nobody even realised that he had died. He just stayed in his armchair all day staring at the television, but I knew something was wrong because he would normally start shouting at the screen when the wrestling came on and today he didn't. He did make himself a cup of tea, but he left the teabag in the mug, drank it scalding and immediately peed it back out onto the floor. My father wouldn't let my mother call the hospital and they had a huge row, after which it was decided that Grandpa could stay for a while so long as he didn't get in anyone's way. My mother refused to change his clothes, but Dad argued that they wouldn't need changing very often as he no longer had operative sweat glands. Still, it was difficult to break the old geezer of his tea-making habit. I guess when you've been making ten cups of Brooke Bond a day for sixty years you don't need motor neurons.

Grandpa wasn't allowed out by himself because he had a tendency not to come back and we would have to go looking for him. Once I was allowed to go on a grandpa hunt with my dad and we had to search the park just as it was starting to get dark. There were dozens of them – Deadies – sitting motionless beneath the rustling plane trees. They were seated in deckchairs around the bandstand with their hands in their laps, quietly waiting for the music to start. Two of them were sitting on the enclosure railings with their arms around each other like lovers, except that the railing spikes had gone through their thighs. It was a strange sight. I stopped going to the park after that.

A few days later I took Grandpa to the cinema. I guess it was an odd thing to do, but I was supposed to be looking after him and there was a film I really wanted to see, one of those slasher films with music that creeps up on you, and I managed to pass Grandpa off as alive, although the usherette looked at us suspiciously. Halfway through the film, just when the heroine had gone to the cellar to look for her cat even though she knew there was a homicidal maniac loose, I turned to find the old man staring at me with wide, flat eyes. He wasn't breathing of course, and his mouth hung open to reveal a thick dry tongue that looked as if it had been carved out of Spam. What bothered me most was the way he repeated one of his living mannerisms, tilting his head slightly to look at me, so that for a moment I couldn't tell if he was really dead. It was just the illusion of life, of course, but an unsettling one.

A few weeks after that, Grandpa took it upon himself to revive another root memory and peel some potatoes. He remembered the peeler but unfortunately forgot to use it in conjunction with a vegetable and succeeded in removing most of the skin from his fingers before I came home from school and found him staring at a set of bony protrusions that looked like badly sharpened pencils. The very next day he sat down on the stove while the burners were lit and branded his trousers. My mother threatened to leave us if my father didn't arrange for him to be put somewhere, so the following morning found me standing on the doorstep waving goodbye to Grandpa as he stared sightlessly back and stumbled off across the flowerbeds, led away by a disinterested hospital porter smoking a joint.

A short while after his departure, I was walking home from late detention and took a short cut past the backs of the terraced houses a few streets away from where we lived. Ahead, only half visible in the grey fading light, a dead man was standing with his head tilted to the sky, studying something. As I drew closer he sat down with a thud, as if his legs had suddenly given way, and I realised that it was Grandpa. He'd come back. It looked as if something had been eating him, rats perhaps. There were little bite marks all over his face and neck, and one of his arms had hardly any skin at all, only shredded brown muscle. Then I realised where we were, and what he'd been looking at.

He'd slipped out of care and returned to the house he had shared with Grandma when they were just married. I knew he'd been standing there watching for the sight of her passing by the windows. But she had died long ago. An idea occurred to me – that I could take Grandpa to the cemetery where she had been buried and that they could somehow be reunited. Perhaps I could explain to the caretaker, and he would allow her body to be disinterred. But I wasn't sure where the cemetery was, and every time I tried to lead Grandpa away he started pulling back. Finally I had to leave him there, standing before the glowing kitchen windows of his youth, staring up through a half-remembered past.

I never saw him again. I rarely leave my bedroom. I don't go to school any more. There are just too many dead people about, and it bothers me. They blunder into the garden at night and follow you to the shops and fall down the steps of public lavatories and float past you on the ferry, and it's undignified. My mother seems to understand how I feel and lets me have most of my meals in my room. She's become overfriendly with the cocktail cabinet these days, anyway. The extraordinary thing is, the living dead don't seem to count any more. It doesn't matter that the stench of corruption is all around us. We've grown used to the smell. The government continues to chair pointless debates and issue toothless white papers. The general public has ceased to care or even notice. The fabric of society is gently rotting through, even if the dead aren't. So I'm formulating a plan, because someone has to do something. Somebody has to care. Somebody has to take affirmative action before it's too late.

Kevin Grady, Upper 4B

'It makes you wonder what he thinks about,' whispered Mrs Grady, pulling the tablecloth in by the corners and removing it. 'He'll sit like that for hours on end, just staring down into the street, watching the people come and go.'

'You should be thankful,' said her neighbour, helping her clear away the cups and saucers. 'My Joey's a holy terror these days, out every night mixing with heaven knows what kind of riffraff.'

She looked across at the chalk-faced child seated before the window, and a cloud of doubt momentarily formed in her mind. It was unnatural for a teenaged boy to sit so still. When you spoke to him he stared back in accusing silence. And the terrible way he looked at you, with murder in those deep-set eyes. 'Joey tells me he's doing his homework,' she continued, 'but I know damned well he's running with that gang of his. I have no control over him, and his father's absolutely no help at all. But your Kevin ...' She furrowed her brow and uneasily turned aside as the boy glanced at her in suspicion. No wonder Kevin's mother was bashing the Bristol Cream these days, with her son wandering about the house dressed in black, narrowing his eyes at every passing adult. He'd probably grow up to be a serial killer.

'Kevin's a good boy,' said his mother firmly. 'He's terribly bright. And sensitive. He and his grandad were very close. He's been a lot quieter since the old man died. Wouldn't even come with us to the funeral. I hope it doesn't have any lasting effect on him.'

'I shouldn't think so,' the neighbour whispered back. 'Children are resilient. He's very quiet, though. He should go outside more and get some fresh air. Mix with the others. Swim. Play football.' She threw the torpid child a look of desperation. 'Anything.'

Mrs Grady unfolded her arms from her ample chest and looked about for the sherry bottle. 'I wish he would, but he prefers to stay in his room watching horror films all the time.' She poured overgenerous measures into a pair of amber glasses. 'It gives him such an overactive imagination. I think Kevin sees the world differently to most children. He has some very odd ideas. I'm sure it's just a phase, but right now, well ...' She turned to her friend and brought her face closer, confiding. 'It's ... the way he looks at us sometimes. Almost as if he wishes we were dead.'

Tales of Britannica Castle :
I. Ginansia's Ravishment

It's not too hard to spot the influence here. I'm a great fan of Mervyn Peake, and a greater one after seeing Physical Theatre's astonishing minimalist production of *Gormenghast*. I wanted to create a series of political and sexual intrigues populated with demented characters, a closed world of dynastic hysteria. I intended the style to be elegant and allegorical, but the word here I think is *lurid*.

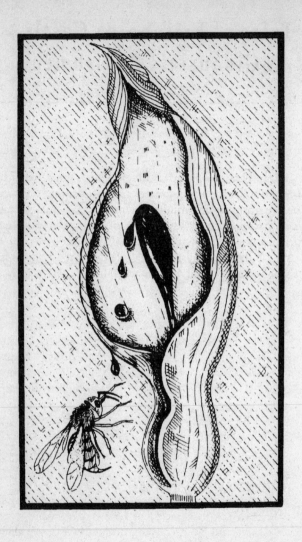

THE PROBLEM with the spiral staircase to the Northeast Quadrant was the plethora of scorpions, small brass ones, set in spiky pairs on either side of each stone step. Their tails tugged at Ginansia's dress, snagging on the sapphire-sewn hem and snatching her back every few feet. Finally she was forced to run with the silken material gathered up at her knee, and run she did because she was late for dinner, and the Great Wound never forgave tardiness when it involved the ruination of sweetmeats.

Although the Princess Ginansia had lived here all her life and knew every room, corridor, staircase, tapestry, window, door and hallway in the castle, she often felt that the building as a whole conspired against her. It was too ornate, as fussy and overdecorated as her mother, filled with dangerous shadows, pools of darkness that concealed sharp little objects that tripped toes, cracked nails and tore skin. In terms of acreage the castle was small, but it was tall. The top five levels had been added by Captain Smackthistle after his legendary victory against the Fire-Tribe Boys of the Infected Mountain. He and his men had returned with all manner of disgusting trophies, parts of bodies which they threaded with gold and silver wire and hung in the heavy blue glass jars that lined the whole of the planetarium.

Ginansia knew no other home but sometimes dreamed of visiting white open spaces, vast halls of light that were free of clutter and gloom, where nothing was more than a few moments old and she could breathe without drawing dust into her lungs, stretching out her arms to embrace the flaring sun.

She tripped on the bottom step and nearly overturned one of the huge cracked Chinese vases that stood on the marble pedestals at the base of the staircase. Catching sight of herself in the vestibule's towering scabrous mirror, she readjusted the dried clematis petals in her hair, carefully tucking them into the auburn folds. She liked clematis flowers because they had no smell; the castle held far too many extraordinary odours to require further olfactory obfuscation by its residents.

Ahead was the narrow, uneven flagstone corridor that led to the Tarnished Hall and the Seven Sepulchres Of Shame, and beyond that the strangely shaped area formerly known as the Heart Of All Sorrow, which was now simply called the Dining Hall. The floor here was always wet and slippery, 'perspiring tears' according to her mother but in reality slick with condensation, because the flues from the kitchen passed across the eastern archway and the fissures in them released steady wisps of steam, wreathing the entire ceiling in swirling mist.

Ginansia was about to open the enormous iron door to the Tarnished Hall when an elegant figure divorced itself from a cobwebbed clutter of crockery and stepped in front of her.

Leperdandy pulled a handkerchief from the top pocket of his purple quilted smoking jacket and flicked it under his quivering narrow nostrils, enveloping them both in an overpowering scent of lavender.

'You're as late as I,' he sniffed. 'Your stepfather went in ten minutes ago. The Great Wound will not be pleased.'

'Have you ever seen him pleased about anything?' she

asked, falling into step beside her half-brother.

'Now that you mention it,' said Leperdandy, 'no.'

'I dread tonight.'

'I know you do. You must be strong.'

They passed across the puddled stones of the angular hall, the damp air clinging to their clothes, fattening the fabric with droplets of moisture. The shadowy stone alcoves on either side mercifully concealed the sepulchres, which had given Ginansia such nightmares as a child. In front of her stood the towering armoured suit of St Ethelbar Squeam, one rusted red arm raised high with his spiked mace still gripped in a battered gauntlet, the other perched effeminately on his steel-lace hip. The mummified corpse of the Squeam himself was still inside the armour, and if you raised the protesting visor and peered in you would see that the rumours were indeed true; the ancient knight had somehow turned himself around within the mail so that he was facing back to front – a sign of cowardice before the enemy, some said.

Opening the doors of the Dining Hall tugged a chain that rang a sharp little bell somewhere beneath their feet, a warning to the kitchen staff to be on their toes. The great table, arranged in cruciform and draped in holly-green cloth, was occupied along its far side, and the inhabitants swivelled their eyes disapprovingly to the latecomers.

'Is it too much to ask that we might share a meal together on the eve of your age-coming?' boomed her stepfather, his sole good eye glaring wetly beneath a bunched, bushy brow as he jutted from the table, an acre of emerald linen splayed at his throat. Globules of venison soup hung in his immense beard. A dripping spoon jutted from his meaty fist. His vast shoulders rose and fell, rose and fell with the wheezing passage of his breath, like an old steam engine labouring with its load. Scarabold the Third of the royal family Bayne, the Great Wound himself, Doer Of Dark Deeds, Rectifier Of Wrongly Wrought Rites, Warrior, stepfather to Ginansia and father to Leperdandy (by a different mother), had watched the severed heads of his enemies bounce down the steps of the Imperial Museum during the Great Siege of '28 with less passion than he now displayed at the tardiness of his offspring.

'The Italian Courtyard is half flooded,' replied Ginansia glibly. 'I had to go all the way around and through the Under-Chapel.' She had, in fact, spent too long at her toilette to register the crepusculation of the hour. These days she was rarely on time for anything. It was one of the few ways she had left of showing dissatisfaction with her circumstance.

'Your father has something to tell you, dear,' called her mother, ignoring the steaming monarch at her side, 'just as soon as you are settled.'

Mater Moribund Bayne had outdone herself tonight. Her sticklike form, so thin that her ribs could be discerned through the purple bombazine of her gown, was bedecked with ropes of jewellery that glittered and shone and swayed about like the lights of a pier in a gale. She was guyed up with so many cascading loops of amethyst and opal that it was a wonder she managed to hold herself erect.

'Come and sit near me, both of you,' said Dwindoline with a kindly smile. Leperdandy's mother was Scarabold's other wife (it being quite legal in these parts for a king to operate a marital duopoly) and, because she was wed to the Great Wound second, occupied a slightly inferior role in the household to Mater Hari (as they called her behind her back).

Plump and lumpen and draped in various shades of pheasant brown, Dwindoline was pleasing and pleasant and resigned to the sidelines of the royal menagerie. She tended her weakling son and her infuriating half-daughter unobtrusively, trying to provide the maternal concern they deserved and certainly didn't receive from Moribund. As the children (children! Ginansia was hours from her eighteenth year and Leperdandy was soon to leave his teens behind) accepted their places opposite, she looked along the table, nodding to the Decrepend so that he might commence the Blessing, smiling blandly at Asphyxia, who was sulking behind her goblet, and at the bulbous, bibulous visage of the Quaff, who had already drained his.

'O Cruel, Cruel Gods, Please Hear The Lowly Call Of This Great Family,' bellowed the Decrepend, who clearly had little faith in the power of prayer and planned to be heard through the more physical expedient of shouting, 'We Give Most Humble Thanks –'

Most humble, thought Ginansia, *the word has been excised from the castle dictionaries.*

'– For The Sheer Lack Of Harm You Have Bestowed Upon Us In Your Infinite, All-Seeing, Wicked Wisdom –'

Ginansia caught her half-brother's gaze and held it. Their aptitude for passing messages was so finely honed that the merest ocular twitch could signify histories. They had grown up side by side in the tall moss-green castle, had hidden together from their ranting, stamping father, had rescued each other from the freezing grip of the moat's shattered crust, had fought secret battles behind the dust-filled curtains of the Red Theatre in the attic. They were childhood allies now standing on the cusp of adulthood.

The Decrepend droned on, his narcotic tone pitched above the sound of falling rain. Scarabold's thick forefinger impatiently traced the edges of the livid ridged scar that crossed his face, the result of a sword blow that had honourably granted him the title of the Great Wound. He threw the Decrepend a look of hatred. The Blessing had to be given again in full if someone joined the table late. Beyond the windows of the tall, narrow Dining Hall, the sky was black and greeny grey, bruised clouds implicitly inclement. Here in the castle the family was safe and secure. Outside the forces of chance raged on.

So did the doddering Decrepend, who suddenly ended his prayers with a thud, smiting the table with a brittle-boned hand in an attempt to drive home his celestial-bound message.

The soup was now cold and curded, and Moribund snapped her fingers at the servants, who scurried to remove the bowls. Scarabold seized the moment to address his stepdaughter. The clearing of his throat was like someone shovelling coal.

'Ginansia, your arrival at the eighteenth year of your life demands the surrender of your maidenhood, and it is my duty as your father –'

'*Step*father.'

'– to appoint a suitably equipped suitor. In short, it is time for your deforestation.'

'Deflowering,' nudged the mater.

Ginansia stared furiously at her stepfather, whom she grudgingly respected as a warrior but considered an odious beast as a human. Since the death of her real father, his every entrance into her mother's bedchamber had multiplied her loathing tenfold. 'I suppose I have no say in this matter.'

'Certainly not,' thundered Scarabold. 'You have no knowledge of allegiances, alliances and allegations. You could not possibly know who would be most suited politically to this penetrative act. The decision has already been made, the bargain struck. The rupturer of the royal crust will mount you at midnight in the appropriate manner, in accordance with the law of the land. The ceremony will commence at half past eleven. Your mother will attend the preparations, and Dr Emeric Fangle will be on hand to instruct you in matters of hygiene.'

'Dando,' hissed Ginansia beneath her breath, 'you have to set me free from this.'

'We agreed you'd go through with it,' replied her half-brother quietly. 'It's an awful obligation, but it's not as if you have to marry him or anything. You never even have to see him again.'

'I know I said I'd do it but I can't. It's a stupid, revolting law.'

'Oh, for God's sake,' snapped the Quaff suddenly, slopping his claret, 'it's just a matter of keeping your legs open and your eyes shut. The women of the family all undergo the ceremony.'

'The women of *this* family,' replied Ginansia sulkily. Somewhere beyond the walls of the castle was another way of living, where families weren't knotted together like rat kings, biting, baiting and barely breathing in the tightest of tangles. Somewhere were places where the young ran wild, where freedom abounded and life was open to an endless azure sky...

'Drifting! Drifting!' screamed Aunt Asphyxia suddenly. 'See, she barely attends to your words, the minx! She needs the member in her fast to take her mind from rumination!'

'Surely you wish to know the identity of your pronger?' asked the Decrepend.

'I wish to know nothing!' cried Ginansia angrily, shoving away from the table and grabbing her half-brother's hand. 'Dando, come with me to my suite.' The boy pushed awkwardly back and joined her, grimacing apologetically to his parents. Dwindoline pouted in sympathy.

'And see she is ready at the appointed hour!' called Moribund, already losing interest as she twisted in her chair to berate the servants for the delay between courses. Behind her, the senior chef bore a huge tureen of bloody meat and knobs of bone, his gore-streaked apron a testament to his bitter, frantic labours. Asphyxia licked her fingers in anticipation.

Ginansia ran. Behind her trailed Leperdandy, the crimson side ribbons on his striped leggings flapping and snapping as he raised his knees in pursuit. 'Gin, please wait, I can't run as fast as you!'

She flew ahead, vanishing around each stone corner with her sapphire gown ruched up around her knees. *She will have to calm herself*, he thought, *or accept sedation before she discovers the identity of her romancer*. Abandoning pursuit, he watched her fleeing figure fold into the misted gloom.

Scarabold was breaking wind in the armoury. His efforts thundered through the filigreed gilt portcullis of the baroque chamber, resonating through the trellis like pummels on a tambourine. A luckless valet named Ratchet shared the room while he attempted to attach a pair of scarlet epaulettes to the fidgeting monarch's ceremonial battledress. The Great Wound raised a cheek of his ample rear and released an alarming fusillade, then fell back against the ambergris velvet cushions on his dressing bench. The valet grimaced and continued thrusting needles into a doublet.

'She has never shown any respect for the traditions of her family,' Scarabold continued. 'And now this unseemly fuss over her Maidenhood Ceremony. She should be pleased to mark her passage into womankind in so firm a fashion.'

'If it please Your Grace,' coughed Ratchet cautiously, 'perhaps the Lady Ginansia has deduced the identity of her suitor and is less than happy to allow him admission.'

Scarabold's face crumpled as completely as if it had been drawn on paper and crushed into a ball. Valets had no opinions, and if they did they should never be allowed to voice them, and even if they *did* voice them should never, ever mention subjects of such indelicacy.

'I mean,' stammered Ratchet, sensing the heat of the royal glower upon his vulnerably thin neck, 'how fiercely she cast her glance aside when introduced to Earl Carapace in the Cathedral of Pons Minor.'

'I do not give a maggot's egg what you think of my choice, you oafish seamster,' he blasted. 'The land is much changed since last they met. Carapace's armies are now the finest warriors in the Dunghills and make better allies than enemies. He has long shown an interest in the youthful glory of the princess.'

The withered valet remembered only too well. During Ginansia's confirmation, on her thirteenth birthday, Carapace had barely been able to tear his gaze from the pale flesh of her bare shoulders. Ratchet gave an involuntary shudder as he recalled the eerie clicking sound the earl made with his throat when considering matters of a carnal nature. Even now he was beetling toward the castle in his iridescent ebony armour to claim the soon-to-be supine body of the princess.

As Scarabold's eruptions, anal and oral, continued unabated, Ratchet returned to work, despairing the fate of females born into nobility. Many years ago he had been employed by the gracious Lady Dwindoline, and look what had happened to her, poor thing, forced to become the Great Wound's second wife because Mater Moribund had failed to secure him a son. Three girl babies had been ceremonially drowned before Dwindoline had finally given birth to the milksop Leperdandy. As the golden needle slithered through his gnarled fingers, Ratchet considered the night that now lay ahead for the princess and her suitor. It was well known that Carapace never travelled without his skittering 'courtiers'. He prayed that Ginansia would somehow find the strength to survive her grim ordeal.

The Great Clock Of Fascinus would have been easier to interpret if it had still sported hands. Unfortunately a slow-turning central spindle and a racing quarter-second arm were all that remained of the timepiece's horological abilities. Ginansia kept it mounted above her bed because the mother-of-pearl face shifted like a sunlit sea. But now the remembrance that Fascinus was a phallic god brought fresh qualms.

'I don't understand why you're so reluctant to help me escape,' she sighed, staring up at the shimmering clock face.

Leperdandy moved the princess's lolling leg and perched himself on a corner of her purple coverlet. 'I don't want you to incur Scarabold's wrath. You know how slow he is to forgive, and a matter such as this bears great importance to him.'

'What about its importance to me?' she cried.

'I mean that the congress carries political weight.'

'And the intrusion upon my body does not.' She sat up sharply and narrowed her eyes. 'Do you know the identity of my despoiler?'

'I have my suspicions.' He coughed awkwardly into his fist.

'Dando, you must tell me the truth. Is it someone I abhor?'

Her half-brother's cough turned into a hacking fit.

'Not that awful man who smelled like a pond and was covered in mud, Plum-somebody . . .'

Leperdandy, crimson cheeked, shook his head and spluttered.

'Or the fat little king who paid court to Mother, the one with the leaky eye . . .' She froze with a sudden thought. 'Not Carapace.'

There was a horrible, confirming silence.

'No, Dando, not the Lord Of Beetles . . .'

'He campaigned long and hard for you,' admitted the boy. 'Scarabold won't be moved from his ruling, and if you fail to abide by his decision he'll treat it as a matter of treason . . .'

'Treasoners must be entombed for life. He wouldn't do that –'

'You are not his blood daughter, Ginansia,' warned Leperdandy, who had once visited the grim, stinking dungeons beneath the castle to see for himself the pitiful bone creatures captured as prisoners of war by the king. These weary albinos with flaking skin and wheedling voices had been forgotten by all except Fumblegut, the jailer, who was rumoured to play elaborate sexual games with his charges in return for food and water.

'Then you must find a way to save me,' she cried desperately.

Her half-brother fidgeted with the quilt, running the fronds of a crimson tassel between his bony fingers. 'There is a way, but you'd be on your own beyond the castle walls. I couldn't come with you.'

'I wouldn't ask you to,' she said, her face softening. 'Just take me to the broad night sky, and I will do the rest.'

At eight o'clock, Dwindoline knocked at the bedroom door and asked to sit a while, but her offer was curtly refused. Ginansia hated to offend but feared that sharing the plan of her escape would place those she loved at risk. Besides, she was not entirely sure that her secret would be safe. As she prepared, she found herself bearing no malice toward Scarabold. Her stepfather had no desire to hurt any member of his extended family, but it was necessary for him to place duty before affection.

At a quarter past eleven, Ginansia rose from her dressing table in a high-necked robe of plain green silk that whispered across the flagstone floor, curling about her like a cubicle. She raised the hook of a slim lead-glass case containing three lit candles and left her apartment, locking the bedroom door behind her, not daring to glance back at her lifelong home.

Tonight the corridors of the West Quadrant seemed alien and friendless. Fewer lamps had been lit than usual, and the leaping shadows were of a deeper hue. The entire edifice was sealed in darkness and cold air like a refrigerator, with the servants waging an eternal battle against rising damp and leaking ramparts. Yet there were pockets of warmth within the castle, and the princess knew them as well as the kitchen cat. She measured her tread to the funereal drumbeat that sounded within the Chapel Of Consummation. The sexangular stone room held a comfortable curtained bed and a basin of warm spring water on an iron stand, having been designed for a single purpose. Mater Moribund had – quite illegally – slept there on those nights when her husband had returned victoriously drunk and muck-encrusted from his pubic skirmishes in the sink towns of the lowlands. As Ginansia approached it now, her heart sank.

The mater was already in attendance, talking softly with Dr Fangle as she watched him wiping his pudgy hands on a strip of linen cloth. Ginansia balked at the chamber entrance. What if Leperdandy had fallen asleep? Consciousness slipped from the sickly youth as easily as an oilskin cloak. She was forever nudging him awake during the Wednesday sermon. What if he failed to keep their finely timed appointment?

'Come, child,' beckoned Moribund, her amethyst wristlets chattering. 'Let Dr Fangle examine you.'

The short, wart-bedecked physician, an unwelcome temporary replacement for Scarabold's dropsical family doctor, revealed an arrangement of yellow teeth and strummed his hand across his housecoat before offering it to shake.

Seated in a wooden-stirrupped chair that seemed to have been designed for the sole purpose of internal examination, Ginansia gave an involuntary shudder as his freezing fingers touched the insides of her thighs. She was frightened that her mother, peering over the doctor's shoulder, would spot the heavy woollen travelling clothes hitched up beneath her gown. A sudden sly icicle ran across her exposed aperture. Fangle grinned into her face. '*Intacta*, veritably,' he whispered. 'Most encouraging.' He reluctantly removed his digit and ran it beneath his nostrils like a fine cigar.

'That's enough, Fangle. Your job here is finished.' Moribund pushed him aside as Ginansia hastily dropped her gown.

'But surely the princess must be taught how to avoid conception and infection,' pleaded the doctor, still staring at her veiled cleft with his forefinger extended.

'Carapace is responsible for the former, and there shall be no need for the latter,' snapped Moribund. 'The earl is also undergoing examination. On your feet, child. You have little time to spare.'

Sweating from her layers of clothes, Ginansia clambered to an upright position. She longed to run screaming into the torch-lit corridor but forced deliberation into her movements so that nothing should seem amiss. In a few minutes she would be on her way to freedom. She took her leave of the ogling physician and fell in behind her mother, who was already retreating from the chamber.

'Of course you're nervous, just as I was long ago,' intoned the mater, swinging her beads. 'Before my coring I presumed all kinds of painful pleasures lay in store. Imagine my disappointment when the great sweating brute dropped upon me like a felled tree and tore at my flowerpot of femininity with a fleshy little twig that discharged its sap and promptly vanished into the shrubbery. No danger of that happening to you, though, as I understand from Carapace's physician that the earl's maleness could steer a tea clipper if raised as a mast.'

Ginansia thought it best not to comment. The fireplace was approaching.

It was common knowledge within the castle that the chimney breasts of all the fireplaces in the Western Quadrant were linked to a central passage lined with ceramic bricks. The original idea had been to light one large fire in the basement boiler and so provide gusts of warm, dry air from fireplaces on every floor, but this plan had been abandoned when the Squeam's mother perished after she fell into the boiler trying to light it. Leperdandy was even now pushing through the elasticated cobwebs of one such passage that ran parallel to the hallway along which Ginansia followed the queen. Separated by a mere three feet of stone, he strained to catch the sound of their progress but could discern nothing.

'I was sure I'd be able to hear them. Bumscuttle!' He blundered into a whiskery nest of spiders, batted the skittering insects from his vision and wiped the webbing from his eyelids. He could hardly see a thing. How would he be able to time his emergence from the fireplace in order to snatch Ginansia?

On the other side of the wall the princess slowed her pace, gradually dropping behind. She needed to put as much distance as possible between herself and Moribund before reaching the great carved maw of the fireplace.

'Don't dawdle, girl!' The queen looked back. 'Carapace is not a man to be kept waiting.'

'I'm sorry, Mother. My hem is caught.' She stopped and affected making a study of her ankle. Leperdandy, hearing the exchange, drew a great breath, burst from beneath the marble mantelpiece in a cloud of soot and grabbed his stepmother, who screamed and stabbed him through the shoulder with one of the many silver hatpins she kept concealed upon her person to deal with Scarabold.

'You've killed me!' gasped Leperdandy, clutching at the protruding pin, his great white eyes bulging out of his sooted face like night-time sea beacons.

'You stupid, stupid boy,' screamed Moribund, whipping the pin from his stinging flesh and tossing it aside. 'This is no time for your idiotic japes!' And with that she seized Ginansia by the wrist and thrust her into the chamber ahead.

'Dando!' Ginansia flung the cry back plaintively as she was swept inside and the door boomed shut behind her. Horrified by his failure, the boy limped into shadow to nurse his burning shoulder.

Moribund was nowhere to be seen.

Her role as procuress completed, she had slipped beyond one of the six chamber walls, leaving her daughter alone with the earl. Carapace stood between a pair of flickering lanterns, barely discernible in his oiled black armour. The susurration of his breath was punctuated with tiny clicks, like an insect rattling its mandibles. Ginansia felt the chill splinters of the door at her back. There were no windows in the cell. Only a bed, a bowl of water, and a freshly sliced lemon set upon the stand 'to cleanse and heal your wound' as Moribund put it. As her eyes adjusted in the gloom, she registered a shimmering movement behind Carapace, as though the purple counterpane was attempting to escape the bed. The earl removed his gloves with deliberation, the leather creaking over his knuckles, and began to unbutton his glistening tunic with a series of little cracking sounds.

'Come closer into the light, my little one,' he croaked,

his throat lacquered with lust.

Ginansia took a small step forward and studied the figure before her. His uncorseted belly hung above his ebony codpiece, but his features were more handsome than she had expected. A goatee hung on his bone-white face like a small black shovel. Elaborate silver rings adorned the rims of his ears. Whatever happened, she would not speak to him. How could the older ladies of the castle have allowed themselves to undergo such an abhorrent ritual? It had no purpose, save to satisfy some ancient law laid down by long-dead ancestors.

There was definitely something moving beneath the coverlet on the bed. As Carapace seated himself in order to remove his leggings and boots, the cloth shifted and rippled around him.

'Come, let me touch you. You have nothing to be afraid of. I am a gentle man.' He raised his arms to receive her. Like a clockwork doll Ginansia shifted forward, her legs moving in tiny spasms.

'If I must be penetrated for the sake of my family,' she stated clearly, 'I will receive no overtures of affection from you.'

'Penetration!' he cried. 'Who taught you to think of love in so clinical a fashion?'

Ginansia was incensed. 'This mockery, sir, has nothing to do with love!'

'But I have loved you from the first moment I saw you, on your thirteenth birthday. I would have broken your hymen upon your communion dais.'

'Oh, this is blasphemy!'

He stopped the shocked oval of her mouth with a searing perfumed kiss. One icy hand slipped into her bodice and cupped her breast, the calloused thumb brushing across the thimble top of a nipple. She tried to pull herself free as he tilted the pair of them back onto the bed.

'This is too intimate – I was not warned –'

'Stay your fears,' he whispered. 'The night is young and we are enormous. We have plenty of time to acquaint ourselves.'

'The night! I was told that the ceremony would last but a few minutes!'

His snickering laugh followed her down as he cantilevered her onto the counterpane. Through the eider feathers she could feel things moving, hard-shelled creatures the size of gravy boats shifting this way and that. Reaching out in puzzlement, she seized a corner of the quilt and peeled it back. Hundreds of black beetles filled the mattress, their polished wing-cases flickering over each other. Recoiling in horror, the princess fought away from the pulsing morass of segmented bodies.

'My courtiers are here to further our conjugal ecstasy,' he hissed, dipping his hand into the heavy, chittering insects and allowing them to run across his arm. 'Now we must obey the natural impulse of their bodies.' One of the beetles was upon his neck, its feelers tentatively entering his mouth.

'Repugnant barbarian!' she screamed, punching at his chest. Her gown tore in his grasp, and the woollen travelling dress beneath slipped free from its silken shell. She fell back from the bed, her shoesoles popping and crunching on the squirming, living floor. Reaching the far wall, she searched for the handle to the door.

'Listen to Lady High-A-Mighty,' laughed Carapace, sitting back on the bed so that the insects could fill his bared lap. 'As if you could afford to choose a suitor for yourself.'

'I will give myself to whomsoever I please!' she shouted, close to tears, scrabbling for the inset brass ring which refused to turn.

'You might try, but who would have you? Who would want someone from Britannica Castle? The door is locked, so calm yourself.'

She turned to face him, sliding her body along the wall. The hidden exit through which her mother had vanished, that was the only answer now. If she could find the door itself she could locate the catch. All secret passageways within the castle opened similarly.

'What do you mean?' she asked. 'Our family is the finest in the land, generations of warriors brave and fair –'

'Is that what they told you? What does the castle look like from outside?'

She caught her breath. 'They speak of golden spires and colonnades so fine that only –'

'They speak? *They* speak? You have never seen the building from beyond it, and do you know why? Because it is not safe for you to leave this edifice. You would be murdered in the winking of an eye. You are prisoners here, outcasts, lepers, Jews. We have left you to peter out, to breed inwards and die. For us to speak with you is taboo, to touch you is punishable by death. Do you know what I risked to be with you tonight?'

'You're lying!' she cried. 'I will not listen to such lies!'

Carapace leaped from the bed in a shower of beetles and pinched her face so hard she squealed. 'Then learn for yourself. Ask your stepfather about your family name, ask him about the noble family from which you are descended. You will find nothing noble beyond the escutcheon that bears your arms.'

Ginansia's Ravishment

'The Baynes are an ancient family, good and wise, just and kind.' She knew this to be true. It was the foundation of all she believed. But she spoke for another purpose; to hold the earl in conversation was to hold him at bay.

'Arrant nonsense, my dear little Ginansia,' he spat, his phlegm-flecked lips an inch from hers. 'Answer me something else. If none of the serving maids dares to enter or leave the castle, how do you think you survive here? What do you live on? What feeds and fattens you?'

'The livestock beyond the river –'

'– are all dead of lung rot and have been for years. No, my dear, you cannot beg the question quite so easily. But surely it is time for you to discover the truth for yourself. Remove the lids of the kitchen cauldrons and look inside if you dare. Or listen to me.'

And he proceeded to tell her what he knew.

'I will not hear this!' The princess buried her fingers in her ears. Carapace reached for her, but she evaded him.

'Ginansia, please believe that I have no desire to hurt you.'

Warily, anxiously, she lowered her hands. 'Do not lie to me in this matter, my lord, I entreat you. This is the only world I know.'

'I merely seek to open your eyes, lady, and to show you what your family will not – cannot.'

But now the passage entrance was at her back with its catch between her fingers, and she fell thankfully into the tunnel, shoving the wall slab shut and running away through the freezing stone space. Behind, she heard him bellowing her name. 'Open your eyes, Ginansia!' came the fading call.

The only light in the dripping tunnel leaked from the cracks between the bricks. When Carapace could no longer be heard, she slowed her pace and drew breath. Wet, steep steps led down, and the corridor curved. She pulled the woollen dress around her, longing for the comforting arms of Leperdandy, the yielding warmth of her own bed. But before that, she had to ascertain the truth. Rest and peace would come only with knowledge that the Lord Of Beetles had lied.

The far end of the corridor was misted with the spicy scent of cloves, revealing the proximity of the kitchens and providing her with a means of irrefutable proof. To her right, a rectangle of buttery light marked the passage's egress. Locating a wooden catch and depressing it, she carefully opened the panel and stepped through. A wall of moist warm air instantly enveloped her.

The crimson-tiled scullery was deserted at this late hour. The gigantic butcher's block table, around which utensils stood in earthenware pots like bunches of steel flowers, had been scrubbed clean. Pulpers, colanders and dough knives dangled in clumps from S-shaped hooks. Light was thrown from the flickering burners of the huge iron stove that extended along one side of the room. Beneath the dull roar of flames below the pots, the princess could hear logs and coals sifting and shifting in the boiler.

She approached the stove, where four great shining saucepans, each of them several feet deep, simmered on the glowing hob. The handle on the lid of the first was too hot to be clasped, so she plucked up a muslin dishcloth and wound it around her fingers. The ring of flame beneath the metal cauldron illuminated her flushed cheeks as she slowly raised the lid.

At once she smelled a dizzying aroma of marjoram, spackwort, cumin and meat, meat most of all as she waved a path through the steam and peered in.

The bubbling brown liquid revealed nothing but surfacing chunks of carrot and fennel. She found a wooden spoon, two feet long and slotted at the bowl, which she carefully lowered into the boiling gravy. The joint within was heavy and hard to raise without slopping juice everywhere, so she was forced to use both hands to balance the spoon.

It was a head, human and male.

Its hair had been shaved away, and the lenses of the eyes had boiled into bulging orbs as hard and white as peppermints. The grey skin seemed loose and ready to separate from the skull. There were no teeth in the mouth, and the lower lip had come loose from the flayed gums. Ginansia screamed and dropped the boulder of meat and bone back into the fragrant depths of the pot, sending its juices hissing and splashing in waves across the burners.

Carapace's words came humming back into her ears. 'For you feed on human flesh!' he had cried. 'The Bayne family, so proud and so regal, are eaters of corpses, devourers of humanity! Why even the name itself is a corruption, from Sawney Beane and his cannibal horde – these are your fine ancestors! And you dare to call me barbarian!'

Bile had risen in her gullet. 'Lies, all damnable lies!'

'Go to the dungeons and see what your father breeds before you damn me treasonous, see what happens to the war prisoners you take. See how their souls reside in the colons of the royal family Bayne! And consider how you yourself have been nourished on the bones of your enemies!'

With a painful howl she ran from the infernal kitchen, leaving the boiling vats of human flesh behind her.

Dwindoline rocked forward in her chair and ran her fingers lightly over her son's fine hair. The boy had slumped his carcass before her fireplace and had barely moved in an hour. Now the apartment was lit only by sinking embers.

'You can't blame yourself,' she said softly. 'None of us can be protected beyond a certain age, and I'm afraid that your half-sister's time had simply arrived.'

'It seems so unfair,' said Leperdandy. 'Why can't we stay innocent forever? Knowledge can only destroy us.'

'You mustn't believe that, child. There always has to be hope for the future.'

Leperdandy raised his head and glared at her. 'What kind of hope? That one day we will be allowed to walk free beyond these walls?'

'Until Scarabold has found success in his endeavours there can be no freedom for any of us.'

'It might help if he didn't cut the heads from those who failed in his negotiations.' Unsnagging his muscles, he rose slowly to his feet. 'I'll go and await Ginansia's return. No doubt she'll need some comforting after her ordeal. Thanks for the advice, Mother, but it's clear you don't have a solution to our predicament any more than I.'

She sighed. 'The young are impatient.'

'And the old complacent.'

Dwindoline watched her son take leave with anguish fevering her breast. She knew she could not change the path of the family, only suffer in silence as each new generation discovered its dark heart.

For the remaining hours of that night, Britannica Castle was filled with tortured bruits: the bitter screams of the mortified princess, the enraged, insane laughter of the beetle earl, the muffled confusions of the boy Leperdandy – and the comfortable, well-fed farts of a slumbering king.

Perfect Casting

This is my first attempt at a noir crime story, and it was such a pleasure to write that I may do some more. It's not a whodunnit, more a who'sgoingtodoit; Edmund Crispin has already covered everything I'd want to do in the former category. Those of you unfamiliar with the creator of the capricious detective-don Gervase Fen should seek out his eleven hilarious, macabre books, or you can borrow mine if you promise to let me have them back.

IT WAS the season of sulphur. The autumn air already held a sharp smell of fireworks. Just beyond the edge of Regents Park, the keepers were raking a bonfire. Peter Tipping noticed spirals of sparks above a sore amber glow of dead leaves just before he turned into the north end of Baker Street. Night had fallen before five. For the next few months darkness would achromatise the days. London was a private city in winter. People remained hidden inside, leaving the buildings to come alive in damp air.

The curving cream stone of the apartment block drew close, and then he was standing below the entrance. Climbing the steps and reluctantly withdrawing his hand from the warmth of his overcoat pocket, he pressed the brass stud and bent close to the intercom, waiting for the familiar sound of Jonathan's voice.

'You're late, Peter.' A hurt tone filtered through. The buzzer sounded, and he stepped into a marble hall. Beyond that, rich crimson carpet and a trellis lift. Chalfont Court was not at home to the twentieth century. There was still a porter's lodge beside the main entrance, still a mahogany box affixed to the wall for the placement of calling cards. The building lodged liverish retired colonels, ancient widows with tiny hyperactive dogs, a couple of discreet escort agencies and a few old showbusiness types.

Jonathan belonged to the last group. His apartment on the fifth floor had been his combined office and home for the past thirty years, during which time business and leisure had lived in easy symbiosis. It would have been impossible to imagine any other arrangement, as the elderly theatrical agent was attuned to receiving lengthy telephone calls near the midnight hour. At this time he would calm his nervous charges, soothe their fears of thespian inadequacy, listen to their analytical appraisals of the night's performance, always reassuring, calming and cajoling.

He wouldn't be doing that for Peter tonight. Peter had let him down again.

'So, you finally made it.' Jonathan pursed his lips and stepped back in the doorway, a balloon-shaped figure balancing on tiny feet, allowing Peter to enter. The passage was lined with posters for shows misbegotten and forgotten, the disco Ibsen, the reggae Strindberg, a musical version of *Bleak House* called *Jarndyce!* starring Noele Gordon, fading signatures from faded stars. Jonathan's fat right fist contained a tumbler filled with gin and irregular chunks of ice, and there were telephones trilling in the distance. Peter was always comforted by the changeless disarray of the flat. This was a place where actors were cushioned and cosseted, heard out and then fed with alcohol. Jonathan puffed past, rings glittering in the dim hall, ready to make Peter a drink even though –

'Even though I'm terribly, *terribly* angry with you.' He entered the kitchen, chipped off an ice chunk and dropped it into a tumbler, pausing to push his spectacles back up the bridge of his nose. Jonathan was constantly in a sweat. It leaked from beneath the auburn wig that fooled no one and trickled beneath his bulging eyes so that his clients were misdirected into believing that news of their backstage woes had moved him to tears. 'One should always be grateful of an audition, Peter, *bitterly grateful*, and you do yourself no favours by acting otherwise.'

Peter had thought the job beneath him, but he hadn't had a decent audition in nearly three months. Playing a jolly dad in a commercial for frozen lasagna wouldn't have been the zenith of his performing career, but it would at least have brought in steady residuals.

'The director was a complete arsehole, Jon.' He accepted the drink and followed the agent through to his desk. There was parkland below the windows of the semicircular lounge, but even during the day it was barely visible through winter mist and traffic fumes. 'I was kept waiting for over an hour, and then asked questions about my motivation by some ad-speaking agency slimeball,' Peter complained. 'I answered him back a little sharply, nothing more, and they told me I wasn't needed any longer.'

Jonathan waved the explanation aside. 'I know, I had them on the phone for half an hour warning me never to send you there again. You're going to be blacklisted by the agency, Peter, the third largest advertising agency in London.' He pushed back-issues of the *Stage* from a leather sofa and sat, daintily crossing his legs at the ankle. 'What have I always said is your biggest stumbling block?'

'Arrogance,' Peter admitted, knowing he was about to receive the usual lecture.

'You've been with me for nearly a year now, and you've hardly worked. You come back with the same story after every audition. You had three – it *is* three, isn't it? – agents before me. You can't go on blaming your representation. It's a matter of learning to handle authority.'

Peter felt the need to explain himself. 'I couldn't see

that there was much authority coming from –'

'*Authority* is anyone who employs you, Peter, and you simply can't afford to alienate them. At least you could wait until you've got the job and you've established a working relationship. Christ, even Larry managed to do that.'

'But you're sending me along for rubbishy little parts directed by ignorant children.' He could feel the gin and the heat of the apartment forcing colour into his face. 'Half of these brats are barely out of film school.'

'You want me to change the system for you? I can't help it if the industry is getting younger around you. That's all there is, you either take it or leave it.'

'Perhaps if I had some new shots done . . .' He had been considering an image change for some time. A new haircut, sharper clothes.

'Photographs aren't going to make any difference, Peter. Let's be honest, you don't look like a classic leading male. Your nose is too long, your eyes are too small and your weight fluctuates. You'd make a good villain, but you're never going to get juve leads. You won't take serious theatrical roles –'

'I can't remember long speeches,' Peter admitted. 'Lots of actors get by without classical theatre.'

'You're not prepared to do panto, so what does that leave? There's no British film industry any more and the network franchises are carving each other up, so you should face the fact that if there's an audition – *any* audition – you have to go for it.' Jonathan wiped the sweat from the edge of his wig. 'That's if you want to work. You're too old to have tantrums, and there's always someone else willing to take the part. As Coward used to sing, 'There's another generation knock-knock-knocking at the door.'

Even though he realised that Jonathan was trying to help him, Peter wanted to punch the smug little man squatting opposite with his empty tumbler balanced on his paunch. He knew the agent meant to shock him into better behaviour but he wasn't prepared to waste his career behaving like a sheep, being pushed about by some snotty MTV kid turned commercials director. Hadn't Hitchcock said that actors were cattle? Had nothing changed since then? It was fine for the pretty teenagers flitting in and out of the office on casting calls, busy enjoying their fifteen minutes of fame, happy to do what they were told, but he was an adult with opinions of his own. He looked across at Jonathan, who was waving his hands as if acting out part of some wailing chorus.

'Oh, I don't know what more I can say to you, Peter. I've always had a lot of working people on my books, some of them very successful –'

'If you're referring to the little queen you placed in the Channel 4 presenter's job . . .'

'That's uncharitable and you know it. He got the part because he was young and he looked right. I mean people like Marc Ford.'

Peter knew all about Marc Ford. Among actors, it was a famous success story. The young player hadn't worked for almost a year. He was down to his last penny, and his wife was pregnant. He'd been offered a small speaking role as a Nazi storm trooper in a low-budget German film being shot in London. As there was hardly any money left to pay the actors, the producer had offered him points at two and a half per cent, and he had accepted. Three weeks' work, standing in a tank of freezing filthy water, then he'd forgotten all about it. The damned thing had won an Oscar for best foreign film and subsequently played to packed houses throughout the world. Marc had retired, a millionaire. He had been advised to take the part by his agent, Jonathan.

'Actually, something did come in today. Not terribly interesting, but worth a bit of money.' Jonathan was a practical man. Having delivered his standard speech he would now attempt to perform some kind of positive deed that would help his boy. They were all his boys and girls. He hadn't much hope for Peter, though. He'd pegged him as one of the bitter ones, an actor who resented success in others and bore the fatal flaw of being unable to acknowledge his own faults. Actors were supposed to see things more clearly. You couldn't trip blindly through life always blaming the director.

He moved back to his desk and unclipped sheets of fax paper from a chrome letter rack, checking through them. 'I had a call from a company called VideoArts. They make corporate promos, and they're looking for featured extras. The first call is Hampstead Heath on Friday morning, early start, dress in your own clothes.'

That means 6 am, thought Peter. *Have to book a cab there, stand around freezing in the pitch dark waiting for the director to show up.*

Jonathan was watching him, waiting for his reaction. It was a test to see if he would show willing. 'Well, do you want it?'

Time to be a good boy. Reluctantly, he agreed to go along.

'Good, now we're getting somewhere.' Jonathan's smile only affected the lower part of his face. He waved the sheet of paper, ineffectually fanning himself. 'The company produces ten promos for the same client every year, and they like to keep their cast consistent. It's just extra work, but they might take you on permanently, which would mean a regular monthly cheque.'

And a regular percentage for you, thought Peter. Another dead-end job that would advance him nowhere. He'd see how it went, but after this perhaps he wouldn't need an agent at all. He had recently heard of a more interesting proposition, a casting call that hadn't come through his agent and had far greater possibilities than a god-awful boring sales promo.

At the Fulham Road gym the following morning Peter checked out the details with Fanny, who worked in the coffee bar. As far as she knew, the rumour she had heard a few days ago was true. One of the actors using the free-weights room had told her – she couldn't remember who. He'd casually mentioned a feature film that was due to start shooting in less than a week. It was being produced by a Dutch, or perhaps a Belgian company, a thriller set in present-day London, but she hadn't been able to understand the title. Filming would take place in central locations for a minimum of six weeks, and because of casting problems a number of male speaking roles were still to be assigned. She remembered the name of the contact but had no telephone number. It would take a bit of sleuthing to find that out.

Fanny was happy to pass on a professional tip, partly because she still hoped that Peter might find her attractive. She was an actress but had been disabled by a childhood illness, and only took roles that allowed her to appear in her wheelchair. The rest of the time she worked at the gym, running the bar, strengthening the upper half of her body with weights and waiting for a man like Peter to ask her out. She had once thought that working here would make her more independent, but the male patrons arrived with inflated egos that pushed her own flimsy sense of courage back into her wheelchair.

Peter tried not to look too excited about the tip. The gym was full of actors who might overhear and get there first. 'You mean it's being shot in English?' he asked, lowering his voice.

'I suppose so. A lot of these people dub or subtitle according to the territory, don't they?'

'Was this guy up for one of the parts? Did he have a script?'

'God, Peter, I don't know. I've only ever seen him a couple of times before. I imagine they'll give the script out to anyone who auditions.' Fanny reached her hand along the counter, hoping he would absently take it. No such luck. She could tell he was already planning his audition piece. She wrote down the name of the production company for him, and Peter headed for the phone booth. At least the kiss of thanks he blew her seemed genuine enough.

Directory Enquiries failed to find the name listed and suggested that he wasn't looking for a company but a specific building. Had he tried the Yellow Pages? He was surprised to find the address registered to a fruit and vegetable market. The woman who answered the number explained that they were indeed auditioning in rooms above the stores. She had an unplaceable European accent, admitted that the film was soon to start production, and agreed to check out his *Spotlight* photograph. If she was interested, she would bypass his agent and call him at home to discuss his CV before making an appointment.

She rang him at seven o'clock that evening and they talked for a full half-hour. Peter exaggerated a little about his recent work and was officially invited to audition on

Friday afternoon. Fighting to contain his excitement, he wrote down the address and agreed to be there. For the first time, he could feel the spotlight shifting toward him through the darkness.

As he entered the southern corner of the park, Peter spotted the other extras. They were standing huddled together in the gloom, like sheep preparing to be attacked. Instantly he wished he hadn't accepted Jonathan's proposal. In a few hours' time he would be auditioning for a real film. He walked over to the nondescript group and stood a little way off. Actors, that is those performers with speaking parts, do not mix easily with extras, whom they consider to be little more than unskilled fans. He knew that they would be forced to speak to each other, though, as there seemed to be no one else around. In the distance bare elms stood on the brow of a hill, thrusting up blackened bones like the spine of some half-buried animal. A sour pink glow edged the sky, the first intimation of dawn.

'Where is everyone?' he asked, breath clouding around him.

'The director's gone with the first AD to sort out payment with the park keeper,' said a small man in a brown raincoat. Shooting on the heath cost two hundred pounds an hour and had to be paid in advance. 'They've already had us rehearsing. There's a lot of mud about. I've just ruined a pair of trousers. Make sure you put in a dry-cleaning bill.'

This was typical extra conversation. They were obsessed with dry-cleaning. Too bad he'd lost the frozen lasagna commercial. At least he'd have had some national exposure in that. Corporate videos never really saw the light of day. Perhaps that was a good thing, though. He wouldn't want some embarrassing early performance turning up to hamper a successful film career.

After a few minutes the director's assistant appeared and explained how he wanted them to move. Lack of enthusiasm dulled his instructions, as if he was being forced to describe the least interesting part of the day's filming. He simply wanted them to move this way and that. Peter's questions were cut short. If actors were cattle, the assistant made it clear that extras were plants.

Half an hour later, Peter could no longer feel his feet. The temperature was hovering around zero. He and the other extras had been running back and forth along the ridge of the hill while the camera recorded their movements from a hollow two hundred yards below them. Peter was taller than the rest of the group and deliberately hung back a little so that he would at least stand out. Occasionally a microphone would crackle and the first AD would warn him to keep up with the others. Apart from commands to go again, there was no other way of telling that they were even being filmed.

'I hate early starts,' said one of the extras suddenly, as if Peter had shown signs of valuing his opinion. 'I live in Barnet, and the travelling does me in. There aren't many showbiz people where I live. You can't buy *The Stage* in Barnet.'

Then they were off again, running up and running back down. No one had told them why they were running, or where they were supposed to be running to. None of the extras had seen a script. Only the main actors were given copies, and they were waiting inside a warm pavilion at the bottom of the hill. Peter could feel resentment building within him. How could the director see them if they couldn't see him?

'Could we go again, quickly please,' called a disembodied voice, as if their movements were being orchestrated by the trees themselves. Peter broke away from the group as it prepared to run once more and set off down the hill holding his arms high, like a surrendering Indian.

'Wait a minute,' he called, 'I have a question. Why are we doing this over and over? You can't possibly see us from down there.'

A bearded man rose from behind the camera and stood with his hands against his thighs. The rest of the crew impatiently dropped their arms to their sides, siding with the director.

'I'm trying to get you lot silhouetted against the rising sun, Mr Whoever-You-Are. Can you go back up *at once* please.' It wasn't a question.

'I appreciate that,' called Peter, continuing nearer, determined to make his reasoning understood. 'You could bring the camera a lot closer and still have the sun rising in the background. At least that way you'd be able to see us a bit better, give us a bit of identity.'

'I don't want to see you any better.' The director separated himself from his assistants and walked up to meet Peter, ready for a fight. 'You're just a group of generic running people. You don't have identities. You could be anyone. That's the whole point.'

'Well, nobody explained that –'

'Because the sun rises fast and we wanted to get the shot quickly.' He looked up at the hill. 'But that was our last possible take, and now the sun is too high. I think you'd better go, don't you?'

It was humiliating, having to walk away from a group of people who were so obviously angry with him. Upsetting the extras didn't matter, but he hated falling out with the crew in case he found himself working with them again. Clapper loaders, first assistants and sound men freelanced in each other's crews, and turned up all over the place. Sound crews were usually men because of the weight of their microphone booms, which had to be constantly held aloft. Peter liked crews and got on well with them. They were professionals, like him. Extras were nothing, star-struck spear carriers who got paid a tenner a night for standing behind a throne through three acts.

He hoped Jonathan wouldn't hear of this latest fiasco too quickly. The misunderstanding could jeopardise his film audition. It would be easy for someone to put in a call and spoil his chances. All work was supposed to go through the agent. Peter was expected to call at the end of the morning shoot, so he went to the public library at Hampstead and hung around until lunchtime, then rang from a pub callbox. He assured Jonathan that everything had gone well, and the agent's replies were relaxed and pleasant, as though the day's first bottle of gin was already improving his view of the world.

Back out in the street it had begun to rain hard. Shoppers loitered disconsolately beneath awnings, waiting for the downpour to ease. Peter kept a beret in his pocket and pulled it on to keep his hair dry. It would have helped to know something about the role he was going for. He checked the address he had written down and headed for the tube station.

The afternoon was already darkening when he arrived at the Edgware Road, skirting filthy puddles to locate a small turning between the kebab shops and falafel bars. Walking to the far end of the street, he found himself in the remains of a cobbled road, facing an old Victorian warehouse of the kind beloved by film location managers.

Heavy steel shutters sealed what had once been entrances for horses and carts. The base of the graffiti-stained building was steeped in rubbish and chunks of rotting vegetable matter, swept from the market that operated inside during the day. Several small windows had been shattered, but all were barred and lined with spikes. For any normal job interview, the building would have sparked feelings of anxiety and revulsion. Peter knew better than to be alarmed. He could see the fierce yellow light shining behind the broad first-floor windows, light that could only be thrown by the 10K lamps of a film set.

As he searched for a door, he marvelled at the extraordinary manner in which film business was conducted. A pretty girl could be picked from the pages of *Spotlight*, her agent called and an appointment made. She could then be sent to an abandoned farm, a lunatic asylum, a den of rapists, and she would happily go along in the hope of landing a film part. It seemed so obviously dangerous he was surprised no one had put a stop to the practice. But that was the way the system had always run. Casting agents were tucked above tube stations. Rehearsal rooms sat behind strip clubs and chip shops. Dressing rooms were converted toilets. But not for the ones at the top. And not, he hoped, for him.

Peter found the notice pinned across a narrow doorway set in the end wall. It read, simply: AUDITIONS 1ST FL. As he climbed to the top of the unlit stairs, he passed a man of his own age coming down. The other actor threw him a cold smile before passing into the street, a sure sign that auditions had started. Pushing open the landing door, he found himself in a vast wood-planked room that ran the entire length of the building. At one end the windows had been whitewashed over, and a simple screen-test area had been constructed. Before it, half a dozen people sat in plastic chairs softly questioning a nervous-looking young man. Peter approached and was waved to a bench against the wall. After a few minutes the actor ahead of him was dismissed, and the team made notes, consulting with each other. Then he was beckoned to the vacated seat, like a patient customer about to receive a haircut.

One of the men rose, shook Peter's hand and introduced himself as Mr Ostendorf. Behind him stood a collapsible plywood table with a single sheet of paper on it. He consulted the typed list. 'You must be Mr Tipping.' His voice bore a trace of an accent.

'That's right.' Peter beamed a smile at the assembled group and shifted in his chair. It was hard to tell which one was the director. Ostendorf ticked his name on the sheet before reseating himself.

'Allow me to introduce everyone. Miss Deitch I think spoke to you on the telephone.' He gestured along the line of chairs, starting first with an attractive young woman who turned out to be the producer's assistant, then pointing to the director (why did all directors have little beards?), the cinematographer, the writer and an arrestingly beautiful woman of middle years, the costume designer. 'I myself,' Ostendorf explained, tapping his chest, 'am merely the producer.' Everyone laughed politely. 'In my own country I have much experience in casting, but here it is more difficult, and you must be patient with me. So –' He gestured about himself with a friendly shrug. 'We are casting now only one role, and we shall perhaps tell you a little of this character and his story. Then we have you read a page from the script, yes?'

'Fine,' agreed Peter, trying to see how many other names there were on the page Ostendorf had consulted.

Christ, it looked like they had seen fifteen people already. All eyes turned to the director. He was an elderly, tanned figure in an immaculate Italian suit and reminded Peter of photographs he had seen featuring Bertolucci's cinematographer, Vittorio Storaro. Could it even be him? But no, the old man introduced himself as Joachim Luserke and had a strong, almost comic German accent. As he spoke, he paused to draw on a heavy, wet cigar that appeared to have burnt itself out.

'We are a Netherlands company,' he began slowly, 'releasing feature films through Columbia Tri-Star in Europe. This film is a modern-day thriller entitled – in your language – *Hour Of The* –' he looked around for help, unable to translate. '*Jackals*' said the writer, an exhausted-looking man in his late twenties.

'There is already a film called *Day Of The Jackal*,' Peter interrupted, then stopped himself from saying more. Better to take Jonathan's advice and get the job first before offering his opinions.

'This was long ago, yes?' Luserke waved the problem aside with his cigar. 'It does not concern us. People go to the cinema for only seven years of their lives, that is the average, and the film you mention is more than seven years old I think.' Peter was impressed. He was not used to having someone listen to what he had to say.

'I explain the plot to you now because not all of the script is translated to our satisfaction. It concerns a wealthy businessman whose son, Jack, is kidnapped one night while working late in his office. He searches for the young man – here, there – but he does not find him.'

The others were watching the elderly director's gestures with amusement. They clearly enjoyed seeing him act out the story. It was probably the sixteenth time he had done so this afternoon. 'Then he discovers the truth. Jack has been taken by –' He checked with the others for the approved designation of the phrase, 'social terrorists, who plan to keep him imprisoned as an example to the complacent business world. They will use his capture as a propaganda weapon that will bring them great power. The police – pooh! They do not believe our hero. He alone must come to the rescue. He finds out where Jack is being held, but it is too late. One of the terrorists argues with the young man about his privileged position in life, secured for him by his father, and kills him in a fit of fury before he can be rescued. Now they will come after our hero's wife, and he must convince the police of the conspiracy –'

'Wait, wait.' Ostendorf raised his hand. 'I think this part is not necessary to tell. Wait until we have the new translation.'

'When could I see a fully translated version of the script?' asked Peter. The project sounded interesting, the plot uncompromising. This was the kind of subject matter European film makers handled so well. It was probably a metaphor for the human condition, very profound.

'We will not give you the complete script unless you win the part, but you may read the pages which feature your role.'

'Which part is on offer?' he asked. Was it too much to hope for the lead?

'I hope you won't be offended when I tell you it is the part of the evil terrorist,' laughed Ostendorf.

'Not at all.' Peter smiled back. Jonathan had thought him perfect for a meaty, villainous role.

He was handed half a dozen pages on which the character of Dr Emil was scored through with a yellow highlighter. In order to provide him with some interaction, the producer's assistant read the role of Jack, the hero's captive offspring. The tone of the piece was sombre and oblique, the exchanges awkward, as though English was not the author's first language. After the read through, Peter raised his hand. 'There's a problem with the English translation,' he pointed out. 'It's very stilted. I could paraphrase my lines and get a better reading out of it.'

'I think for now it would be better if you stayed with the words you have,' replied Luserke firmly.

Peter could take a hint. Tidying the pages, he sat back and waited for a response. The group talked quietly among themselves. Heads were nodding. Only the art director seemed to be in dissent. Finally Ostendorf rose and turned to Peter with an outstretched hand. 'We believe we have found our evil doctor,' he said, smiling warmly. 'You are happy?'

Peter thrust his hands in his pockets and beamed his thanks back at the group. 'I am very happy.'

'Good. Now we take some test pictures of you to show our backers.'

'What do you mean, they're shooting before signing your contract?' asked Fanny. 'I've never heard of such a thing. Your agent certainly wouldn't allow it.'

'My agent is never going to find out about it.' Peter reached across the counter and emptied a container of apple juice into his cup. The gym was empty and about to close. Rain pattered against the skylight far above them. 'The guy playing Jack is a big-deal star in the Netherlands and they only have him for four days. It's not a large part but it's the key to the film. I'm going to be playing my lines with a stand-in. Obviously I have to do it before the set is struck, so they'll film my performance at the same time.'

'Then why not put the two of you together in shot?'

'For Jack's scene with me he's tied to a chair with a bag on his head. He doesn't need to be there.'

'Just make sure you get the contract signed as soon as possible.' Fanny was growing bored with all this talk of Peter's success. He never asked her how she was doing, why she still spent her evenings serving sandwiches to walking lumps of muscle tissue when she could be pursuing her dream, running a course for disabled actors. She had known all along that she would never be much of a stage success, but she was sure she could teach. She was prepared to settle for something more satisfying than pouring coffee. What she needed now was advice.

'But you'd advise me to do it even though the contract's not through, wouldn't you? I mean, they seem like pretty trustworthy people. It's a big company. They're not going to run off without paying me.' He was looking at her intently, waiting for an opinion. She threw up her hands, knowing that he would only hear what suited him. So many actors were like that. 'Sure, take the job. It's what you want.'

'I knew I could rely on you to steer me to stardom.' Peter reached down and kissed her on the forehead. 'I'd better go. Big day tomorrow.' He swung his gym bag onto his shoulder and headed for the door.

She could have killed him. It was the forehead kiss that made her most angry, as if he didn't see her as a woman, or the possessor of any kind of sexual identity. Grunting furiously, she wheeled her way back behind the counter and began turning out the lights. Peter was a typical bloody actor, completely closed to the real needs and purposes of other people. She hadn't seen it in him before, or perhaps she'd hoped that he would be the one to break the mould, but he was the same as all the rest. She didn't mind them lying, but it was boring when they lied to themselves. No wonder his girlfriends never stayed around for long. She certainly wouldn't be there for him after tonight. Far too much acting, she decided grimly.

Rain blanketed the city, sheathing the rooftops in a grey shower curtain of mist. It flooded the gutters, coursed over pavements, breached the drains and ruined Peter's chances of making a decent impression with his new shoes. Filming was about to commence in another old warehouse. This particularly run-down specimen was tucked behind the tube station in Tufnell Park, hidden by a row of shops that were either covered in For Sale signs or were already derelict and seemed to be spouting water from a thousand broken pipes.

Peter looked for the telltale glare of the spotlights, but found none. Studio lighting was always turned off between takes because of the intense heat it generated. Besides, the set was supposed to be low lit, so he doubted that anything could be seen from the road. He found the producers waiting on the second floor with a small crew (below British union requirements, certainly) and a simple set of rubble and straw, in the centre of which was a single wooden chair. Bound to it with ropes around the torso and legs was a rather unrealistic dummy, intended to represent the young hostage. Luserke came over and greeted Peter warmly.

'I hope the late hour does not upset you, Mr Tipping,' he said apologetically, 'but we have been having some trouble with the lights.'

'Nothing serious, I hope?' Peter looked over at the

single cable trailing behind the set. There didn't seem to be enough lighting here to go wrong. But then, the scene they were about to film was an intense one, and every element had to be exactly right.

'You will be pleased to know that our "Jack" is so far very good,' the director continued, anxious to please. 'He finished his part of the scene today. I would have liked him to stay here for your lines, but he is a big star in his country because of a television show, how you say *sitcom*, and he will not sit with the bag like so.' He indicated the linen sack gracing the head of the mannequin, whose left leg looked as if it was about to detach itself completely. Wherever the money was being spent on this production, thought Peter, it certainly wasn't going into the props.

'The dummy doesn't look very convincing,' he complained. 'Couldn't you make the scene more realistic by getting someone to take its place while we film?'

'I think we will not need to do so. Watch please.' Luserke gestured to one of the crew and the set lights came on, throwing a dingy blue haze across the chair and its occupant. With the figure half buried in indigo shadow, its imperfections were lost to the darkness. 'I am more concerned with your close-ups tonight, and your speech, which we will do in one take. I think we will not need to feature our Jack in clear focus. If you would like to take your mark on the set –'

'I haven't been made up yet.'

'Made up.' The phrase seemed new to him. Luserke looked over to his producer, who said something in German. 'Now I see. This was not made clear to you before I think. No make-up for this scene. The light, the blue light, will be on your face.' Peter looked back at the low glow of the set and hoped it would be bright enough for his facial expressions to register. This was to be an emotionally draining moment. He didn't want his performance to be lost in the gloom, like it had been with the extras on the hill.

He made his way past the shattered-looking writer who was sitting with his head in his hands, nodded to Ostendorf, who was whispering into his mobile phone, and found the gaffer-taped cross on the floor of the set. Ostendorf had told him that he needed to learn only two pages of dialogue for this first night's shoot, which involved the end of his scene with the hostage and the moment of fury in which he kills him. The producer felt that, as he would be addressing a plastic dummy rather than a live actor, it would help to start with the least interactive part of the sequence.

Peter studied the lolling, strapped-up figure and rolled the handle of the carving knife between his fingers. Although to his eyes the set appeared absurdly unrealistic, he knew that through the camera lens it would take on a strange reality, so that even the luminous turquoise lighting would somehow be appropriate. The lengthy scene was divided into sections, the last part involving a ranted monologue from Peter which culminated in him stepping forward and thrusting the knife into the mannequin's chest.

By the fourth rehearsed take of his 'fury' speech, the crew were egging him on and applauding. Encouraged by Luserke, who sat forward on a stool beside the camera studying Peter's every movement with glittering eyes, he grabbed the chair back with one hand and with a despairing scream thrust the knife deep into the gut of the dummy, splintering the plastic shell to bury his fist deep within the kapok and foam interior. The director wanted his inner rage to surface, to slam against the floor and walls until it exploded into unstoppable violence.

During the final rehearsal Peter caught himself thinking, *This is what it's really about, to be in the centre and in control, to reach inside and draw emotion from the heart, to feel the sheer naked power of performance.* He had reached this point by his own efforts, not through some agent looking to cream off a percentage. This was just the start, a glimpse of the future making itself clear to him, a fabled city appearing through a calming sea. *Enjoy the moment*, he told himself. *Make it last.*

They took a short break and the film magazine was loaded for the first take. Peter returned to his mark and stared across at the battered dummy strapped to its chair, chunks of torn rubber clinging to its cream plastic chest.

'Peter, could you come here a moment please?' Luserke called him over to query an inflection at the end of the monologue, tapping the speech with a nicotine-stained finger.

'I can handle it that way if you like,' he conceded, 'but it's a long speech, and by the time I get to the end my voice has risen so high it's hard to control.' Peter promised to try his best, but he knew that he'd do it his way. The matter was out of his control. He could only give his talent full rein and shape the power as it grew within him.

'Your mark, please. Quiet everybody.' The crew quickly returned to their places.

Peter reached his spot and looked up. Rain still blurred across the skylight. The knife handle was warm in his hands. The lights dimmed even lower than in the rehearsals, and the room fell silent, so that the only sounds came from the rain above and the breath catching in his chest. He could see nothing beyond the shadow of the dummy and the straw-lined edge of the set.

Slowly, carefully, he began the speech.

The anger flowed from him as he accused the captive young man of having all the things he could never have, of squandering his inherited power, of wasting a life that paid lip service to truth and decency while perpetuating an immoral, divisive society. He felt the bile rise within him, felt real hatred for this golden boy who knew nothing of the real world, who had never tasted the hard lives of working men and women, and forward he ran with the knife at his waist, thrusting it out into the bound ribcage of his captive in an explosion of bare rage.

The first spray of warm liquid jetted into his face, blinding him as the next boiled hotly over his fist, which still clutched the knife. He tried to pull his hand free from the dummy's chest but it was trapped, caught between the flesh and bone of the hostage's ribcage. There were no lights at all now, only the scuffling of feet and the slamming of a distant door. As he fell to his knees he knew he had cut into a real, living body with the foot-long blade and that even now the roped-up figure was sinking fast within the coils of death, leather-soled shoes drumming madly on the floorboards until the chair toppled onto its side and the form bound to it lay still and silent, but for the steady decanting of its blood.

The crawl across the room in darkness seemed to last a lifetime. When he finally found a light switch he was frightened to turn it on. Two bare bulbs served to illuminate his blindness. He looked down at his shirt, his hands, his trousers, at the gouts of blood, as if someone had emptied the stuff over him in a bucket. The camera, if that was what it had been, had gone. There was nothing left in the room except the 'set', a pile of bricks and straw, a pair of gel-covered standard lamps set on the floor in either corner, a wooden chair and the cooling corpse of a young man, bound at the hands and feet, and taped at the mouth.

It took him a moment to realise that the room wasn't quite empty. Something else was over everything. His fingerprints – on the body, the chair back, the floor, the walls, the knife.

And even as his confusion lifted to be replaced with mounting fury, he wanted to know not why but how. How had they come to choose him, of all people? Because even now he could not see the blindness in himself.

And then what hurt most of all, what really cut into his heart and burrowed into the little soul he had, to lie there stinging and burning in a wormcast of purest agony, was the disappearance of the audience who had witnessed his greatest performance, and the knowledge that his moment of triumph had not been captured.

It was a pain he had only just begun to nurse when the police broke in the door.

Tales Of Britannica Castle:
II. Leperdandy's Revenge

This began as a separate Britannica story, but preceding events had clouded the characters' minds; it would have been unfair of me not to provide some kind of resolution. Exotic grotesquerie becomes hard to sustain without collapsing into caricature, and I'm not sure I'll do any more. Peake fans will find parallels once again.

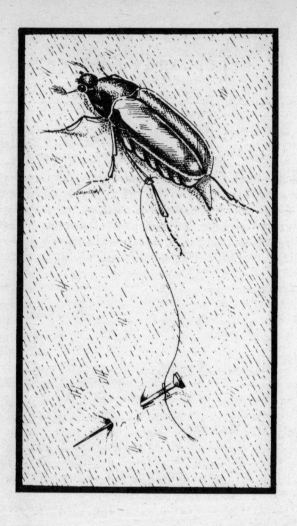

'YOU MUST eat something,' coaxed Dwindoline, raising the steaming ladle of bone broth to her half-daughter's parched lips. Ginansia coughed and knocked it aside, spattering an Arthurian arras with ruby droplets and shreds of gristle. She dropped back onto the bed, sinking into the dull-gold pillows.

'How can I eat, knowing what I now know?' she asked. 'My bile rises. I shall never eat again. The shame of it, to think we are descended from common cannibals!'

Dwindoline knotted her dimpled hands in her lap and sighed. 'So many generations ago,' she whispered, her breath clouding in the chill bedchamber, 'and born of desperate necessity. How could we help but follow their tradition when it was all we ever knew?'

'Decency should have told you to desist. I despise the entire Bayne dynasty.'

'Then you must despise yourself, my dear,' said Dwindoline gently, 'for you were fattened on the braised flesh of traitors, just as we all were.'

Ginansia's opal eyes turned to her. 'Did you never think it was wrong?'

'I thought it the way of the world.' Dwindoline tugged at a stray brown thread poking from her dirndl. 'When we are children, we assume that everyone else is like us. When we discover the truth, we have to adapt.'

'Then I shall adapt as well.' She reached down beside the bed and pulled out a raffia parcel of carrots and radishes that Leperdandy had thoughtfully delivered. 'The family has found its first vegetarian.'

'Your father won't be pleased.'

'My father is dead. Killed in the stupidest of all the stupid wars. My stepfather can be buried alive by the blind gravediggers of St Minch for all I care.' She bit disconsolately into a carrot. The sound was like snapping wood.

'Scarabold is too angry to countenance your presence at table. He has allowed Carapace to stay on at the castle and is attempting to placate the earl, whose alliance he needs. Your maidenhood ceremony may yet take place.'

'Not while this body has a breath left in it.' The girl flummocked onto her side, the bedsprings chiming. The wind moaning through the arrow slits of the East Quadrant turrets sounded like a distant mad organist. Dwindoline felt she should deliver a warning.

'The Great Wound will not wait for your agreement in this matter, Ginansia. As I try to placate him, Mater Moribund goads him on.'

'I can fight my own battles.' Ginansia raised herself on one arm, studying her stepmother with returning affection. 'Don't fret. I'll meet with Scarabold and disarm his argument.'

'That, my doveling, is something warrior kings have failed to do,' said Dwindoline, sadly stroking her hair. In these grim times, she seemed to be forever comforting her disillusioned offspring. Outside, the wind wailed in sympathy.

'I must see for myself,' said Ginansia firmly, 'and you must take me.'

Leperdandy uncrossed his skinny legs and rose from

the marble dais, pacing to the window and staring down through the smeary stained-glass at the weatherbeaten hedgerows lining the moat. His face was as pale as lightning. 'I once descended deep into the heart of the prison chambers,' he murmured, 'and it is not a sight for female eyes – nor any who value their sanity.'

His ears pricked, and he yanked open his bedroom door before the second knock. Aunt Asphyxia, all velveteen and liverspots, stood with her bony fist still raised.

'Conspiring!' she cried, the word emerging from her frayed vocal cords as a muzzled scream. 'Always tucked away, the two of you, whispering and plotting!'

'How could we be, Aunt Asphyxia, with you lurking around to spy on us?' asked the boy in mock exasperation. 'Ginansia wants to visit the dungeons. Shall we let her?'

'Germs!' screamed the old lady. 'Disease, deformity and diarrhoea! No woman is allowed to take such risks!'

'Did you want something specific?' asked Leperdandy, looming in the doorway to prevent her entry.

'Tell the girl she must acquiesce!' Asphyxia suddenly screwed up her eyes and scratched her mottled nose to prevent a sneeze. It gave her a face like a diseased parsnip. 'She must apologise to Carapace and beg for his carnal attentions!'

'I don't think there's going to be much chance of that, Auntie.' He started to shut the door, but she thrust at him in an angry cloud of mothball musk.

'You have no inkling of the consequences, you useless young fop! We cannot afford to make an enemy of the earl! Loyalties must be forged!'

'Then the Great Wound will have to exercise some diplomacy for once.' With that, he slammed the door shut.

Leperdandy raised a slim finger to his lips, halting his half-sister's laughter. 'She'll be hovering outside for ages yet,' he whispered, 'and she's not as harmless as you might think. From her ears, straight to Britannica's war room.'

'Will you take me down to the prison cells or must I go alone?' his half-sister asked.

'Fumblegut will never admit you, and you should be glad of that. His tastes are more exotic than the excesses of your imagination. Better by far to begin with Scarabold.'

'Do you really think so, Dando?' Her headstrong ideas were usually mitigated by Leperdandy's guidance. 'Then I should go to him now. Reparation without surrender. I will have my wishes observed.' She rose from the bed with a creak.

Leperdandy worried a cuticle and watched as she washed her cheeks in rosewater and donned an evening robe of deepest sapphire. She showed her mother's determination, even if she lacked the authority to access her desires.

'Gin, if Scarabold consents to a confrontation, you will try to be –' he searched for a word that would not annoy her, '*reasonable*, won't you?'

'Reason is as reason does,' she replied, clasping a gold opera necklace over her breastbone. It was a family heirloom, a pendant chain hung with six flawless cabochon-cut rubies, Scarabold's favourite. Leperdandy furrowed his alabaster brow. The princess was unversed in the art of discretion, and her stepfather would not take kindly to accusations. He began to regret suggesting a meeting so clearly fraught with dangers ...

The Great Wound had wondered how long it would take

his errant stepdaughter to come a-creeping back in abject apology and gave a smile of satisfaction to see her humbly seated on the edge of the battered crimson recamier in the reading room. He strode across to the vast granite fireplace and scratched a match into his overloaded briar, filling the chamber with a smell akin to burning sweet wrappers. Ginansia had woven tiny violets in her hair and laced them through her bodice, appearing an image of innocence in the mistaken hope that it would sway Scarabold to her argument.

'Gad, you're a headstrong minx and no mistake,' he complained, 'but I'm prepared to bygonify your quarrelsome attitude if you are willing to renounce your vestal status and comingle with the earl Carapace.' He tamped down his pipe bowl with a fat sepia-tipped thumb, clearly expecting no response.

'That is quite out of the question,' the girl replied hotly. 'I came to speak of another, far more serious matter.'

'What could be more serious than the perpetuation of our line?' The Great Wound hissed and sucked at his pipe, peering at her with his good eye through a cloud of cinders as though discoursing through a raked bonfire. 'If we fail Carapace now he will deny us the alliance that secures our future. Don't you see, you silly girl, how our fate is entwined with his?'

'You hated him once,' answered Ginansia. 'You told me that the iron rule of the Bayne dynasty held the entire valley in its grip.'

The old king softened as he remembered. 'The world has changed, my petal-pudding, and we are driven to befriend our former enemies. That is why I ask your help and pray that you can understand our predicament.'

Ginansia had no wish to hurt her family; her life knew

no one else, for the castle had few visitors. She began to appreciate her role in the destiny of the Baynes – and to understand the bargaining power it afforded her.

'I shall attempt to do as you wish, stepfather – on one condition.'

'Condition?' asked Scarabold suspiciously. 'We don't have conditions.'

'I must visit the dungeon chambers wherein you keep our war prisoners. If you deny me this, I would never surrender myself to the Beetle Earl in a thousand years.'

'But why would you wish to enter such a dreadful place?' demanded her stepfather, genuinely confused.

'To meet the people we eat,' she replied, trembling with indignation. 'I wish to see the men we breed like cattle and slaughter to fill our bellies.'

Within the undergrowth of his vast beard, Scarabold's lips were pursed in anger. Who had informed the child, and to what purpose if not to upset her? Even he could see what damage the knowledge might have on one so lacking in the family ways.

'So you know,' he said simply.

'We are butchers of men and that is all you can say?' cried Ginansia, ending her determination to remain calm. Before Scarabold could formulate an appropriate attitude, the princess burst into a furious fit. She accused her stepfather of treason and murder and much worse besides, of lying and hiding, of cowardice and bestiality. She said many things she had no intention of saying and wrecked any chance of a reconciliation between herself and the king. More harmful still, she ended the diatribe by renouncing her name, something no member of the family had ever dared to do.

Scarabold was apoplectic. In a fiery cloud of briar

embers he banished the girl from his limited sight and ordered that she should remain confined to her quarters. Ginansia ran from the room in a flood of tears and ransacked most of the East Quadrant searching for the bonily comforting arms of Leperdandy, but he was nowhere to be found. She returned to her chamber and fell onto the bed, drifting quickly into a bitter, miserable slumber.

An hour later she was awoken by the sound of nails being heavily driven into her bedroom door. She counted forty of them, long iron shards that protruded through the oaken piers of the door arch. She tried the handle but it would not budge even a tenth of an inch.

She was sealed in.

Forced to reply to her bellowed questions, two servants shifted from spandrel to keyhole and admitted that they were carrying out Scarabold's wishes. Her meals would be delivered through the gap beneath the door, and she was to remain incarcerated until she saw the error of her ways – however long that might take.

Spackle and Peut were running through the corridors of the castle's skewed seventh floor playing Dead Man's Sting, a game requiring intimate comprehension of its convoluted rules and an attitude of extreme spite. The twin progeny of Aunt Asphyxia were spoiled brats with barely a single original thought to share between them, and were consequently used by their mother to spy on the rest of the family. Asphyxia was not, in fact, a genuine aunt but an embittered widow inherited by Scarabold after he had made a promise to her dying husband on a gore-soaked battlefield. In the emotional turmoil of the moment, the Great Wound had forgotten that his old friend's wife was pregnant and so had found himself providing for the only family inhabiting the castle that was not directly blood related. He did not approve of the twelve-year-old twins; their sly, underhand meddling offended his warrior sensibilities. He would have approved of them even less now, for they had been sent at their mother's command on a spying mission. Spackle stood at Earl Carapace's door, and Peut stood on his brother's shoulders, peering through an engraved blue crystal transom. The cut and thickness of the glass gave him only the vaguest of refracted views but magnified the voice of the Beetle Lord into reedy sharpness.

'There must be a way to make her see reason,' he was insisting, unaware that she had already glimpsed it after unsealing the kitchen's cooking pots. 'Why, she's no longer a girl but a mature woman, luscious, full, bulging, a fragrantly moist plum, ripe for plucking and peeling.'

'Your trousers, sir.' That was the valet's voice. 'The buttons are undone.'

'Is it any wonder,' sighed the earl, attending to his groin.

'He's smitten with Ginansia,' Spackle whispered downward, always prepared to state the obvious. He resettled his boots on either side of his brother's spine. 'I don't know why he doesn't force himself upon her and have done with it.'

'Not everyone's like you,' hissed Peut, arching his sore back.

'And now that the Neanderthal Scarabold has sealed her up inside her bedchamber, how am I supposed to plight my troth?' There was a rip of silk as Carapace put his elbow through his shirt. The exasperated valet was attempting to dress his master as he paced. 'His loyalty to me is touching, if transparently political. Presumably the

Great Wound hopes to curry my favour by punishing the child for refusing to succumb. His actions have left us all without a choice.'

'Do we have to stay here much longer?' croaked Peut. 'My bones are cracking.'

Beyond the door, Carapace's valet offered a solution. 'If I might be so very bold as to make the tiniest of minuscule suggestions,' he began, the servant deferring to nobility with the acquiescence of a whore collapsing into bed, 'why not perform a service for the princess and endear yourself to her by fulfilling her desires? She's locked away; there must be something she needs, and such an act will confirm your allegiance to her against the wishes of her stepfather.'

'Now I remember why I keep you on!' cried Carapace. 'For someone who lives in a world of socks and silver polish, you occasionally produce a superlative idea. I'll venture to her rooms at once.'

'He'll never be able to get her door open,' sniggered Spackle, hopping down. 'Come on, let's get there before him.'

As silent as a sunset, they entered the wet stone corridor running behind the panels of the fifth floor and made their way through the maze of dripping brick. It was within these walls that Suppurus, the disgraced Knave Of Chaucery, had avoided his scheduled beheading by remaining hidden for five days and surviving on his own regurgitated vomit. Although that was nearly a hundred years ago, his person, mummified by the crosswinds of the rumbling latrine flues, could still be found in the passageway with the index finger of its right hand wedged firmly in its throat.

The twins arrived minutes before the earl and secreted

themselves in an alcove opposite Ginansia's room, behind a weevil-chewed tapestry celebrating one of Scarabold's most senseless massacres. Ginansia's door looked as if it would not be opened without the aid of a battering ram. Shortly, Carapace strode up, ran his tapering fingers across the pounded nailheads and brought his lips to the edge of the keyhole.

'Ginansia,' he called gently, 'I am mortified to find you imprisoned like this. Perhaps there is something I can do to secure your release.' The twins failed to discern the princess's reply as the draughts blowing along the corridor rattled and banged the tapestries, obscuring all sound from within her apartment. Peut peered out through a tangle of rotted stitches. Carapace seemed to have been granted an audience, for he was listening intently at the mortice and nodding to himself. He shifted position, listened some more, then wrinkled his forehead in alarm as a small sheet of folded paper was slipped to him from beneath the door. Gingerly, he unfolded the page and studied it with augmenting consternation.

'What you are asking is utterly impossible,' he cried, refolding the sheet. 'If the king found out he would have me killed in some brutal, lingering fashion.' He hunched against the door again.

'Of course I desire it, with all my heart, but how can I –? Yes, most certainly I wish to prove myself to you, but is there really no other way that I can help –'

A boot kicked at the door from within, sending Carapace reeling. It was clear that whether Ginansia's terms were met or not, she meant business. The earl deposited the slip of paper in his jerkin and set off at a lick.

*

Spackle and Peut were stumped. As spies, they had failed miserably. All they knew was that Carapace might or might not have agreed to aid the princess in some treasonable enterprise of her own devising. Asphyxia would be far from pleased by this incomplete bulletin. Spackle scraped a curtain of ragged black hair from his eyes and stared at his brother. Whatever Ginansia had requested of the Beetle Lord, it was sure to cause upset in the rest of the household.

'We'll have to follow him everywhere,' said Peut, 'use our initiative. Either he'll do as she requests and antagonise the crown, or he'll rat to the Great Wound and lose her forever.'

'What about the princess?' asked Spackle.

'Forget about her,' came the reply. 'She's not going anywhere. Few would help her, and they dare not risk the anger of the king.'

'What about Leperdandy?'

'Pouting milksop!' Peut snorted derisively.

'Wheedling catamite!' added his twin.

'Simpering sodomist!'

'Bulgy bilge bottom!'

How they laughed as they crept back into the brick-bound rookery that would lead them once more to Carapace's quarters.

Ginansia paced the floor, wringing a yard of olivine damask in her pallid hands. Outside, rain sprayed from the buttresses and leaked through the broken tracery of the stained-glass windows, discolouring the herringbone parquet upon which she stepped. To have defied her poisoned family and be rendered so completely powerless! Leperdandy meant well but could only fail her, and even the

Beetle Lord had quailed at her demands. She had simply entreated Carapace to prove his love by visiting the dungeon chambers and arranging for the immediate release of all the prisoners held there. Was that too much to ask for? The family would be forced to curtail its cannibalistic behaviour, and in the ensuing aura of normalcy Ginansia would at last be heard. She would be a clear voice of reason, someone to lead the Baynes out into a bright new dawn.

Or so she thought.

In truth, Scarabold was not prepared to heed his errant stepdaughter, even if the direst of circumstances demanded it. Fate had always ruled the castle, her broad dark wings smoothing and combing out the terrible events of the years, and that was not about to change.

Fumblegut was pounding a mouse flat with an iron mallet. Two more and he would have enough for a hat. Too lazy to bother with skinning them, he simply smashed away at the pinioned rodents until their guts had departed their hides. He flicked the mouse innards from his pudgy fingers, then buried his hand down the back of his trousers and gave the sweating cleavage of his rump a good scratch.

As he rose and kicked the mallet aside, he decided that it must be time to eat again. Below ground there was no telling night from day. The only source of illumination came from flesh-tallow torches, and the only whisper of the outside world descended from the distant hissing of rain on tin gutters. Nobody bothered him down here. Nobody wanted to know what went on. Nobody dared to take even the smallest peek. And that suited the jailer down to the straw-strewn gore-soaked ground.

Fumblegut wondered about the boy in cell 71, a

spirited young colt who had followed his father into pokey by admitting a minor act of vandalism against the Bayne escutcheon. A rowdy lad, he was, forever hammering his food plate against the bars, but of tender appeal. Fumblegut fancied burying his teeth into the child's plump buttocks but was forced to content himself with a cold tongue sandwich and a pot of porter. Although some dank recess of his mind had registered the increase in the number of cockroaches and stag beetles scuttling over the flagstone floor of the dungeons, Fumblegut failed to spot the spindly form of Carapace. The earl was sliding from shadow to shadow as he unlocked the prisoner's cells with the iron hoop of keys he had found tossed on a nearby table by the careless jailer.

Carapace had determined to do the bidding of his beloved; well versed in the ways of darkness, he slithered through the stinking cubicles like a passing eclipse, so that when the gloom lifted from each holding pen, the inmate within could discern a door now standing ajar.

Fumblegut had no idea he was being robbed of the castle's future meal supply. Ensconced in his private chamber, he focused only on the bottom of his draining pint pot.

Carapace could see that many of the dungeon's denizens would be unable to leave unaided. Some had been fattened up so much that they could barely raise themselves on their pustulant haunches. Crimson sores on the legs of others forced them to remain in strange static positions. Flesh had withered and rotted on arms too long chained together. Here were diseases and tortures beyond imagining, and the results of these twin horrors lay moaning in their own filth. But the earl had obeyed Ginansia's edict, and thus his mission could be counted a success.

A further torch-lit cell stood alone at the end of the muck-plastered corridor, separated from the rest. Carapace looked back anxiously at Fumblegut's closed door, convinced that any minute now all hell would break loose; the dazed prisoners were starting to emerge, and the sound of their shuffling movements would soon reach the jailer's ears. But curiosity had bettered him and, determined that his liberation would not be incomplete, Carapace approached the distant lone receptacle with key hoop cocked.

He reached the single jail room and read the notice pinned to the lock:

FEED BUT DO NOT TOUCH
By Order Of His Majesty The King

He tipped his ear and listened to a laboured wheezing, then squinted inside. For a moment the cell's darkness refused to yield the figure within. But as the poor inmate's features clarified in torch light, everything became apparent.

What little colour there was in Carapace's face drained as he took a stammering step back. Someone clearly knew about this; someone would pay, and someone else would have to be told. He reached out to unlock the door but the keys jumbled themselves together in his hands, and then Fumblegut was emerging from his room to find himself jostled within a swirling cotillon of crazed inmates. It was clearly time to leave. Storing away the sights he had witnessed, Carapace searched for the entrance to the passageway that the princess had so carefully described. Ginansia possessed hand-drawn maps of almost every area in the castle, even though she had ventured to fewer than half of them herself, and had passed one to him beneath her bedroom door. Now he prayed that he could decipher it with enough speed to make good his escape. As he hunted the secret alcove, he forced himself to remember that any risk was worth taking for the warming glow of the princess's approval.

Imagine this: As Carapace was making his way back through the castle armed with his explosive nugget of hitherto hidden knowledge, Leperdandy was undertaking his own carefully plotted revenge for Ginansia's sake. Following a secret plan of his own devising, he first visited Dr Fangle's temporary office just beneath the leaking roof, then he crept unseen into the kitchens to fiddle about in the scullery, and finally he made his way to the Heart Of All Sorrow for a last-minute amelioration of the dining table. Satisfied with his arrangements, Leperdandy prepared himself for the evening meal.

For the past two hours, Spackle and Peut had been annoyed and confused. After trailing the Beetle Earl from Ginansia's apartment, they had lost him somewhere within the corridor walls. It was as if he had been provided with secret knowledge neither of them possessed, almost as if he'd been given a map. Peut slapped himself on the forehead; what about the paper that had passed beneath the bedroom door? It meant that Carapace was doing the princess's bidding, which somehow, obliquely, spelled trouble for them. And now he was back outside her chamber, angrily removing each of the forty nails with a hammer claw.

What in the name of Beelzebub Bayne was going on?

The Dining Hall was illuminated by forty-one tall candles,

the number of days into the year. The candle boy dreaded December. Scarabold, always the first to table, was seated between Mater Moribund and Dwindoline. The Quaff had been sequestered in a poorly lit corner, the better to hide his bibulous demeanour. Aunt Asphyxia, unusually, had brought the twins to her side. They slouched to the left and right below her like a pair of badly potted ferns. Leperdandy, resplendent in a silken-starred waistcoat of midnight blue, touched his hair nervously as he watched and waited.

The Decrepend was droning on through the Blessing even though two further place settings had yet to be filled. He stopped so abruptly that everyone in the room looked up.

Ginansia was standing in the doorway on Carapace's arm.

Scarabold's mouth fell open. His stepdaughter was wearing a floor-length cream lace gown interwoven with honeysuckle buds. Their scent quickly filled the room, banishing the reek of candle tallow. The earl was bound into a corsetted leather military suit ornately knotted with lengths of polished steel, darts that had been removed from the bodies of his enemies.

As the couple took their seats, no one could think of a single thing to say. Scarabold's immediate reaction, to blaspheme foully and throw his fists about, quickly subsided. Mater Moribund's eyes settled on the couple and narrowed slightly before she turned her attention to the pouring of the soup. Leperdandy, however, was shocked into another century. He had expected – counted on – Carapace to appear, but couldn't imagine what Ginansia thought she was doing. Ginansia knew very well what she was doing.

After he had removed the last of the nails, Carapace had informed the princess of his trip into the dungeons, and as he described his freeing of the prisoners she had seen a saviour's light aglow in his eyes. She felt sure that the mission she had given the earl had changed his nature, although she was a little surprised by the success of her pleas. And if she had not consented to marry him, she had at least agreed to go through with her deflowering ceremony.

But first there was a matter of proof. She had made Carapace promise that he would reveal his act of liberation to the Great Wound before announcing that he was now willing to form an alliance with the family Bayne. This way everyone would achieve a limited degree of happiness. Scarabold would have a strong new ally, Ginansia would have ended the castle's dependence on human livestock, and Carapace would have somewhere to bury his virtually permanent erection.

If only it had worked out that way.

At first, the only sound in the room was the clicking of spoons in bowls. The soup appeared to be cream of turnip, but Ginansia pushed hers to one side in case there was something of a more human nature lurking at the bottom. The Beetle Lord ate heartily, ignoring the fascinated stares of Asphyxia and Leperdandy, then smeared his napkin across his shovel beard, cracked his knuckles in a series of tiny pistol shots, and requested everyone's attention. A cockroach fell out of his tunic and was hastily flicked aside.

It was a moment upon which the future of the great and damned Bayne family hung. For Carapace was about to reveal the one discovery he had so far withheld from the princess – a discovery that would reshape the destiny of this dynasty.

Ginansia's worst fears were realised as the soup plates were efficiently replaced by steaming platters of grey stew. Nausea caressed her belly as she recalled uncaulking the steaming kitchen pots. Carapace, a lump of gristle already pendent from his fork, spoke out.

'My Lord, Ladies, Your Grace, you might well be wondering how I come to be seated here at table with the princess.' He lowered his fork in the ensuing uncomfortable silence. 'The fact is that Ginansia agreed to my terms on the fulfilment of a certain condition. Namely, that I should enter the dungeons below us –' a silence deeper and more horrible than the previous one ensued – 'and free the prisoners held therein.' He looked around the table, confronting a set of stony glares. 'You all know the purpose of penning up those poor unfortunates, even if you prefer to turn a blind eye.' He paused for dramatic effect before preparing to deliver his bombshell. Even now, those prisoners were presumably burrowing up toward the Dining Hall and were about to burst through the doors. He could not know that Fumblegut had successfully halted the mass escape by flooding a section of the dungeon passage. Carapace held the sweetness of the moment. 'But,' he was about to say, 'there is one prisoner kept in a solitary cell whose flesh is not for the delectation of his betters.' Indeed not, for at the far end of the dungeon he had discovered none other than Ginansia's real father, the Pater Moribund himself. Carapace slid the meat-laden fork into his mouth, savouring the taste of victory.

The earl was an ambitious man. He had affected to enjoy Scarabold's company so that he might receive the attentions of his stepdaughter. But his discovery opened up another possibility; by revealing that the Great Wound had locked away his rival and lied to his family, he would earn Ginansia's gratitude and Scarabold's enmity, both of them desirable commodities. Better still, he would shatter the family Bayne forever, watching as it descended into a bitter web of hatred, suspicion and treachery.

'Now I am able to reveal the truth,' boasted Carapace, chewing slowly. He took a sip of cloudy water, enjoying the looks of puzzlement that surrounded him. Revenge was truly a dish best served cold.

But not served as stew.

For suddenly he began to cough, then to choke, and then to scream out. And thick dark blood started to stream from his ears. Everyone watched in horror except Leperdandy, who stared down at his plate. The powder he had removed from Fangle's poison cabinet had been liberally shaken over Carapace's dinner plate. Poison dusted his cutlery and glittered at the rim of his water glass. And what an awful poison it was, capable of causing epilepsy in a month-old corpse as it dissolved each internal organ. Leperdandy had won a terrible, bloody revenge for himself and Ginansia. Now there would be no dynastic alliance, no deflowering ceremony, no reconciliation with his elders. Scarabold would no longer see him as an ineffectual fop but as a powerful political force to be reckoned with.

Things would have to change.

He smiled to himself as the earl sprayed gouts of blood about the place before vanishing backwards beneath the table with a disgusting gurgle. Silence fell once more as Ginansia gingerly raised the tablecloth and stared slack mouthed at the cascading blood fountain that had been the Beetle Lord until a few seconds ago.

Leperdandy had prepared a short speech to explain Carapace's alarming demise. He caught Scarabold's good eye and was momentarily shaken by the Great Wound's odd reaction.

The king was smiling.

Then he lowered his fork once more, dug into a mound of streaky red meat and shovelled the lot into his mouth. 'Well,' he burbled, speaking through fat and gristle, 'it's a bloody shame the earl got took sick. I wouldn't touch his portion if I were you. S'pose we'll never know what he was going to talk to us about.'

Leperdandy sat back, appalled. What had he missed? Where had he gone wrong? Scarabold was pleased to see the earl murdered and clearly wasn't prepared to be bothered with details. Slowly the suspicion dawned on him that someone else's plot had interfered with his own.

The Great Wound sat back and chewed happily. His kingdom was safe and sound once more. Carapace had discovered the truth about the pater, but fate had lowered her ebony wings across his path, bearing him away into a land of eternal night. There was no need for the others to know that the old king still lived. He glanced absently about the table, wondering which of them had done the murderous deed. But what did it matter, so long as life continued without change?

In Britannica Castle that terrible stormy night, Ginansia howled in rage and grief, Leperdandy was tangled in sheets of nightmare guilt, and the king slumbered peacefully on, his log-saw snores shattering the nerves of his two exhausted wives and just about everyone else within earshot.

The Most Boring Woman
In The World

There's an advertisement for running shoes or sausages or something that reads, 'Wherever you are, be somewhere else.' Surely most people are anyway. J G Ballard was once described thus: 'He doesn't care where he lives, because he lives inside his head.' It's impossible to know what others are thinking, or whether their self-evaluations are accurate. That gap in perception gave me this, which led in turn to my most recent novel, *Psychoville*.

I CAN'T imagine why you'd want to interview me, I'm the most boring woman in the world.

I'm nobody. Nothing interesting ever happens in my life. I live in a house like thousands of others, in a banjo crescent called Wellington Close in a suburban part of South London, in a semidetached with three bedrooms and a garden filled with neatly pruned roses that have no scent and a lawn covered with broken plastic children's toys. I have a labrador called Blackie, two children, Jason and Emma, and a husband called Derek. I keep my clothesline filled and my upstairs curtains closed (to protect the carpets from the sun – blue fades easily) and my days are all the same.

Derek works for a company that supplies most of Southern England with nonflammable sofa kapok. I met him when I was a secretary at Mono Foods, where he was senior floor manager. One afternoon he came by my desk and asked me out to the pub. I'll always remember it because he drank eight pints of lager to my three Baby-chams and I'd never met anyone with that much money before. Six weeks later he proposed. We were married the following June and spent two weeks on the Costa where I picked up a painful crimson rash on the beach and had to be hospitalised in a clinic for skin disorders.

Before that? Well, nothing much to report. I was a happy child. People always say that, don't they? My older brother, to whom I was devoted, died in a motorbike accident when a dog ran out in front of him, and at the funeral they muddled his cremation with someone else's, an old lady's, so that we got the wrong urns and her family were very upset. Also, the dog was put down. Things like that were always happening in our family. On Christmas Eve 1969, my father got completely drunk, fell down the coal-hole chute and landed in the cellar, and nobody found him until Boxing Day. His right leg didn't knit properly so he had to walk with a stick. One day the stick got stuck in a drainage grating, and he had a heart attack trying to pull it out. My mother passed on a few weeks later. They say one often follows the other, don't they? I lost a cousin around the same time, when a gas tap jammed in a Portuguese holiday villa.

No such calamities ever occur now. Now my days are all the same.

When I was young I was a pretty girl, with straight white teeth and hair that framed my face like curls of country butter, but I didn't know I was pretty until I was thirteen, when John Percy from three doors down tried to rape me in exchange for a Chad Valley Give-A-Show projector. I told my mother and she went over to the Percy house. They moved away soon after. They had to. John came around and hit me when I opened the front door to him. He broke my nose, and I wasn't so pretty after that.

When I was sixteen I wanted to go to art college, I wanted to be an artist, but my father said there was no call for it and I would be better off in an office. So I went to work for Mono Foods, met Derek, got married. I didn't have to or anything, it just felt like the right thing to do. He seemed interested in me, and nobody else was, so I said yes. My father joked about it being a relief to get me off his hands, but he wasn't really joking.

For a while we moved in with Derek's mother, but that didn't work out because she hated me for taking away her son and stood over me in the kitchen while I cooked, saying things like, 'That isn't how he likes his eggs,' until I felt like strangling her. Then I fell pregnant and we moved here. We put her in a very nice old folks' home, but the first night she was there she wrote and told me I was cursed for stealing her boy, that she was going to die and that it would be on my conscience forever.

The awful thing was that she had a stroke that night and died, and I had to go into therapy. Derek took his mother's side, and while he didn't actually call me a murderer to my face, I knew that was what he was thinking.

Since then I always joke that I'm not addicted to Valium, I just like the taste.

My days are all the same.

Here's my routine:

The white plastic radio alarm goes off at seven-fifteen. The DJ makes jokes about the day's newspaper headlines as I rise and slip into a powder-blue dressing gown covered in little pink flowers. I'll have been awake since five, lying on my back listening to the ticking of the pipes as the boiler thermostat comes on. Derek sleeps through the alarm. I wake him and he totters off to the bathroom moaning about his workload and complaining about people at the office I've never heard of because I'm just a silly housewife who can't retain any information that isn't about the price of fucking washing powder.

I drag the children out of their beds and pack them off to wash and dress, make them breakfast (cereal and toast in the summer, porridge in the winter), check that they're presentable and send them to school. Derek usually finds something to bitch about, like I've ironed his shirt with the creases going in the wrong direction or there's a button missing from his braces, and tuts and fuffs until I sort out the problem. Then he takes the Vauxhall, leaves me the Renault and the house falls silent. And I sit down with a cigarette, a nice glass of Scotch and a Valium.

They don't know I smoke. I have to wash the ashtrays and open the windows before the kids get back.

During the day all sorts of exciting things happen. Last Tuesday the knob came off the tumble dryer, on Thursday next door's cat nearly got run over, and on Friday I found out that my husband was having an affair. Her name is Georgina. She works in his department. His pet name for her is 'my little Gee Gee', and she explains all of the awkward, stilted phone calls that take place here in the evenings. If you're going to have an affair it's a good idea to remember to empty the pockets of your trousers before you give them to me for dry-cleaning, that's all I can say.

I don't get on with the neighbours. The stuck-up bitch next door won't talk to me because I once got a little soused in the middle of the day and fell into her fishpond. Sometimes I sit in the car and rev the engine just to blow smoke over her washing.

Jason and Emma come home and lie on the floor on their stomachs in that curiously impossible position children use for watching television. They remain glued to cartoons, space serials and Save The Fucking Zebra updates, all presented by some perky fresh-faced teenager I'd secretly like to ride naked.

I cook. I make sausage, egg and beans with chips, and fishfingers with chips, and beefburgers with chips, and chop, chips and peas. Everything comes with chips at number 11 Wellington Close. I'm the only one who doesn't like chips. I'd like to cook *langoustine* swimming in garlic, *loup grillé* with capers and shallots. But you can't get *langoustine* around here, just *doigts de poisson avec frites*.

I don't eat with the others. After the smell of frying has permeated my clothes I'm no longer hungry. I have a brandy. I keep a bottle at the back of the sink. Sometimes Derek comes into the kitchen to refill the saltcellar and finds me on all fours with my head somewhere near the U-bend, and I tell him that the waste disposal is playing up again.

Then I clear away the dinner things while Derek provides more news about the people he works with and who, for me, only exist as a series of names with personality quirks attached. The Byzantine intrigue of the sofa kapok world is such that if Lucrezia Borgia applied for a job she'd barely make a secretarial position.

I don't wash up very well. By now the kids are yelling and I'm getting jumpy. Anything I drop goes in the bin. Nobody notices. Nobody notices anything. My days are all the same. I listen to the pounding in my head and watch as the lounge fills up with blood. You can't see the telly when there's blood in the way.

At the weekend I go shopping. Sometimes I go shopping in my mind, but I don't come back with anything. Oh, how we love to shop! B&Q, M&S, Safeway, Tesco, Homebase, Knickerbox, Body Shop, we just wander around lost in amazement at the sheer choice and ready availability of luxury products at the end of the twentieth century. If the excitement was running any higher it would be leaking from our arseholes. Derek doesn't come with us, of course; he stays behind at the house to creep around making furtive phone calls from the bedroom. He says he's 'doing the accounts', presumably a coded phrase that means 'telephoning the trollop'.

On Sunday mornings we rise later than usual and I prepare a cooked breakfast before Derek heaves his flabby body from the chair and chooses between the pastimes of straightening up the garden and hoovering his floozie's hairpins from the car. Do they still have hairpins? I can't remember the last time I saw one. There are so many things you don't see any more. Those little pieces of green string with metal rods at either end that used to hold bits of paper together. Animal-shaped Peak Freen biscuits. Jubblies, sherbet dabs and Jamboree Bags. You never see any of them any more. Instead I see the white plastic radio alarm clock and the powder-blue dressing gown and the hairs on Derek's indifferently turned back.

The first time I took speed I got all the housework done in under an hour. It was great. But I felt so tired afterwards that I couldn't cook, and Derek had to go and buy us all fish and chips. Speed helped me to organise the household. Thanks to the speed, which I got in the form of prescription diet pills, I not only started collecting money-off coupons, I catalogued them all in little boxes according to date, value and type of offer. I just never got around to using any of them.

I have never hit my children. Not even when I caught Jason smoking in the toilet and he was abusive. It would have been hypocritical of me. Is punching hitting? Sometimes I don't remember things very well. I have lapses. Little bits of housewife downtime. Sometimes the children tell me I did something when I'm sure I didn't. The dog won't come near me any more, and I think it's something to do with one of those vanished moments. I think I fed Blackie something bad.

When we argue, which is quite often these days, Derek always tells me that I never learn. I try to learn, but it's hard to get motivated when you're alone all day and you know exactly what's going to happen from the minute the white plastic radio alarm goes off until the time you set it again at night. I don't like the nights. It's when I feel most alone. We go to bed, read magazines and sleep, but we don't speak. I lie there listening. Derek's furry back is turned away from me, the children are unconscious, the streets outside are black and silent. It's like being dead, or being buried alive, or some damned thing.

Wait, here's something new I learned. Cocaine, Valium and Lamb's Navy Rum don't mix at all well. I got the cocaine from a man at the shopping centre because I'd just had a huge fight with Derek and it seemed like a good angry response to his wheedling, wide-eyed denials. I'd already drunk half the bottle of rum to get my nerve up, and the Valium was a matter of habit. I opened the little paper packet of coke and chopped it finely on the breadboard with my M&S card, then snorted it up through a Ronald McDonald straw. The kids were in the lounge watching adults get green slime tipped over their heads on TV, and I was off my face in the kitchen. I threw a careless glance at the lasagna filling the oven with dense grey smoke and thought, hey, it's takeaways again tonight, kids!, chucked the burning lasagna in the dog's bowl and crawled under the sink for another hit of rum. Derek was at the office 'attending an extracurricular staff meeting', which roughly translated as 'bunging the bimbo one in the photocopying room', and I no longer gave a toss about the world or anything in it.

I love my children because they're my flesh and blood. But I don't really like them. Jason, without intending to, has learned to be sly and grasping and is already watching his father for tips at gaining a better foothold on the easy life. Emma is, well, *bovine* is too unkind a word. Slow to catch on, shall we say. She stares slackly with eyes like chips of glass and only becomes animated before certain TV programmes. These children are from me, but not of me. Each day they become a little more like Martians, shifting away from my embrace with each incomprehensible new habit learned in the school playground. And as their language grows more alien, as the cults and rituals they design to be misconstrued by adults grow more elaborate, I lose them a little more each day, meal time by meal time. Every mother knows that her children eventually leave. I just hadn't expected the process to start so fucking early.

Derek works on winning the kids over to his side, of course. He can only allow himself to be seen as a hero. He teams up with them against me. Fathers often do that. Nice habit.

The house is quiet now. But then, it always was quiet. Our fights were conducted in a series of controlled explosions that wouldn't wake the children, muted insults escaping like hisses of steam.

It was important to Derek that we also presented a unified, peaceful front to the neighbours. It didn't take them long to cotton on, of course. The bin bags filled with bottles were a giveaway. Well, Mr and Mrs Rodney Boreham-Stiff next door can go and fuck themselves as far as I'm concerned. They're dead from the wallet up, like everyone else around here; you want to talk about politics or art, they want to ask you how you get your windows so clean. Everyone's a Stepford Wife. We have television to thank for explaining to us the importance of germ-free, pine-fresh tiles in our lives.

I'll admit it now. At some point, I lost the plot. I could no longer remember my set routine. Housewifely duties became unfathomable to me. When the alarm went off I would rise and stand at the bedroom window, looking down into the deserted dawn streets, wondering what on earth I was supposed to be doing. How to function as a mother and a wife. Was it get up, wash the kids and iron the breakfast, or make dinner, fry the dog and kill the husband? I asked the children, but they didn't know. Just got frightened and ran to Daddy. Big brave Daddy.

When Derek came home early one day and told me he was leaving for good, heading off into the sunset with his little Gee Gee, I was heating oil in a copper-bottomed omelette pan. Bad timing, big mistake. The pan left a series of concentric rings on the side of his face, and the oil badly burned his neck. The second time I hit him it dented the back of his head with a crunch, like putting a spoon through a soft-boiled egg. He dropped to his knees in complete surprise and pitched onto his back. I wanted to make sure he was dead, so I cut open a cushion and stuffed his mouth with kapok. I expected my civic-minded neighbours to call the police any minute, complaining of hearing 'raised voices', as if such indications of human life should never be given, and I began to panic. I imagined being led away through a crowd of gawping, tutting onlookers to a waiting car. But before agreeing to go with the police, I would tidy up the kitchen and tearfully say goodbye to the children. And I thought to myself, if only one of you could have met me halfway, just to show that you cared, I wouldn't have had to murder someone. But I had, and he was lying on the kitchen floor, a halo of coagulating blood expanding on the diamond tiles, and I had to do something about it.

So I put him in a bin bag.

Well, not one, about three, but it wasn't at all difficult. I did it without thinking, as though it was the most natural thing in the world to do. Derek wasn't a large man, and I was used to manhandling sacks of rubbish, and before the kids were back from school I had him trussed up by the back door ready for collection. I squeegeed up the blood, rinsed the mop and replaced it, then showered and changed and came back downstairs just as Jason walked in, asking what was for dinner.

That night after the kids were in bed I entered the garage from the house, put the bin bags in the Renault and drove over to the edge of the estate, where there was a gravel pit that the council were landfilling so they could built yet another Tesco nobody needed but would soon be hypnotised into using. I dragged the bag across the back of the carpark and gave it a good shove down into the pit, then kicked a load of rubbish on top of it. Then I went home and watched 'The Late Show'.

I didn't plan any of this, you understand. I simply acted without thinking about it. The police would turn up and arrest me and that would be that.

But they didn't. The next morning, Derek's office called to find out where he was, and I told them I had no idea. The kids asked in a half-hearted way, and I told them the same thing.

I didn't go to the police and report him missing, because if they came calling I knew I could say he'd run off with his mistress. Instead I opened a fresh bottle of rum, got pissed watching 'Pebble Mill', and got away with murder.

When I was a little girl, I believed that you got what you deserved. If you were very good, you were rewarded with a lovely house, a husband and children. If you were disobedient, you would never meet anyone and die a bitter, loveless death. Now I know that it's the other way around; you get what you don't deserve. And I didn't deserve this frozen life where my days are all the same.

Oh, but they *are*. You think they should be different since I murdered my husband? And you wonder why I chose to confess to you?

Well, because I only just made the murder part up.

I didn't really kill Derek, even though I had the opportunity. He's still alive. We did have a row about his fancy woman, but he promised to put an end to the relationship. He hasn't, of course. And I missed my chance to conk him on the head.

But it's always there in the back of my mind, the knowledge that one day I might just go berserk with the Black & Decker. Hack his dick off, saw the dog in half, drink rat poison and set fire to the house while the children are in bed. Sometimes I get up in the middle of the night and watch them all sleeping, and I wonder if they realise how much danger they're in. I stand above Derek as he snores lightly, his head buried deep in the pillow, and I want to pour lighted petrol into his mouth.

Each day they bring themselves closer to a reckoning with me. And they have no idea, because our days are all the same. Soon there'll be screams in the night, power knives, lamps being overturned, doors slamming, flames and madness.

Or perhaps there won't.

I have to go, my husband will be home from work soon and the dinner isn't on. I don't know why you wanted to interview me, anyway. I'm just like everyone else around here – more so. I'm the most boring woman in the world.

At the moment.

The Unreliable History Of Plaster City

The history of a small American town may only span a couple of centuries, but it's liable to be a colourful one. It may be peppered with those By-Jiminy tall tales beloved by settlers, marked for infamy by white supremacists or born-again fanatics – or steeped in the kind of supernatural shenanigans that seem so appropriate to wide, western spaces. This is my venture into Stephen King territory.

WHEN OTIS Dagg decided to swat blackflies from the wall of his motel room he shouldn't have used the butt of a loaded twelve-bore shotgun, because the damned thing went off and some of the pellets perforated the plaster-board room divider, rupturing the left eardrum of the woman next door. Her name was Betty Segal, and she'd been resting her head against the wall watching a game show, trying to think of a six-letter country beginning with *M* and waiting to see who'd won two weeks of amoebic dysentery in Mexico, when suddenly she found herself smothered in specks of blood, and buzzing in the ears like a nest of pissed-off hornets had been tipped over her head.

It took Betty a while to figure out what had happened, but when she finally did she went even crazier, physically attacking poor confused Otis, who was still casting puzzled glances from the end of his gun to the ragged hole in the wall when she burst screaming into his room like a Valkyrie in a nylon housecoat. She managed to bite him on the face a couple of times before one of the porters pulled her off, and later successfully sued his ass in a brief but embarrassingly ugly court case.

Naturally, Otis didn't have too much to lose – he wouldn't have been staying in a joint called the Forty Winks Motor Lodge if he had – but he skipped town at the first available opportunity just to get away from the

Neanderthal brothers of the woman he had rendered deaf, both of whom looked like members of the World Wrestling Foundation and had threatened to tear his arms off if he failed to meet his payments. Since Otis Dagg didn't hang around long enough to cough up any compensation money, the court took away the only piece of property he owned, a small clapboard building with a collapsed front porch that stood at a crossroads in the industrial end of a small town called Plaster City, 217 miles from Los Angeles, and they granted the deeds to Betty Segal.

Betty had spent all her adult life in a trailer park and the prospect of living in something that didn't have wheels appealed to her, so she moved in. She passed her time happily there, leaning out of the slanting porch window to watch the trucks roar by, and eventually compounded this pleasure by finding a man uglier, deafer and richer than herself to marry. Tony Marco sponsored the local basketball team and made his money in the furniture trade, so when he rebuilt the old Dagg property he turned it into the only furniture store in the area that had a full-sized basketball court in the car park. The parents of the players attending Plaster City Junior High could often be seen leaving after a game with armoires and dining chairs loaded into their station wagons, and pretty soon the old store sold anything you could name, provided there was a demand for the item and it could be turned around for a profit.

And so it was that, twenty-two years later, after a spectacular vein-ripping heart attack had slam-dunked Tony Marco out of life's final quarter, his widow took to her room above the store and left the daily running of her business in the hands of an experienced manager who had recently relocated from San Diego.

The manager was a tall, stooped man with narrow eyes and an uncomfortably furtive attitude that made his customers think he was in the Witness Protection Programme. His name was Taylor Hollings.

By this time the property sported a large red and yellow plastic sign reading VALURAMA, which sounded more like a Hindu god than a discount furniture store, and until 1987 it functioned as the Plaster City equivalent of a shopping mall. Extensions had been added to the front and back in violation of every known zoning law, which was okay because the councillors all shopped at Taylor's store and knew that if they complained about what he was doing with the property he'd accidentally cease to stock their favourite monthly magazines. Business was good and life went on, most of it bypassing Plaster City completely and barely bothering to call in at any other town before hitting the West Coast.

Taylor met a widow called Barbara Stokely, who was driving through in a beat-up Oldsmobile Cutlass one summer and made the mistake of stopping for gas and directions. Something in the store window caught her eye, Taylor probably, and she married him and pretty soon had three kids, Big Joey, David and, with a sigh of relief, Julie. Shortly after this her biological clock threw a cog and she became tranquilliser-dependent. But in the meantime there were golden years, while her three children grew up in and around the old store.

To an impressionable youngster the place was a spidery Xanadu, filled with corridors that led nowhere and storerooms full of forgotten end-of-line items, stuff that didn't sell and hadn't been returned. Behind the stacked boudoir chairs and plastic-covered vanity bureaux were all manner of hidden delights: X-ray goggles, Aurora model kits and packets of dried sea monkeys, BB guns and useless boxes of magnets, Hallowe'en masks, back issues of *Aquaman* and *Famous Monsters Of Filmland*, and giant weather balloons that no one knew how to inflate. The building even provided its own scary monster in the form of old Mrs Marco, still deaf, still crazy and still living in the room at the top of the house. Barbara fed her and changed the bed, and the children took turns to visit her in the evenings, but the room smelled of piss and lavender and she never did anything except complain about the weather and how terrible the TV shows were and what a lousy hand life had dealt her, so going upstairs to see her became something of a reverse lottery.

David Hollings used the make-believe possibilities of the furniture store more than anyone else in the family. Although he hero worshipped his older brother, Big Joey was practical and unimaginative and spent his spare time helping their father with deliveries, and Julie was an asthmatic china doll who wasn't allowed to play near dust, which ruled out all of the downstairs storerooms.

It was a lucky thing David enjoyed staging complex battles in the labyrinthine depository, as Plaster City had little else to offer a hyperactive child. It wasn't a proper country town with a summer creek you could jump into from a rope and winter hills designed for tobogganing. The only river ran past a factory that made rubber grommets for faucets, and nothing with a central nervous system could survive in it for long. There was a large, perpetually arid park, mainly used by Mexican families for barbeques, and a lookout point that didn't look out over anything and should have been renamed Drop Point, considering the amount of dope that changed hands out there. This was where most of the town's kids went to lose their virginity, and on Sunday mornings the grass around the car park was slick with knotted condoms.

More than anything Plaster City was like a suburb, but there was no nearby metropolis to which it could attach itself. For many years the nearest place with a population of over five thousand was Bakersfield, and that was a damned long way off. Every August, choking grey dust blew in from the distant fields, and the furniture store became Flies-R-Us. Every January, shiny new snow-ploughs came out to clear the streets, only to return to their garages when the powder failed to settle. Still, there was always religion to keep idle souls occupied. Plaster City was a Baptist town with a vengeance. It seemed like there were more churches than any other kind of building and twice as many preachers as believers. Everyone could offer an explanation for the extreme zeal of the religious community, but no two explanations were the same. Some said the area had once been designated a holy ground, but if there was any evidence of this, it had long since been covered over.

At some point in the early eighties the main street became notably more prosperous as the chain stores moved in and VALURAMA became as anachronistic as a tram token, a twilight zone of a store, in which you half expected to find old geezers playing checkers on a cracker barrel, now stranded between a pair of mammoth glass and chrome retail outlets staffed by relocated New Yorkers.

Those were the bad years, when the old customers died and moved away, and business dried up like a high-season river bed. Taylor lost weight and developed a peptic ulcer. Barbara cried all the time. The store seemed to shrink in the shadow of its competition, and the children, now teenagers, grew claustrophobic and trapped and angry with each other.

Two days after his eighteenth birthday David left home, but he didn't leave town. Los Angeles was just too big a jump and there was nothing much else on either side of the freeway to interest him so he stayed on, renting an apartment with an old school friend over near the freight yard on the other side of town. He told himself that he hated the idea of not being near his brother, and Julie needed him to help her out with homework. But he also knew the truth, which was that he felt safe here, in a place he understood, in a town that underpinned his life.

By this time, Plaster City was in danger of turning into a real one. It was nearly ready to be designated one of the new edge cities, racially integrated and classless, vaguely liberal, slowly replacing its farm hands with computer punchers. Property developers built a kind of yuppie Olympic village called Greymeadow at the edge of town, and then came a mall that had Tower Records and Sharper Image and Radio Shack and an ice rink, and soon the main street began to look just like everywhere else. David was nineteen years old and working in his father's store when his life arrived at its purpose and conclusion.

The most famous thing about Plaster City is that Ethel Merman once made a phone call from there when her car broke down. She probably couldn't get out of town fast enough. Back in the sixties there was nothing to see but a main street composed of the usual mix, dry-cleaner's, food store, garage, diner, and rows of neat ranch-style houses with carports, yapping hounds and lawn sprinklers. On the road out of town a crazy old guy called Elmer Boricswyn had spent his retirement years building the

House Of Mud, a grotesque clay outhouse studded with thousands of crimped bottle tops that he charged people two bucks each to photograph. According to Elmer, whose conversational English was exactly like that of Mr Rogers, it was the only one of its kind in the entire state. When you saw it, you had to ask yourself if you were entirely surprised.

The nearest thing Plaster City had to a nightclub was the Hot Spot, a joint appropriately situated down by the coach station in an area that boasted a lone Catholic mission run by Mexican nuns, an old wino called Stick who lived in an abandoned dumpster and spent his days outside the truck depot telling people he could talk to the devil, a couple of seventies time-warp topless bars, one of which was actually, honest to God, called the Boom-Boom Room, and a single adult book store populated by perspiring kids with poorly forged IDs.

The neon sign outside the Hot Spot showed the profile of a woman poised with a phallic cigarette holder, and the name of the place uncurled as if she'd just blown it out in a puff of smoke – real sophisticated stuff. David had been there a couple of times with his roommate. Brett wasn't a very social guy. He spent most of his time watching uncut horror videos and hardly ever went out, except to go to the Safeway for beer and to hide when his creepy mother came by to leave him some money and see if he was okay. David had never been invited into his room, which was fine because he probably had a dead body in there or something. Brett was kind of involved in a romantic relationship. He dated a tiny blonde girl with a squeaky voice who lived outside Phoenix on the Gila Bend Indian Reservation, where she was studying anthropology, and as the Colorado Desert stood between her and Plaster City they didn't get to see a whole lot of each other.

Thinking about it later that night, David was careful to recall every detail of that freezing Saturday in late October. It was a couple of weeks before the bad weather settled in, and he and Brett had been drinking in a fake Western bar called the Twisted Wheel over on Third and University (typically there was no university on University, just like there was no plaster industry and it wasn't a city). The Just Say No To Alcohol campaign hadn't made its mark in town – everyone was still slamming the stuff back as though the end of the world had been scheduled for a midweek appearance. The two young men recognised everyone's faces in the Twisted Wheel and, worse still, were recognised in turn, so they decided to head over to the Hot Spot, where there might just be someone from out of town on the dance floor.

Brett was a year older and a foot taller than David, with the burnished complexion you get from using too much spot cleanser and the kind of thin sandy hair that leaves you semibald by the age of twenty-five. He could always be spotted across a crowded bar because his wardrobe consisted of fluorescent tour shirts advertising bands he had never heard of, let alone seen. He worked for a company that made portable office partitions, so if you rented floor space and didn't want to sit looking at the guy next to you, you'd call up Brett and someone would come and construct these chipboard dividers to cut you off. The company motto was something like 'Integrated Wall Systems For A Divided Environment', but only David could see the sad side of it.

It began with a tingling in the pit of his stomach, the kind of feeling you get when you realise you're about to have a terrible fight with someone. Brett had gone ahead, and he was left walking alone toward the club, a low brick building blocking off the end of the road. It had been built away from residential properties so that they could keep the music cranked up until 2 am without getting complaints. The night winds were wild, thumping at the ground in smudges of dust, and the neon flickered through the trees, tall beaten pines with top branches that thrashed in the turbulent darkness and sounded like TV static. For a moment it seemed that someone was following him. David stopped and turned around, half expecting to find something dark and heavy descending from the sky, but there was nothing to be seen. The highway was deserted for miles. It was a clear night, and a chain of cross-street lights wound all the way across town, swinging green bulbs that made it look as if the earth was moving.

Every Saturday the club found an excuse to have some kind of theme party, and tonight's was billed as 'erotica', presumably because the DJ remembered that Madonna had once chosen the title for an album. In the car park, among the chopped hogs and tinted-glass RVs, there were plenty of new Datsuns and Mazdas, a sure sign that the Greymeadow yups had ventured over for the evening. The building's entrance corridor was designed like a space-shuttle ramp, a reminder of the club's previous incarnation as a Trekkie hangout called the Final Frontier Disco. David caught up with Brett and they paid ten bucks apiece, for which they were each given an indelible-ink hand stamp and a drink ticket.

They never had much to say to each other. Like a lot of the people in town, Brett wore an expression of perpetual dissatisfaction, because he was pissed off with his job, his folks and his life but didn't seem capable of changing anything. Although he was technically an executive he wasn't a business graduate and was aware that he had no real skills or qualifications. He'd once considered moving away, until he realised that the money he'd make in San Francisco or Los Angeles wouldn't leave him enough for an apartment, so why swap a solid, predictable existence for a set of unknowns? Plaster City had become enough of an urban area to stop them from feeling like hayseeds. There was a mall and a multiplex; it wasn't like they were homeboys or anything and yet – there were those who left. Guys you went to school with who couldn't wait to get out, girls whose idea of heaven was Plaster City in their rear-view mirror. Sometimes David envied them, in the summer when the store was empty and the streets were hot and still, and there was only enough air to breathe if you stirred it yourself. Other times he was happy in the knowledge that his life was unlikely to hold many surprises, either good or bad ones.

David could see his roommate on the other side of the dance floor with a girl called Kathy who sold condos on the Greymeadow estate. She dressed like an anchorperson, pastel suits and big gold earrings, and drank spritzers with a bunch of man-hungry women in property sales, and he was surprised to see the two of them talking.

The main dance area was illuminated by a large rotating silver light bank, another remnant of the building's former Star Trek theme, and crimson velveteen banquettes were arranged in horseshoes all the way around the room. At one time the place must have been a movie house because there was still a stage area separated by heavy black drapes, from which the heady aroma of dope billowed constantly.

The guys David and his brother had gone to school with still came here at the weekend because this was the closest they could find to any place fashionable or disreputable. Just lately, some of the girls from Grey-meadow had been spotted slumming, mainly because the promised Greymeadow Leisure Center never got built and there was nowhere else for them to go at night. There were also the ageing Lotharios, overtanned men in silk shirts and cream suits, Wayne Newton lookalikes who shot each other finger .45s and drank bourbon like it was tap water. The music wanted to be West Coast fresh but was a little too far from LA to stay current, so the DJs opted for a loud nondescript techno drone with a bass beat you could feel pulsing in your belt buckle.

David checked his watch and made it nearly midnight. On the suspended screens above him were endless MTV clips and Nike ads. The place was full but uninteresting, as if everyone wanted a good time but couldn't be bothered to help create it. Brett came over and stood nearby, something he usually did when he'd run out of drink money.

'What's the deal with Kathy?' asked David. 'I didn't know you guys even knew each other.'

'It's nothing.' Brett dismissed the idea and held his friend's beer up between two fingers to see how long he would have to wait before David offered to buy him one. 'All she ever talks about is real estate, like she's had a character bypass or something.'

'Maybe she's offering you a piece of her property.'

'Hey, I'm not proud,' Brett admitted with a shrug. 'I'd take her up on the offer. It's your turn to go to the bar.'

'It's always my turn.' David pulled a squashed ten from his pocket and stuck it in Brett's hand. 'You go.'

The music had become a series of modulated thuds offering no hint of a tune. David walked toward the dance floor and studied the stage beyond. The black velvet drapes were slowly undulating back and forth. It looked like the wall was gently tipping, as though they were all on board a ship. A sharp tingling ran across the ends of his fingers, and tiny, painfully bright lights spackled the edges of his vision, causing the room to shift. In the middle of so much movement he felt more than mere alarm. He was suddenly disturbed that he was alone. No one else seemed to notice him. Perhaps they could no longer see him. It was as if for a moment he had slipped into an entirely new realm of existence. Then, as quickly as it had appeared, the tingling and the lights receded. The music, the cigarette smoke and the fake painted-marble walls of the Hot Spot closed in around him once more.

When Brett returned with the beers David asked, 'Did you feel anything just now?' and Brett just screwed up his face.

'What, you mean like an earth tremor or something?' After all, the town was near a couple of dormant fault lines.

'No, it was more ... I don't know. Something shifted.' David shook his head and squinted around, hoping to see some remaining effect.

'You sure you didn't smoke a joint before you came out?' To Brett, getting stoned could explain most of life's confusions.

'You know that stuff makes me sick. This was – different. Skip it.'

He stayed watching the dancers for a while, but the evening's experience had unsettled him, and he soon decided to leave. Brett was nowhere to be seen, so he walked back to his car alone. He rounded the mud-splashed hood of the old blue Chrysler, and his heart thudded hard in his chest as a figure lolled forward from the shadows.

'Jesus, Stick, you nearly gave me a fuckin' heart attack. Ain't you in the wrong end of town?'

The old tramp thought for a moment, then remembered. 'I just heard the news. You best get back to your daddy's store, boy, an' be quick about it.' Stick heard voices all the time. They were always telling him to warn people about the devil's return to earth, or some damned thing. Stick was mostly harmless. People liked him and often left food packages by his dumpster.

David checked his pockets for the car keys, making conversation. 'Why, what's happening this time?'

'Bad things comin', the worst you ever saw. Worst since – since – hell, I can't remember when.' That wasn't surprising. Stick couldn't remember anything, not even where he lived.

'You've been drinking, haven't you, Stick? My pa leave you out a little drop of whisky tonight?'

The old man threw his hands wide and nearly fell backwards into the rustling hedgerow. 'No, I swear! It's the people from inside the ground, coming to take back the town. Didn't you feel 'em arriving a few minutes ago? I sure as hell did.'

David stopped halfway into his car and stared back at Stick, who was trying to look as serious as a man could be wearing a floor-length raincoat and a back-to-front truck cap.

'I felt something, yeah. You're trying to tell me that was a train coming in?'

'Jeez, you think these people travel by train? They don't catch no trains, and they don't *drive* here neither! They just – just –' he gestured drunkenly at the night sky, 'open up th' air and step through. That's what you felt. The air tearing open to let 'em in.'

'I thought you just said they lived in the ground.'

'They do – that is, that's where we nailed 'em. Jest ask your daddy if you don' believe me!'

This had gone far enough. David climbed into the car and tried to close the door, but the old man moved with surprising agility, catching him by the wrist. 'You get back to your store, boy, an' you look after your family. They're gonna try and take down Plaster City tonight, you just watch an' see!'

He'd seen Stick drunk plenty of times before, but the wino's urgency was beginning to rattle him. 'Why would anyone want to take over Plaster City?' he asked, pulling the car door shut. 'There's nothing here worth having.'

'I didn't say take it over, I said take it down – down into the ground. Plaster City's time just ran out. Tonight we're all gonna burn in hell!'

The engine turned over first time. David gently edged the Chrysler forward around Stick, who was twisting his head into the wind, listening. David knew he had to ask as he passed.

'Why, Stick? If that's gonna happen, why this town? There's plenty of other crummy places this side of the state line that no one would ever miss.'

'Talk to your old man 'bout what they're doing here – he knows the reason good enough. And so does that old deaf bitch your ma takes care of.' As David pulled away into the road, Stick stumbled after him. 'Ask Taylor about the spike! But you'd better do it quick 'cause I hear 'em coming, right around the next hill!'

David cruised up through the speed limit as he hit the empty highway. Behind him the stars were blotted out by the encroaching black outline of the hillside. He could feel it now, the change in air density, the faint humming that didn't come from the telephone wires. Something had been displaced. A coldness spread across his chest, filling him with panic. Something terrible really was coming; he could feel it inside himself – and outside the car.

The crosswinds were whipping his radio antenna so much he couldn't get a fix on any station, not even WX-GOD, the twenty-four-hour evangelical hotline run by the indefatigable Reverend Lowe, who tub-thumped the coming battle with Satan night and day, interspersing his sermons with depressing country and western songs no one had ever heard of. David hit the Plaster City turn-off at forty plus, wheels barely locking on the dirt-covered shoulder. Sloping away in the distance, the town looked as if everyone in it had died or simply vanished. Only the swinging green lights gave any suggestion of life.

He reached the crossroads where the fitful buzzing of the VALURAMA sign had drawn him home, the only light in a row of glass and concrete boxes, and wondered what he was going to tell his parents once he had managed to wake them. He hadn't brought his keys to the store, and the front bell hadn't worked for years.

The problem of entry was solved when he saw the flashlight skittering through the ground-floor windows. Either his father was still up or the place was being burgled. He pulled into the customer car park and turned off the engine, vaulting the door and running lightly past the faded backboard of the basketball court. As his trainers touched the ground the soles grew warm, as if the earth itself was changing. Beside a low hedge he saw a body sprawled face down on the concrete. The fawn pants and navy-blue shirt identified him as one of the sheriff's men. A black pool of blood several feet long blossomed from his crushed head. Fighting his fear, David ran on. The porch steps groaned as he climbed them, but the sound was lost in the rising wind. Taylor was moving around inside the store, but he hadn't turned on the overhead panel lights. David pushed against the front door, and it swung open to his touch. As he entered, the smell of fresh wood and packing cardboard brought back a thousand childhood memories. His father was standing at the rear of the room, by the entrance of the depository, his torch beam slowly traversing the floor.

'Dad?' he called softly, 'What the hell is going on? There's somebody dead outside.'

'David? That you?' The beam came up into his face, forcing him to shield his eyes. 'You shouldn't be here, son.' He knew. David could hear it in his voice. He knew what was going to happen to the town. 'Close that door quick and come over here.'

David obeyed the command and joined his father. Taylor looked wearier than he had ever seen him before. He swung the torch beam back and forth as if looking for something but not knowing where to begin.

'What's going to happen to us?' David studied his father's face. Taylor was anxious to talk to someone, even if he would have preferred it not to be his son.

'That kind of depends how much you believe, David.' He flicked his hand nervously across his forehead. 'But you can feel the bad energy, can't you?'

'Sure, it's coming from outside, like it's in the air or under the ground or something. You feel it?'

'Yeah, and I guess a lot of other folks do too, but they're staying indoors, too frightened to come out into the street. I got through to the sheriff's department, told them they're a man down. Last call I managed before the lines went dead.'

'I came past there a few minutes ago. The place is dark.'

'Listen, you can see for yourself something terrible is goin' on, David. They're gonna take Plaster City back, unless we can stop them.'

'Who? No one can take a whole town anywhere.'

'Listen to me.' Taylor pulled him over the step of the depository. 'I would never involve you in anything dangerous, you know that. But I need your help.'

'Just tell me what to do and I'll do it.'

Taylor pointed back at the stairs to the first floor. 'Go on up and look after the women. The wind is frightenin' them. Keep 'em away from the windows.'

'I want to be down here with you. What are you doing?'

'I don't suppose you'd believe me if I told you. Now go on upstairs.'

David wasn't happy about it, but obeyed his father. Deaf old Betty Marco had been brought down to the lounge that overlooked the main street. Julie was sitting motionless with her feet pulled up under her, watching TV from behind a stack of cushions. His mother came from the kitchen and threw her arms around him.

'David, I've been so worried. The lines are down. I couldn't get through to you or your brother.'

There was no point in telling her what had already happened. He prayed she wouldn't see the shattered body lying at the rear of the house. 'I haven't heard from Joey,' he admitted. 'Everyone else okay?'

'Julie's acting strangely. She hasn't said a word for the past hour. Nobody knows what's happening. Taylor won't tell me anything. I looked out of the window a few minutes ago and you know what I saw? Rats! Thousands of them, like a brown carpet, running across the highway. Do you suppose there's an electrical storm coming? Aren't animals able to sense these things first?'

Behind them, the television signal fuzzed and flared, the picture alternately glowing and dying.

'I don't know, Ma. Dad says Mrs Marco can explain all this.'

His mother was fretfully twisting a dishcloth around her hand. He had never seen her looking so frightened. 'What could he mean?' she asked, confused. 'She talks all the time but she never makes any sense, hasn't done for years.'

'Let me try.' David walked across the room and knelt before the old woman. She had been staring out of the window, listening to the rising wind just as Stick had done, but as she turned he sensed a sharp intelligence behind the cold blue eyes that watched him. Slowly, she reached down a thin, freckled hand and slipped it into her bed jacket, twisting a dial, raising the volume of her hearing aid. Her deafness varied according to what she was prepared to hear.

'You know what happened, don't you, Mrs Marco?' Either she had told his father, or it was something Taylor already knew about.

'Nobody ever listens to me,' Betty Marco began, clearly relishing the notion of being in demand. 'Nobody ever wants to hear what I have to say.'

'I do, Mrs Marco, I want to hear. Tell me.'

Her hand snaked out and seized his shoulder, pulling him closer. 'Then you better listen good,' she said. 'I'll tell you what I told your pa long ago, see if you believe me any more than he did then. It was back in the nineteen twenties. A government brush clearance scheme uncovered a settlement out here at the crossroads. Wasn't much left of it, just a few old bits and pieces, rags and bones and burned rocks. Archaeological value, they said. The town was tiny then, barely more than a few shacks. The local people examined the site and decided that the settlers were bad. They'd been without religion – or perhaps they'd chosen to follow some older religion of their own. Early settlers was free to choose back then. It wasn't all damned Baptists, like now. Anyway, there was artifacts, unholy symbols, and weapons, like the stuff you'd use for animal sacrifice. I don't know what else. But the settlers had claimed the area for themselves.'

'What happened to them?'

'I have no idea – I guess nobody will ever know. Maybe they got drove out, maybe they just died off. All that was left was these signs that they'd once occupied the site for a while. Perhaps they moved on, further west.'

'I don't understand, what has this to –'

'Just mark what I'm saying.' She raised her head for a moment and listened. Outside the wind was growing again, hammering the window frames. From behind her fortress of cushions, Julie released a squeak of terror.

'The townspeople was all God-fearing Baptists, so they covered up the site and acted like it had never been there. They couldn't have pagan worshippers laying claim to their town, this was where they was going to raise their kids an' build their churches, so they plastered over the remains of the settlement, then later they concreted it into the highway.'

'What happened to the artifacts?'

'Maybe they found their way to museums, who knows?

Problem was, the Baptists couldn't reconsecrate the site. They didn't know how to go about doing such a thing, so they came up with a special service of their own. They held a big prayer meetin', and then they hammered a spike into the freshly covered ground, right in the centre of the settlers' camp. It was a foot-long iron spike like the ones the railroaders drove into the land to break new territory. On its flat head they engraved the whole of the Lord's Prayer, and they surrounded it with holy symbols. I guess everyone forgot about the site after that. The thing was barely noticeable, and as it weren't near any big roads, no one had reason to go by it. Wasn't until the fifties, just before the highway department was due to lay the new interstate, someone came and stole it, dug the blasted thing right out of the ground. Just think, all that time it'd been in the soil, holding back trouble and protecting the town. It was dug up by Otis Dagg's no-good father who thought it might be worth somethin'. He tore it out of the site and damned us all.' She pointed up at the ceiling, illuminating cracked plaster as pale as bone. 'I been up there all this time. I watched from my window and seen the changes in this place as it went from good to wicked, and I knew about the spike 'cause Otis inherited it when his pa died. I tried to tell people that the town started goin' bad the day the spike was pulled, but nobody believed me. They just carried on buildin' their fancy homes.'

'That's crazy,' David whispered, but even as he spoke he acknowledged the truth.

'I know it's true,' the old lady was saying, 'because the spike is right here, down in the storeroom, where it's been for the past forty years.'

Now he remembered seeing the spike as a kid, even recalled turning it over in his hands. It lay somewhere in the back of the store, among the hundreds of boxes of toys and tools, just another childhood plaything.

'But why tonight?' he asked. 'Why would they return after all this time?'

'They been waiting to gather their strength, until they was strong enough to take the whole town back in one go.'

'And you believe all this?'

She narrowed her ice-blue eyes at him. 'Don't you?'

David took the stairs two at a time, reaching the depository just as a cry from outside brought his father running to the windows. He could see his roommate's Camaro parked outside, at a sharp angle to the road. Then he caught sight of Brett himself, spinning and shoving at something formless as his coat was pulled up about him and the wind plucked at his legs. He was trying to reach the front of the store but was being pushed back, shoved and grabbed at until he screamed and lashed at the swirling darkness in the air. There were slashes of blood across his face and chest. As David ran toward the door, passing the scene from window to window, he saw the boy outside lifted from the ground, pulled and stretched and finally ripped in half by figures barely visible in the raging turbulence.

'We have to find the spike and put it back in place,' he shouted to his father.

Together they tore the cluttered old depository apart. On the floor above them, David's mother forced a chair against the door that led down to the store and fearfully waited with her daughter and the old woman.

The task ahead of them seemed hopeless. There was no way of knowing where the spike could be. They heaved aside spider-filled cases of linen and crockery, gate-leg tables and tea chests smothered with termite eggs, decades of untouched bric-a-brac. David wanted to call his brother, but with the telephone lines dead there was no way of contacting him. He forced himself to think, to try and remember those rainy afternoons passed in the back of the store, playing complex solitary games of make believe – cowboys and spacemen, firemen and sheriffs, werewolves and vamp–

Dracula.

He had always used the spike for Dracula. It looked just like a stake, and it had religious stuff all over the head. Christ, he hadn't thought about the horror games for years and now here were the memories as vivid as the fantasy had once been, waiting to be dusted off and relived. He set off through the maze of furniture, sure of himself.

'Give me a hand with this.' Thousands of issues of *National Geographic*, standing in stacks and glued together with mildew. They weighed a ton. Behind them were dozens of hat stands, clumped together like a winter forest. And at the foot of these was a box, a big old tea chest filled with black curtains – vampire cloaks – that had stood in for a coffin until he had grown too tall to fit it any more. The spike still lay there, wrapped in rotting folds of fabric. Although the years had tarnished it, the Lord's Prayer was still completely legible. Perhaps that was why these pioneer spirits or whatever the hell they were hadn't returned earlier to take the town. The spike had been removed from the site, but it was still here at the crossroads, still protecting, even if it only retained a fraction of its power after being uprooted. He lifted it in his right hand, slowly rotating its octagonal stem, and could feel the angry winds suddenly changing direction around the house, as though the ancient settlers could sense that this most hated of religious artifacts had been rediscovered.

'We have to return this to the settlement fast,' said Taylor, shining his torch down into the crate. 'I don't like the sound the timbers are making.'

'It's all highway out there now,' said David. 'How are we gonna find the right spot?'

'We've got the co-ordinates,' his father replied. 'They blacktopped the crossroads over the exact centre of the site. We just have to follow the centre lines.'

In the front of the store they found a pair of heavy steel sledgehammers. Taylor waited for a moment, thinking, then ran back into the depository. He returned with a handful of cheap Mexican-gold crucifixes and threw some to David, who slipped them over his head.

'I don't know if this'll make much of a difference, but it might keep them away long enough to reach the site. I mean, if the Lord's Prayer has such a strong effect.'

The crossroads were a good hundred-and-fifty-yard sprint from the store. Between the porch and their goal, David could make out several hunched black figures picking at the remains of his butchered roommate.

'The longer we leave it, the worse it's gonna get,' said Taylor, pulling open the front door. Instantly, the air was filled with the shrill squealing of the dead. Father and son ran out into the storm, the wind almost lifting them from their feet. They had barely descended the steps and reached the forecourt before the dark creatures fell about them in a fast-closing ring. Instantly, David could see that they had no chance of reaching their destination before being brought down. The things were scuttling toward them on blackened spindles, their fleshless arms pumping back and forth as they flexed and clasped their fingers. They moved at great speed, like clustering insects. David skidded to a halt as he realised the path ahead was already blocked. Taylor was behind him, preparing to swing the mallet as the first of the settlers approached.

Just as the ring seemed about to collapse on top of them, a shaft of bright light fell across the ground and the circle suddenly widened amidst much hissing and crying. David looked back at the house, where Mrs Marco and his mother had turned on the lights of the main store, the first floor and the attic. Thank God his mother had followed his lead and had finally listened to the old woman; the illuminated rooms formed a perfect cross. Seizing their chance, David and his father ran upwards along the lengthy path of light to the top of the crucifix, then on into renewed darkness and the hard tarmac of the highway.

David knew they had only a matter of seconds to spare. Out of the protecting light, they were prey once more to the rallying creatures. His trainers pounded along the central markers leading to the crossroads. Taylor arrived moments after, wheezing badly. He fell on his knees at the spot, barely able to catch his breath.

'Give me the spike.' Taylor held out his hand. 'I'm stronger than you.'

Together they set the tip of the iron rod at the exact point where the road lines crossed. David steadied it as Taylor raised his mallet for the first blow. Behind his father, one of the creatures was already dropping down to attack. He threw his own mallet at the figure with all the strength he could muster. The steel head smashed through its skull as if the bone was just a shell, like the head of a burnt match. Taylor slammed his hammer down on the spike, sinking it two inches into the tarmac. The noise around them became insane, a raging storm of death.

David gripped the spike as his father swung again. The blow connected, thrusting it deeper into the blacktop. Taylor had raised the shaft for a third time when the creatures reached out their melanistic arms and grabbed him, wrenching his head back until the neck broke with a sound that could be heard above the maelstrom. David screamed into the gale, starting toward his fallen father, but the malformed spirits dragged the body back and fell upon it in a frenzy. Grabbing the fallen mallet, David swung at the spike again and again, hammering it deep into the crossroads until the head was flush with the surrounding tarmac surface.

Sweating, he fell back onto the highway and dropped the sledgehammer. The banshee shrieks that had accompanied the first of the blows had died away now. The worst was over. He raised his face to the night sky and felt the wind in his hair as it began to lessen.

And rise again.

Puzzled, he looked back at the highway. His father's body lay eviscerated and ignored as the pagan spirits now advanced on him in a ragged line, stalking forward like shore crabs avoiding the surf. He crawled back to the glistening stud set in the highway and examined it as the air pulsed in a wild roar, and the rocks themselves were unanchored from the surrounding hillside.

In his determination to slam the spike back in place, he had completely flattened its head with the mallet, obliterating the protective prayer. Instead of revealing a statement of faith, the smooth, shiny surface of the spike blankly reflected an idolatrous moon.

In the moments that followed, David's short life shifted before his eyes, the events of the night recurring as if they had taken place an age ago. He cried now, unleashing his anger in a wail of sorrow not for himself but for his family and the terrified, helpless inhabitants of a town about to be reclaimed by an apostate enemy in the eternal war of the gods.

WELCOME TO PLASTER CITY says the twisted tin sign, but there's no town to be seen any more, just dusty brush and broken concrete, summer scorpions and flies. Stray from the highway, though, and you'll catch a glimpse of something that once existed, the bleached awning of a corner store, a shattered backboard from a basketball court, a piece of kerbstone, now the rubble of history. Who knows what terrors the inhabitants of Plaster City endured that night? None who saw the tragedy remain alive to tell.

These days the nearest town is Greymeadow, smart and fashionable, growing fast, sporting a finally completed leisure centre, one of the finest golf courses in the country, and churches – you never saw so many churches. Although Greymeadow is becoming increasingly popular with God-fearing young families, they would do well to examine the ruined site five miles down the road and learn from the mistakes of their old neighbours.

They should find a way to plug the fissure and seal off the pagan terrors of the past. Because Greymeadow will soon be crossing city limits, to where an unforgiving hunger waits. And the acolytes of a disrespectful god will once again appear in Plaster City.

The Young Executives

For young and old, the ageing process involves a growing impatience between differing generations. The young can't understand why the old must be so slow and set in their ways, while through older eyes the attitudes of the young often seem derivative and ill informed. That's only natural; but now we have the profit motive preventing either side from learning about the other. If it isn't a conspiracy, it certainly feels like one.

I **WAS** watching television the other day, one of those black and white science fiction films. Aliens had landed in the Nevada Desert, and a young man (I assume he was young – a trilby puts years on anyone) saw this humming silver spaceship land. When he took the town sheriff back to the site, the ship was gone and no one believed it had ever been there. At the end of the film the hero was left running about in the street trying to warn people that they were being taken over, but everyone thought he was crazy.

I know now how he must have felt.

When my husband finally died of lung cancer, I was relieved. It had been a long illness and he had suffered greatly, as much from the treatment as the disease. During the last few weeks of his life I nursed him at home. The doctors knew there was nothing more that could be done, and I wanted the hospital bed to be used by someone for whom there was still at least the hope of recovery.

William had very much wanted to live. Some people let go easily, but not my husband. Most of all, he worried how I would manage without him. I told him that everything would be fine and refused to discuss financial arrangements. It was impractical of me, I know, but I felt it was unseemly to speak of money with a dying man, even a man to whom I had been married for thirty-three years. I had been raised to believe that such talk was vulgar and quite avoidable. My mother always said that money was a subject best discussed at a racetrack. All in all, I'm glad she didn't live to see our modern world; she would have been simply unbearable.

I tried not to consider what would happen after William died. Our savings were gone and the house was mortgaged to a level that would necessitate its immediate sale. We owned little of value, certainly nothing that could be sold for a profit. I could see there were difficult times ahead and knew that I would have to face them by myself. William was not an articulate man, and his state of partial sedation hampered our conversation. In our final hours together I knew there was much he wanted to say, important questions we had never managed to answer, but we contented ourselves by joining our hands on the bedspread and sitting quietly, waiting for the time to arrive, as if death had made an appointment.

Well, the appointment was kept that October afternoon. William's departure was as imperceptible as the autumn sun slipping into the trees, and I was left alone in a darkening bedroom. During the funeral I made a vow to carry on in strong spirits. I was determined not to be one of those weak wives who throw themselves on the mercy of disinterested relatives. I moved into the spare room because our old bedroom held too many memories, but apart from that I tried to continue my life with as few disruptions as possible.

It didn't really seem that William had gone until I sold the house and moved into a modern flat nearer town. I took very little of our old furniture with me, knowing that it would be harder to imagine him walking around a corner with his newspaper tucked under his arm in such different, new surroundings. He would not have approved of the flat anyway, too expensive, too much glass, too bright and sunny, but it lightened my mood when I looked from the windows and saw people crossing the street below, and looking from the windows was unavoidable because they covered one entire wall of the lounge.

A lady from the council came to see how I was coping, and although I suppose she was trying to help, I did find her rather patronising. A neighbour had arranged her visit. She wanted to leave leaflets and told me that I could still lead a useful life, as if I had suddenly ceased to do so. I was polite but firm, even when she suggested that counselling could show me how to visualise my 'lost one' in order to minimise the effects of bereavement. I told her I considered it healthier to try and gently release one's grip on the past. Hold on too tight and you make a ghost. She gave me a look of utter confusion.

Shortly after moving into the flat I spent an evening with our remaining accounts and made a decision to return to work. Some silly creatures are content to live through their TV sets and follow the affairs of fictitious television characters as if they were real. I have never been like that. I have no trouble filling the hours of the day – but the narrow margin of my finances demanded that I return to work.

I had done so once before, after our boy was old enough to be left alone, and had trained as a medical secretary. My excellent shorthand was largely redundant now, and like many people of my age I was a little daunted by the prospect of learning to handle new technology. Peter, my son, is a victim of this fast-changing business world. He lives with his wife and daughter in Melbourne and found himself jobless after the aerospace company for whom he worked had been bankrupted by changes in the development of computer hardware.

Peter was unable to attend William's funeral. He offered me money that I knew he could ill afford, and I refused it. However, I accepted his kind offer to attend a company course in word processing here in London, and I found the lessons easier and more enjoyable than I had anticipated.

After finishing the course I applied to an agency for work and was encouraged to find that older women were welcomed into certain areas of the workforce because they weren't likely to run off and have babies. Decent medical positions were still hard to find, so I accepted a job typing letters for the head of a worldwide delivery-service company. I started on a bitter Monday morning exactly three months to the day of William's death.

I had read enough magazine articles to know that offices had changed in the last few years, but my initial experience at DMK was heartening. Rooms were 'open plan', light and bright. Young executives were 'power dressed' and 'groomed for management', which simply meant they were ambitious and careful about their appearance, the same as we had been in my younger days. The general office work flow was faster and there was less waste, but much had remained constant; gossip in the coffee break, routine jealousies and rivalries, shows of strength as people tested the boundaries of their power. I was surprised by my own confidence and pleased to be part of the workforce again. And it was fun playing den mother to the young typists.

If only it could have remained that simple.

It wasn't until the end of the first week that I noticed how differently most of the younger executives behaved from the rest. People like Mr Gould, Mr Nash and Miss Kidston, all in their twenties, seemed pleasant enough at first but kept a certain distance between themselves and the older employees. They dressed elegantly, worked late hours without complaint and performed their allotted tasks quickly but without rush. They were methodical and thorough, anxious to help the company achieve greater profits and rarely discussed anything but the work in hand. And yet it seemed to me that they lacked passion, the spark of enthusiastic imagination that stops a man from being mistaken for a piece of wood.

Then there was the business of the biros.

In my first week, I made a friend. Her name was Rose Tippet. She was a true Cockney, and she was three years younger than me. She had an alarming blue tint to her hair that she called a Wapping rinse and told the sort of jokes that made you throw your hand across your mouth, and the sadness that sometimes appeared in her eyes was explained by the fact that she had lost her own husband the previous year.

We sat opposite each other, outside the offices of our respective bosses. My desk wasn't the tidiest, but Rose's appeared to have suffered a direct hit from a bomb. She always had at least two pencils in her hair and dozens beneath the paperwork, and Post-It notes were fanned across her work station. She seemed able to lay her hands on anything she needed, though, and was allowed to keep her own 'system' because she was extremely efficient.

It was she who pointed out how the younger executives kept their biros. They each had six, three blue and three red, squared off neatly to the left-hand side of their terminals. Nothing odd in that, you'd think, but it was the exactness that seemed strange. Rose said you could measure their placement to a fraction of an inch and it never changed. And the coffees. They stood their coffee mugs with equal care, three inches in from their telephones. Coffee was always drunk at the same times, and the mugs always occupied the same spot.

At first I thought Rose was being silly, but once my interest had been piqued I started to notice other things. For example, their handwriting was similar. Not identical – various flourishes and curlicues distinguished them – but it was as if they had all studied with the same teacher. I could tell that their extreme capability made some of the bosses feel uneasy and threatened. It wasn't just that they were young and ambitious; when they presented their work to senior members of staff at the weekly strategy sessions, tension filled the air. They would tonelessly read reams of numerical data to Mr Franklin, the managing supervisor, who never caught their eye and seemed to agree to anything if it would help to conclude the meeting more quickly.

Diane Kidston was the worst.

She always made me feel untidy. She would stride past my desk in her charcoal-grey suit as she returned from the photocopying machine, squaring her documents neatly at the corners, and make some sharp remark about the seniors being inefficient or slow. Everything about her implied that she was more suited to the company than I, less likely to become obsolete. There's a word for it now; *ageist*. I didn't know it then.

One morning I had trouble locating a copy of her status report, and she informed me with a blood-freezing smile that she had requested I be formally warned about the state of my desk. I knew that keeping a neat appearance would have no effect on my efficiency, but I cleaned up my act quickly enough. The job was too good to lose over a little mess. Rose managed to remain exempt from the order because her boss was capable of overriding any demands made by the younger executives. One day she had a shouting match with one of the juniors who had complained about her untidiness and came off the winner, much to Miss Kidston's disgust. Oh, the Jacobean intrigue of office work!

Computer classes were mandatory for all employees. Some of the senior staff still refused to change systems and made a great show of failing to appreciate the use of computers, so the tutors would set them up with simple puzzle programmes while they taught the rest of the staff, rather like giving children colouring books to shut them up. That way the senior executives could complete their computer literacy courses and go back to work without losing face in their departments. I didn't have to do that. With my son's help, I was ready for the future.

The technology boom had certainly smartened companies up since my last bout of full-time employment. There was little need for paperwork now. All internal memos were passed on as E-mail. Of course, there were no ashtrays around, either. The few employees who still smoked had to leave the building and skulk about in the quadrangle below, puffing furtively. That part seemed a bit unnecessary to me, particularly when it was clear from investment reports that the company, which was owned by an American corporation, had links with the tobacco industry. But that, I concluded, was the modern business world for you; everyone is owned by someone else. Everyone's hands are slightly soiled.

Signing on with the company had meant reading through a sixty-page manual of do's and don'ts. When I started work at sixteen in a tiny nicotine-coloured insurance office in Oxford Street, our bosses weren't listless managers but enthusiastic owners. The typewriters we used were enormous steel machines that gave us sore fingers from hammering the keys, and we shared telephones three to one. Thinking about this, I put the distant attitude of the younger working generation down to the wide age gap between us (I remembered my own respectful horror of the elderly as a child) and forgot about it when I went home.

Until the matter of Mr Nash's computer.

One evening I agreed to stay late. Overtime pay was good, and I knew that the extra would come in handy for a new winter coat. We were opening a new delivery route to the Far East and there were feasibility studies to be typed and printed. Rose had offered to stay behind with me, but as I knew she was supposed to be babysitting her granddaughter I insisted she went home. The younger executives would often still be in the building at eight or nine o'clock, but on this particular night there was a company squash tournament, and they seemed to take their sports very seriously.

I was watching the rain tacking across the windows while I waited for the machine to carry out a command. A beep drew my attention back to the screen. I had been loading old files onto a diskette but had run out of memory space. The DISK FULL sign winked back at me like a little neon hieroglyph. I searched my drawer for a fresh box of disks but couldn't find any, so I went to Mr Nash's terminal and borrowed one of his.

I checked to see if it was correctly formatted and called up the file directory to ensure that it was blank. Instead of an empty column, I found myself looking at a special document that read like a staff list. One of the files was labelled *Tippet, Rose*. I couldn't resist taking a peek and opened it.

There, laid out across a spreadsheet, were all kinds of private details about Rose, medical and financial things that should only have been in the hands of a personnel manager. It got worse. Under *Evaluation: Work Attitude* it said *Cantankerous*. Beside *Level Of Efficiency* it read *F***king Awful*. Under *Personal Habits* it said *Slovenly*. I wondered; had times changed so radically that such insulting language could be used in an unprotected file? Below this I was shocked to read another line which said simply *Course Of Action: Termination Of Employment*. Mr Nash had no jurisdiction in this area. Hiring and firing was not his responsibility. Had I invaded his privacy by reading a note intended to be kept solely as a record of his personal frustrations? Eventually I decided that he must use private files to vent his spleen on employees for whom he did not care. What other explanation could there be? I returned the disk to its place in the box and for the next few days watched my colleague's impassive features for signs of discomfort when he was drawn into conversation with Rose. If he really hated working with her, he certainly hid it very well. But that was the thing about the younger ones; you could never tell what they were really thinking. They never stopped being *corporate*.

One Friday evening after work Rose and I went over to the local wine bar, imaginatively named Corks, and shared a bottle of plonk. Something had clearly been troubling my friend all day, and I waited patiently for her to come out with it.

'I don't understand,' she said at last, running a finger around the rim of her glass. 'I've been with DMK for four years now, and I've always enjoyed the work, but just lately –' She stared into her drink.

'Yes?' I prompted gently.

'They seem to be deliberately getting at me, Harriet.'

'Who do you mean?' I asked.

'The younger ones. People like Mr Gould. He keeps piling on typing just as I'm about to leave for the night, waiting for me to refuse to help him. And Miss Kidston – I was coming back from lunch the other day and I saw her deliberately knock a folder of papers from my desk into the bin. If I hadn't seen them fall I might not have found them before the cleaners came around. There were signed cheques and all sorts of things. I would have lost my job.'

'Are you sure she did it on purpose?' I asked.

'There are other oddities, too,' she said, barely hearing me. 'Have you noticed how quickly they talk to each other? And they use this funny code, so you can't understand what they're saying. I'm sure they talk about me behind my back.'

'They're much younger than you or I,' I explained. 'They have different tastes, go to places we've never heard of, lead faster lives. You know how the young evolve their own way of speaking. It just shows that we're getting older. We don't keep up with their private jokes – we used to have our own.' I tried to make light of it, to stop her from looking so depressed. 'Then again perhaps they're aliens from outer space, planning to take over the planet. They're going to enslave the human race, but first they have to commandeer the nation's delivery systems.'

Rose laughed. 'No,' she said, 'I don't think they're aliens. Miss Kidston's from Leeds. They're definitely a new breed, though, different to us.'

'I should hope so,' I replied. 'Our generation made quite enough mistakes, thank you very much.'

'We won a world war. I doubt we could do that again.'

'I don't know. I think Miss Kidston has enough moral

fibre to lead a few regiments. But I hope we'll never have to worry about such things.'

'Don't be so sure.' She took a sip from her glass. 'Perhaps there are other battles still to be won.'

It was an odd thing to say, and I didn't recall the remark until the following Thursday, when Rose failed to show up for work. It wasn't until after lunch that we heard about the heart attack. Apparently it was severe and she was on the critical list. The hospital wouldn't allow her to have any visitors. She was still unconscious.

Rose lived alone. A neighbour had found her on the floor of her kitchen. As I typed my way through the afternoon's correspondence, I looked up and saw that someone had placed a rose on the opposite empty desk. I remember thinking what an inappropriate gesture this was, because the rose is a symbol of silence. Then I recalled the note on Mr Nash's file, the one about her termination of employment.

Well, wouldn't it seem like an odd sort of coincidence to you? I didn't see how it could be anything else, and I imagined Mr Nash must have felt terrible when he heard, knowing what he'd written about her. The odd thing was, I'm sure I heard him mention Rose's name to Mr Gould and laugh. Why would he do that?

I started to imagine all sorts of conspiracies. Rose's dirty coffee cup had inadvertently been left on her desk. As I started to wash it up I nearly wiped a thick white residue from the bottom of the mug and was already mentally accusing Mr Nash of poisoning her before I remembered how much sugar she always used to shovel in. Still, I returned the mug unwashed to my bottom drawer as a memento of our friendship. She'd been so nice to me. It didn't seem fair.

The next morning I called the hospital. Rose's condition had stabilised, but she wasn't up to seeing people yet. Her attack had been very serious and would leave some permanent damage. At the office I saw them huddled around Mr Nash's desk, the young executives, talking quietly together. I moved a little closer and tried to hear, but they noticed me and suddenly dispersed, shooting their cuffs and straightening their skirts and ties, as guilty as school children caught with cigarettes.

At the end of the day I arranged to take over some of Rose's work until Mr Franklin could get Human Resources to provide a replacement. That meant working until late, after the others had gone. Well, I had to do something, if only to prove to myself that I wasn't imagining some giant conspiracy against the older members of the company. I'd always had an overdeveloped imagination.

Still, that night I decided to take another look at Nash's file and make a copy of it for myself.

The office was silent but for the humming of the air conditioners. I missed the sound of traffic. The fourth floor, where I worked, was empty but for the supervisor, Mr Franklin, who was working in his office with the door closed. I could see him bent over his desk through the smoked glass, never shifting his gaze from the oblongs of paper neatly arranged before him. I went over to Nash's work station, removed his disk case and prepared to take another look at the file I had opened from the unmarked diskette.

I clipped it into the IBM and accessed it, looking through the list of names. Everything was just as it had been before. It would take too long to read through the files now, so I decided to copy the relevant sections onto the hard disk of my machine. It was then that I noticed my own name. I couldn't open the file while it was copying, and it had only just finished when Mr Franklin came out of his office to get a coffee. Panicking, I removed the diskette and hastily returned it to its rightful place in the box. My heart was thumping beneath my cardigan. Anyone would have thought that I'd done something highly illegal, and that's how I felt, like a detective breaking and entering without a warrant. As soon as Mr Franklin was safely back in his office with the door shut, I opened the copied file and scrolled down the list. There it was, plain as eggs, my name, *Harriet Sinclair*. I decided to take a look at what Mr Nash really thought of me. Beneath a host of personal details about my financial state I found a category marked *Evaluation: Work Attitude*. Next to this it said *Servile*. Under *Level Of Efficiency*, it said *Too Damned Slow*. And under *Course Of Action* there was the awful phrase again, *Termination Of Employment*. I didn't understand. I could feel tears welling up in my eyes and I didn't want to cry, but I hated the idea that someone thought I was past the age of usefulness because I knew that I wasn't. I saw how the other girls worked and I matched them easily. On some jobs I was much faster than them.

'What on earth's the matter?' boomed a sudden loud voice. Mr Franklin was staring over the top of my terminal, trying to look concerned. I hit SCREEN CLEAR faster than I've ever moved in my life.

'I have hay fever,' I said sharply. 'I'll be fine in a minute. I have some work to finish.'

'You should go home, let one of the younger girls do it for you in the morning,' he offered vaguely before returning to his office. Closing the file I switched off my machine and covered it. I felt alone and depressed.

That night I looked in on Rose at the hospital. We were only allowed to speak briefly because the nurse didn't want her tired. She asked me to collect her belongings from the office because she would not be returning to work. It seemed to me that there was something else on her mind, something she wished to speak of but found difficult to express. I filled the minutes with mundane office gossip, waiting for her to formulate the thought, but it eluded her. The medication wasn't allowing her to think clearly. Tucking my hair beneath my hat, I rose and promised to return in a day or so. She seemed very sorry to see me go.

When you live alone you sometimes find yourself dwelling on silly things, speculations you would dismiss from your mind if only you used your common sense or had someone to talk you out of it. I thought about the behaviour of the youngsters at the office, unable to decide whether or not there was any real cause for alarm. If William had still been alive I would have told him about Rose's hospitalisation and Mr Nash's file, and he would have dismissed the whole thing as a nonsensical coincidence. But I couldn't do that by myself.

So the next day I returned to the office a little warier than before, and I worked hard and stayed out of trouble. After the flurry of workload changes caused by my friend's sudden illness, things quickly returned to normal. A week later Rose was released to recuperate at home, and I visited her with flowers and sincere-sounding Get Well cards from members of staff.

That was when Danny joined the firm. I arrived one morning to find a tall ginger-haired boy sitting at Rose's desk emptying out the drawers. He had a gold front tooth and freckles like you'd never seen, even on his eyelids.

'Who are you?' I asked rather more sharply than I had intended.

'The new temp,' he explained with a smug grin. 'I suppose you're going to show me the ropes. Just don't tell me you have to be crazy to work here.'

I hadn't expected them to employ a boy and tried not to look surprised. 'Has someone shown you where everything is?' I asked him.

'It's okay,' he replied, casually flicking on the computer, 'I've handled secretarial work on every system they could throw at me, IBM, Apple, Microsoft, you name it. This should be a piece of piss.'

'Don't bet on it,' I said, objecting to his language. 'The last person who sat there had a heart attack.'

But Danny turned out to be completely different from the first impression he had given. Each morning he would arrive slightly behind the rest, his ginger hair fanning up uncombed and uncontrollable, and plonk himself down at the seat with a paper bag containing two polystyrene cups of cappuccino, one of them for me. He would never let me pay for mine, so eventually I started buying an afternoon treat, bars of chocolate, mints or biscuits. And I began to look forward to my cappuccino. His unremitting perkiness was a cross to bear at times but the young are like that of course, so sure are they of their invincibility. I couldn't hold his age against him. Quite the reverse; his steady stream of jokes and anecdotes finally wore down my resistance, and we became friends. Danny was twenty-two but seemed wise far beyond his years. He was earning some money before returning to university to study Bulgarian history, of all things. Over the next few weeks he became my lifeline to the world of the young. Through his eyes I could understand them once more, by seeing what excited or upset him and his friends.

'What do you think of this?' he once said, pulling off his Walkman headphones and letting me listen. A hammering tempo sounded in my ears, electronically generated drum effects.

'A bit repetitive,' I replied.

'I know,' he said, smiling. 'Nice though, isn't it?' And he was right, it was.

One afternoon, after being briefed on the typing of a document by Mr Gould, Danny turned to me and pulled a gargoyle face.

'What's the matter?' I asked.

'Does the Ghoul remind you of anyone?' He had nicknames for most of the people on our floor. I shook my head.

'You know that John Betjeman poem, "I am a young executive, no cuffs than mine are cleaner"?'

'Oh yes!' I agreed, thinking for a moment and placing the line, 'He is a bit like that, isn't he?' I was amazed that someone like Danny knew any poetry at all.

'A bit?' Danny cried out incredulously, 'It could have been written for him. He's like the others; you get no sense of a moral dimension from any of them.' And he was right. After this they became known to us as the Young Executives, Mr Gould, Mr Nash, Miss Kidston and the rest. It was us against them, just as it had been with Rose. I had found an ally. It meant that I wasn't imagining things after all; somebody believed me because they could see what I saw.

I wondered if I should confide in Danny about the comments on the private files. Mr Nash had taken to locking away his diskettes now, almost as if he suspected that someone had been checking them, but I had the copy on my machine's hard disk, tucked away under a password.

I was still trying to decide whether I should tell him when the matter was decided for me. Rose developed complications from her heart attack and died quite suddenly. Danny asked if he could join me at the funeral. Her old boss, Mr Davison, was the only other member of staff to attend. Afterwards, Danny asked me if I would like to join him for a drink at his local pub in the Edgware Road, but I declined the offer. Rose's death had greatly saddened me, and I didn't want the boy to become infected with the sense of mortality that hung in the air that day. He was too young to be hanging around with an old fogie like me, I explained, packing him off.

Instead I decided to attend Rose's wake, which was held in the house of her next-door neighbour, a pragmatic Irishwoman of indeterminate age. Her name, as far as I could gather, was Nessie, and she had sometimes cleaned for Rose.

I sat in the gloomy front parlour with a whisky and a plate of dry sandwiches and listened to the neighbours talk as their children chafed and scratched at their constricting smart clothes. You could see they longed to be outside, and should have been, but it wasn't my place to say.

'She was a good-hearted soul,' said Nessie, folding her hands in her ample lap, 'and her in so much pain.'

'I don't think she was in pain,' I said.

'Oh, I don't mean at the end, love. She was always in pain but hid it well, terrible for her it was. The night cramps in her legs, and her nerves in such a bad state. Ever since the old man went.'

'I had no idea. Wasn't she given anything for it?'

'Indeed she was. Did you never see her with the little box of pills she always carried?'

I thought back. I vaguely recalled Rose sitting at her desk, toying with an opaque plastic cylinder that rattled. 'What was she taking?' I asked.

'Calcium tablets. She had a deficiency, poor woman.'

'I didn't know that,' I added lamely, and the conversation moved on to the grim details of a neighbour's gallstone complications.

The next day, for reasons I myself was unsure of, I decided to confide in Danny about the private files.

'Taken by themselves they don't mean much,' the boy agreed. 'I mean, I don't like the Young Executives any more than you do, but are you saying they murdered Rose? Don't you think it's a bit unlikely that they'd find a way of bumping her off just because she kept a messy desk?'

'I know,' I said with a sigh, 'it's absurd. I don't know what I was thinking of. Forget I said anything.'

Just as I was preparing to leave that night, Miss Kidston came by and left me with a three-hundred-page document to type. Three hundred pages!

'Better wake your ideas up, Harriet,' she said, slapping the paper onto my desk. 'There's a lot more where that came from.'

For the next three days she applied the pressure, piling up work that kept me typing late into the night. Actually, it suited me well enough. I had nothing to rush home for. Besides, I was being paid overtime and was happy to earn the money. But by the end of the week I was arriving two hours earlier than the rest of the staff and knew that I could not keep up the pace.

'They're really piling on the pressure, aren't they?' said Danny, setting down my cappuccino. He reached over and took a thick file from my in-tray. 'Here, let me do this one for you.'

'No, it's my work, I can handle it.'

'Absolutely not,' he said, holding onto the file. 'Can't you see they're deliberately trying to wear you down?'

'I know that,' I replied carefully. 'But I'm not going to let them beat me.'

'Then at least let me help. Nobody will know.'

Between us, we finished the work on schedule. Just in time for Mr Gould to dump a stack of Dictaphone tapes on my desk. I thought of complaining to Mr Franklin, but since poor Rose's departure he had been oddly subdued in front of the Young Executives, as though he no longer felt like facing them. Over lunch one day, Danny and I tried to figure out what motivated these soulless creatures, these junior-assistant-vice-presidents, armed with their pompous work titles and their productivity quotas. Danny told me that many of his own friends pushed hard at work because they were frightened of failing, an idea that profoundly depressed me. Twenty-two is no age to become frightened.

Friday evening arrived, and rain was falling hard around the building. I decided to finish Mr Gould's tapes, hoping that the downpour might have eased by the time I was ready to leave. Danny wished me a pleasant weekend and left, and soon I was the only one remaining on the fourth floor. I was nearing the end of my final tape when the earpiece of the Dictaphone crackled and packed up. I remembered that Rose had kept a spare, and that I had asked Danny not to throw it out, so I went over to her old desk.

I found the earpiece. I also found a plastic tube of tablets stuck at the back of the drawer, behind the box containing her Dictaphone equipment. I read the label, which referred to the treatment of something called hypocalcaemia. Calcium deficit. There was a warning not to exceed the stated dose because of the danger of respiratory acidosis. Now, I remembered from my days as a medical secretary that respiratory acidosis led to cardiac arrest. It immediately made me wonder if she had somehow overdosed on calcium.

I don't know why I made the connection then.

I looked down through the work room, with the neat desks and the emptied bins and the angle-poise lamps throwing cones of light in the dimness, and I listened to the distant falling rain. Then I returned to my own desk and withdrew Rose's unwashed mug from the bottom drawer. The white coating at its base had dried to a hard sediment, like congealed chalk dust. I crumbled one of the white pills from the vial and compared it to the residue, touching both on the tip of my tongue.

They were identical in texture, taste, everything.

It was perfect. Calcium is a natural body product but lethal in overdose. Someone had seen her taking the pills, had checked out their content and added the medication to the coffee mug. It sat on her desk throughout the day. I wondered if they had also worked out the exact hour of her death. She took the medication for night cramps. With the contents of the mug still active in her system, the tablet before bedtime would have tipped her well over the limit.

I sat at my desk with the damned rain drilling against the windows, and I didn't know what to do. *Termination of employment*, Mr Nash's file had recommended. It hadn't specified how. *This is not my overactive imagina-*

tion, I thought. They killed her, the Young Executives, because she was old and they hated her, and they were going to do the same to me.

I had to do something, tell someone. I wrapped the mug and the pillbox in a plastic shopping bag and took them home while I considered my next move.

I felt that going to the police would be a bad idea, that they would listen with amusement and merely humour me. Discussing my views with senior management would probably get me fired, and I couldn't afford that. Which left positive action on my part or continued silent observation. I couldn't see myself skulking around the building in a balaclava sabotaging the terminals, so I elected to remain silent.

Well, not completely silent. The next morning Danny arrived at his usual time, slightly after me, marching to his work station with his hair in his eyes, whistling off key, paper bag clutched in his hand. He took one look at me and asked what was wrong.

I'm ashamed to say that I burst into tears. When I could catch my breath again, I told him what I had discovered. About Rose being killed by a deliberately administered calcium overdose, and how I couldn't tell anyone because they'd think I was deranged. I asked his advice. When I had finished I looked at him for help, waiting while he fumbled with the paper bag.

'What do you think we should do?' I asked.

He removed a single cup of cappuccino, set it down on his desk and crumpled the bag into a ball.

'What do you mean, *we*, you deranged old bitch?' he asked.

Then he rose with his coffee, took a sip and sauntered contemptuously away between the desks. With a pounding heart I grabbed a few belongings and left. As I passed the closed door of Diane Kidston's office I could see Danny through the glass, laughing with her. I wondered what sort of offer they had made him. I never dared to go back, not even to collect the wages they owed me.

The security guards have all been warned to look out for a crazy old lady, of course, and who's to say that I'm not? I spend my time planning devious ways to take revenge for all the people like Rose, for anyone whose death was hastened by the young. I see them all around me, regiments of marching ebony suits and skirts, carbon-copy men and women culled from the fashion pages of glossy magazines. I loathe the stare of their frozen flat pupils, the supercilious look that says *You are not a part of our fine modern world*. I watch them and I long to see a hair out of place, a stumble in their step, a glimpse of humanity and freedom. I long to suppose that they dream of something other than mere success at the cost of all else, that they secretly hope to do more than just fit in. But I know they don't. To them, imagination isn't a profitable commodity.

The thing I most regret is that I'm always suspicious now – distrustful of their youthful intentions toward me. Perhaps all older people are to varying degrees. Long life makes everyone a little crazy.

It's getting dark. I sit in the lounge and watch from the window until the sun has vanished behind the rooftops. Sometimes they slip pieces of paper under my front door. The neatly blocked lettering on yesterday's note read simply, Why don't you kill yourself?

I tell the police they are after me. They're very sweet about it; they want to send me a social worker. They wonder why I won't talk to a nice, smart, ambitious young social worker. Young executives. Why am I such a thorn in their side, I wonder? How much damage can one old lady do? Perhaps they hate us because the past is another country, and I am a citizen of that country. If this war must be waged and this murderous new breed is really here to stay, the old ways need to be forgotten quickly. And I will become like that man in the flickering film print, forcing drivers to stop in the rush-hour traffic, begging someone to believe that the invasion has already begun.

Jouissance de la mort

I make no apologies for this extremely odd tale; there's joy in telling an absurd story which seemingly has no direction or solution, only to tie it up with a punch line that (hopefully) explains everything. The title refers to the almost sexual pleasure in death that signifies the curse of the Condorcet family.

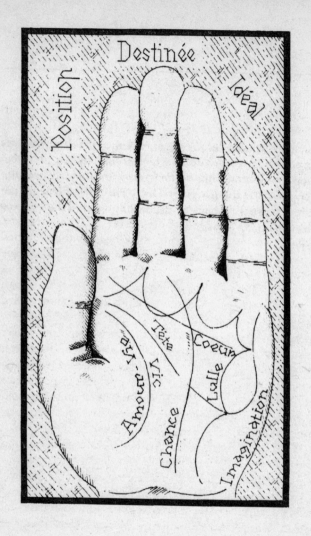

IT WAS a cool unmisted morning in the rich green fields beyond Rennes. Swallows filled the trees above the Château Saint Vincent as M. Jean-Luc Condorcet set off through the loamy pasture towards his herd. He preferred being in the open air; the château's atmosphere was damp and unhealthy. For decades the building had been shunned by those villagers old enough to remember the Condorcet family's dissolute flirtations with satanism. M. Jean-Luc was the last surviving member and preferred the bucolic delights of animal husbandry to the arcane interests of his forebears.

The farmer paused and listened; a distant aircraft. An unusual sound in this area. No commercial flights passed overhead. Several cows looked up as the engine noise grew. He searched the sky and glimpsed the tiny silver plane, a customised private Lear jet, banking above a crest of white cloud. The aircraft had been chartered to bear a dance band from Carcasonne to its first public appearance in Nice. Thanks to a leaking fuel lead and a drummer who insisted on smoking in the toilet, they never reached their destination. The plane exploded in midair.

After the bang there was a shocked silence. Everything was still. A black ball of smoke and debris hung motionless in the sky. Then M. Condorcet was hit on the head by a falling cocktail cabinet with chromium legs and gold glass doors. One of his cows was knocked unconscious by a trombone. A bottle of Remy Martin demolished the

Jouissance de la mort

henhouse, and two chickens were impaled by drumsticks.

M. Condorcet was in such a terrible mess that they had to cremate him. His staff consulted an ancient family manual, then inscribed four lines from a poem, the first of which was '*Les mouches bourdonnaient sur ce ventre putride*', on the side of the brass urn containing his ashes. Unsure what to do next, they parcel-posted him to the surviving member of his family, an English aunt living alone in a flat in Bayswater.

Elizabeth Fritton had been dismissed by the education board after losing a child on the Northern Line, and the incident had destroyed her life. She and another teacher had set out with a crocodile of pupils heading for an exhibition of molluscs at London Zoo but had disembarked the train to find themselves one short. Extensive searches were made in the tunnels, but no explanation for the disappearance was ever uncovered, and Miss Fritton assumed that the boy must have drawn the attention of a molester, who had stolen the lad away when her back was turned. The police found a French essay book inscribed with the lad's name on the tracks at Camden Town tube station and returned it to the school, whereupon it fell into Miss Fritton's possession. On the last page was part of a poem that began '*Les mouches bourdonnaient sur ce ventre putride.*'

Miss Fritton had not seen her nephew for some years and received nothing in his will, the château being sold to cover debts. What little monies remained from the sale of the property fell to the staff in descending order of loyalty.

When the urn arrived she set it upon the mantelpiece in her sitting room, where it gathered dust for several months and became stuck to the paintwork. Miss Fritton had few acquaintances and fewer visitors. The only woman she permitted within her fringed baroque apartment was an impoverished family friend named Maria Brown, who was Antiguan by birth and longed to return there. Kindly Maria convinced the wheyfaced ex-schoolmistress that she should get out more and cajoled her into visiting the seaside one August Bank Holiday.

The morning of their departure, Miss Fritton tried to move the urn but found it stuck fast. Finally she was forced to use a chisel to release it from the paint.

Bedecked in postcards and candyfloss, Miss Fritton strode the seafront and found herself having fun for the first time in years. She even suggested that the two of them should relive a childhood memory and ride the switch-back. Unfortunately, the switchback operator had tempo-rarily left the attraction in the hands of his dimwitted French nephew, who noticed an unused car on the side rail and pressed it back into service.

The car's base was faulty, having lost a number of screws in the recent poor weather. In the middle of the first big drop, with the car travelling at forty-five miles per hour, Miss Fritton went through the floor, losing both her feet to the scything sleepers. Due to the centrifugal force of the ride there was scarcely a drop of blood that had not been forced from her by the time the electricity could be turned off.

Maria Brown was deeply traumatised by the accident, but her misery was partially mitigated by the fact that Miss Fritton had left her a considerable amount of money, on the condition that she would take care of the apart-ment and its contents. Maria Brown dutifully did as she was bid, then booked her passage back to the West Indies.

She returned to a wooden house in St John's, Antigua, with almond trees, a pink and green verandah, a VCR and a cellular phone system imported from Montserrat. Feeling guilty but faced with no other choice, she left the urn and the rest of Miss Fritton's belongings in the care of her cousin Bill in Notting Hill.

'Calypso' Bill was considered a bit of a ne'er-do-well and lived up to his reputation by promptly selling off the old lady's furniture. He couldn't get anything for the urn and still had it under his arm wrapped in newspaper when he accidentally incurred the wrath of an obeah man in a local pub called the Albatross.

The furious obeah man accused Calypso Bill of trying to steal his woman, which may have been true, and with a mystic pass of the hand 'turned his eyes'. Bill, who believed in the witchcraft of the old country, was instantly blinded, his eyes turning over in their sockets, and stumbled out into the street to be knocked down by a truck delivering skimmed yoghurt from Northern France. On the dashboard of the truck was a copy of Baudelaire's *Les fleurs du mal*.

In the confusion following the accident, the urn was knocked from the bar and burst open, its contents clouding out onto the folded jacket of a young man named Simon Turner. Turner was a frustrated insurance clerk who had long considered leaving his job to live a life unfettered by convention. He wanted to be an artist but lacked the necessary bravery to break free. That afternoon, though, he dusted off his jacket and returned to the insurance office with a determined look in his eye.

He demanded an interview with his superior, resigned on the spot, received a cheque for his back pay and walked from the building a liberated man.

Within a month the change in Simon's appearance and personality was remarkable. He rented a tiny studio apartment in Shepherd's Bush, filled it with art equipment, dyed his hair into a red and yellow striped mohawk, put a silver pin through his nostril and strolled through the market in purple tartan bondage trousers. He was not a very talented artist, but at least he felt like one.

Simon's former colleagues would never have recognised him – and in fact, they didn't when they staggered out of a local wine bar called Vive La France late one night and saw him standing on Shepherd's Bush Green studying the configurations of the stars. Irrationally annoyed by someone who clearly dismissed notions of conformity by refusing to wear a regulation grey suit and black nylon socks, they drunkenly kicked him to death.

Simon's jacket, still heavily impregnated with the urn's contents despite a visit to the dry-cleaners, was given to Oxfam and bought by a girl called Amanda, who worked for a Bloomsbury publishing house. She embroidered an ornate collar around the jacket, tutting at the greasy grey dust that emerged from the unpicked material, and wore it to a smart French restaurant that was hosting the launch of the publishing house's most successful author.

Being a lowly assistant, Amanda's job was to stack the author's new book – a poetic romance set in nineteenth-century Paris – in attractive piles that would draw the attention of reviewers and photographers. The room was filled with literary celebrities, magazine writers, minor television personalities and tabloid journalists, in that order, and Amanda, taking time off from her stacking duties, enriched her vocabulary by chatting amiably with the first group.

Returning to her book display to straighten a wayward

pile, Amanda was shot in the face by an assassin's bullet that had been intended for Salman Rushdie. She died instantly, and Mr Rushdie was safely hustled from the rear of the building into a waiting car. It seems callous but necessary to mention that Amanda's jacket was ruined. As her broken body was removed from the restaurant, the embroidered collar became detached and landed under a table, where it was later discovered and pocketed by one of the cleaning staff.

The cleaner, a young French girl named Gabrielle, was visiting London with her mother and had taken a temporary job to earn a little extra cash. She sewed the dusty collar onto a white work blouse but, failing to find pleasure in the effect it produced, folded the garment away into a valise that her mother was sending back to France. Two weeks later, the package containing the bag was delivered to their gloomy apartment in Paris and taken in by Alice, a friend who was staying there.

Alice had been dating a jazz musician who was killed in an air crash on the way to his first professional performance. One night, a heroin addict named Charles broke into the apartment and ransacked it, looking for money. Alice, returning late from a poetry reading, surprised the thief in the act and was clubbed to death with the nearest weapon to hand, a ceramic chamber pot. The addict grabbed a gilt mantel clock, a jewellery box and Gabrielle's package, and fled down the fire-escape.

Charles bought his fix by fencing the contents of the jewellery box, then boarded a train and alighted at Rennes, where his former girlfriend worked, cleaning house for a young farmer who was purportedly the master of the Château Saint Vincent. However, when he reached the château he found the building locked up, the windows barred and bolted. Although the property had been sold, the new owner had become seriously ill and was, as yet, unable to take possession.

Charles sat down on the overgrown steps of the building to think through his next move. He could not return to Paris, for he was too well known to the police, and they would now be searching for a murderer. He studied the crusted needle marks on his arms and knew that he would soon be needing another fix, another chance to keep himself suspended between pleasure and death. What was there left for him to barter now? In the back of his brain, a strange fragment of poetry surfaced; something to do with flies humming over the guts of a corpse. *Les mouches* ... The words were buzzing in his head like the insects themselves.

He still had the package containing the valise and opened it once again to see if there was anything at all that he could sell. But there was not. Angrily, Charles tossed the case onto an iron drainage grate at the foot of the steps and searched his waistcoat for a joint. He found a squashed brown stub and jammed it in the corner of his mouth. Then he scratched a match against the heel of his cowboy boot.

He would not have done so had he known that several months before, his former girlfriend, being the last of the château's departing staff, had failed to turn off the kitchen gas taps, and the pipes beneath the house were now filled to capacity with highly flammable vapour.

The force of the match igniting the combustible mists leaking from the drain upon which the valise stood blew Charles into the air like a mad rag doll. He landed on his head in an ornamental garden seventy feet away. The explosion shattered a stained-glass window in the small chapel, which stood to one side of the main building, and blew the contents of the case through it, so that Gabrielle's white shirt with the embroidered collar fluttered down upon the chapel altar with a silken sigh, to drape itself neatly over the upturned brass crucifix, which stood there patiently awaiting the arrival of the damned surplice.

The satanic history of the Condorcet family is well documented. Of less common knowledge is the fact that, in exchange for their success in the black arts, the Condorcets were not permitted to leave the Château Saint Vincent. It was written that if they did so, catastrophe would befall all who impeded their restitution and that even in death they would be forced to return and remain, whole or in part, on the ungodly site. The prophecy was now fulfilled.

Evil Eye

I was commissioned to write this for an anthology of superstitions, but as I'm not superstitious I decided to tackle a related area. The best tale of misunderstood omens is Daphne Du Maurier's 'Don't Look Now'. After all, why should we grasp the significance of future events if we're not used to reading the signs?

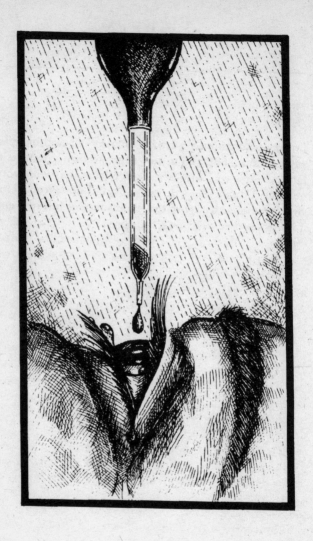

SIXTY-FIVE MILES on the wrong side of Rancho Mirage, Todd Cartland began to fall asleep at the wheel. The incessant thrumming of tyres on tarmac dulled his mind and closed his eyes as the Chrysler LeBaron drifted slowly toward the hard shoulder, spraying dirt against the wheel arches. This time he managed to snap himself awake in time. Another few seconds and the car could have finished up just another overturned rusting wreck by the side of the highway. He was still a hundred and ninety miles from San Diego. Time to take a break. The glowing green numerals of the dashboard clock clicked over to 10.15 pm. He checked the gas gauge. Less than a third of a tank left. There was nothing to see through the bug-spattered windshield, just the road ahead and a dark patch at the horizon where the hills met the stars. Once in a while a stovepipe truck rolled by, a wall of shiny rib panels and amber lights, like the side of a ship. He reached across the seat and yanked his map back into the dash light, tracing the route with his thumb. He had not planned on breaking the trip until he was clear of the desert, but what the hell; for once he wasn't on any schedule.

There was a diner sign approaching on his left, vertical letters in yellow neon blinking out an illegible message, a gas station beyond that. He slowed the car and swung it onto a brush-covered slip road, gently fishtailing the vehicle as the rear tyres slipped on sand.

The diner was called Buddies, enough of a fifties design throwback to have been considered retro-fashionable in the city. Out here it was just another truck stop, with red and blue plastic seats, stay-hot lamps above the meal point and ancient waitresses in tennis shoes.

Cartland pulled into the lot beyond the picture windows and turned off the engine. As he opened the car door the cold desert air hit him, a clear fifteen-degree drop from his last step outside. Still dressed in jeans and a short-sleeved shirt, he removed a chilled sweater from his bag in the trunk, slung it over his shoulders and entered the diner.

The waitress, a plump late-forties blonde with 'Myra' stencilled on her badge, checked out his designer shirt on the way to the booth in the nonsmoking section, probably thinking he was a little uptown for the establishment. She dropped a well-thumbed menu in front of him. 'Your waitress will be with you in a moment,' she said, displaying her dental plate. 'That'll be me again.'

'Thanks. Where's your men's room?'

She hiked her thumb. 'Out back and left.'

He walked to the rear of the overlit diner, taking in the Muzak version of an old Willie Nelson song. Eight people in the place, including the two waitresses. A blackboard hanging over the counter; 'Today's Special – Meatloaf & Gravy'. This was good. Diners had a reassuring home-liness that hotels lacked, even when they tried to copy it. He was glad to be free of Phoenix. Free. It was a concept that would take some getting used to. He cupped his hands in the washbasin and splashed icy water on his face. His reflection stared back, tan and forty, a little lost.

He wondered how long he'd be able to hold out, firing off toward the coast with no real purpose. He'd called the office, told them he was taking the rest of the week off, and it was only Monday. What else could he do?

Staying on at the house was out of the question. Amy would never have allowed it. Anyway, the place was in her name. He knew that by now all the glass would have been swept up. She'd probably have arranged for the chair to be replaced, too. Amy was infinitely sensible, always practical. He dried his face and returned to the table, taking his time with the menu.

'What can I getcha, honey?' The waitress was back, pad poised.

'You still have the special?'

Myra looked at him with the wisdom of ages. 'Honey, we *always* have the special, only by this time of night it ain't so special.' Her eyes flicked to the chef, who was scratching himself with a spatula. 'Steak's good.'

'You sold me.'

'Comes with fries or jacket potato, sour cream.'

'Fries. And a beer.'

'Miller, Coors, Budweiser.'

Behind her, headlights crossed the glass as a steel-sided big rig pulled in and doused its engine.

'Miller's fine.'

'Be right up.' She packed her pad and went for the ice water.

The entrance door opened and closed. A young man in a cowboy hat and a canary-coloured truck jacket took the nearest counter stool. He was in his mid-twenties, dressed for riding distances, blue jeans and worn boots. Handsome. Vaguely familiar.

The waitress set out his beer and cutlery. It was a slow night. He could tell she was going to talk to him.

'You headin' for San Diego?'

'How'd you know?'

'Ain't nowhere else to head for on this route. You got the desert on either side, Palm Springs if you play golf and you're real old, a few small towns but nothin' you'd want to visit. You come from Phoenix?'

'Guess you must be clairvoyant, Myra.'

She looked up and smiled, creases through make-up. 'Not me. I leave that stuff to Sasha. She's good, too.'

'Who's Sasha?'

'She's kinda like a palm reader, she lives out back o' here. She came from Russia originally. They hounded her out 'cause o' her powers. Said she had the evil eye on her.' She looked around the diner. 'Guess this is about the farthest away you can get from Russia.'

Cartland was intrigued, but mostly he was killing time until his steak arrived. There was no one else waiting to be served. The cowboy had ordered direct from the cook. 'So, can she tell me my future?'

Myra rested one hand on her hip. 'Up to about five years, she reckons. All depends. She says it gets hazy after that. I says to her, "Sasha, I can't even remember *back* five years, I don't know how you can manage it forwards."' Shaking her head, she went for the steak platter.

The cowboy took a sip from the neck of his beer, set it down and surveyed the room, sharp blue eyes shining in the shadow of his hat brim. For a long second he caught Cartland's gaze and returned it. Eyes like the tinted glass of a Mercedes windshield. A relaxed face cut in neat, tan planes. Then he turned back to his beer.

'Enjoy,' said Myra, placing an oval plate before him. The steak was vast, the gravy elastic. For the next twenty minutes he chewed and watched, chewed and thought. Mostly, he just chewed. Amy sponging the wine from the wall and the carpet, Amy emptying the dustpan into the bin. Maybe he should have stayed to help before taking off. No, she wouldn't have wanted him to. Too much had been said to resume conversation. Funny, for weeks they had barely spoken at all, then this fountain of anger erupting between them, shattering the uneasy truce. A few home truths, a few nerves touched. A point reached where real damage was done, even if they'd both taken back their words.

The pie looked good. It was under glass on the counter. The cowboy had some, forking each mouthful thoughtfully. Cartland ordered a piece and coffee to flush it down.

'Myra, is there a decent motel around here? I don't want to drive on tonight.'

'Sure, at exit fifteen, about eight miles west. It's all lit up, you can't miss it. You wouldn't want to take a picture of the place but it's clean.'

'Perfect.'

His pie arrived as the cowboy laid down some change and slowly rose from his stool. By the time Cartland looked up again, he was gone. He turned away Myra's offer of a refill, asked for the bill instead. Somehow the place seemed less interesting now than when he had walked in. He left a large tip, feeling vaguely sorry for the waitress. He took a mint from the tray and looked back, watching her clear his table. She smiled thanks across at him.

'Don't forget what I said about Sasha,' she called. 'She's got your future all laid out, I'll bet.'

Curiosity got the better of him as he walked back to the car. He turned back around the side of the diner and spotted the low wooden building hedged with cacti. The hand-painted sign on the porch read, 'Madame Sasha sees the truth – $25.00'. It seemed a reasonable deal. The sign was decorated with the usual astrological crap, glowing eyes, stars, electric flashes. Beyond orange wool drapes the lights were on. As he walked toward the building he fingered the billfold in his pocket, smiling to himself. If Madame Sasha could figure this one out, she knew a damned sight more than he did.

'Kindly sit over here on the cushions.' The woman waiting in the lounge was old and tiny, jerky in her movements, like a long-neglected doll. If she really came from Russia, there was no evidence of it in her voice. Her speech had the Lone Star twang of a Texas preacher. The room was bright, decorated in earth tones. Clay pots, Navajo rugs and too many cacti, most of them marked with For Sale tags. Cartland settled into the cushions and sat back. There was no table between them. Wasn't there always supposed to be a table? As if reading his mind the old woman slowly shook her head.

'I don't see your future by studying palms or laying out cards. You can pay me first if you like. Cash.'

Cartland dug out two tens and a five. She pocketed the notes in her dress and seated herself in a kitchen chair opposite. Her slippered feet barely reached the floor.

'Then how do you do it?' he asked.

'I'll show you. Come, sit forward. D'you have a lucky object on you?'

'No.'

She released a crackly sigh. 'You're one o' them rational types, I suppose.'

'I don't believe in trusting things to luck,' he said.

'What, you never bet on a grey horse because it felt right? In my country, there's a fair amount we believe in that ain't rational to the Western mind.'

'We have that kind of thing too.' Cartland shrugged. 'Step on a crack, seven years bad luck – kid stuff.'

'You believe?'

He hauled short a laugh, scratching the side of his nose. 'Uh, no, not exactly.'

'You should. It never hurts to keep an open mind.'

'Right.' He had been expecting some kind of full-blown mystic preamble to her routine. Instead, Sasha became brisk and businesslike, as if she was running some kind of homeopathic medical practice. He pulled himself to the edge of the cushion as she manoeuvred a metal lamp stand between them and switched on its small, bright light.

'We'll do it this way,' she said. 'I read eyes. In the old country there were many beliefs concerning their power. Often the eyes were cut from the newly dead and kept. I saw my father do it once. A distant uncle, he lay on the bier in his black suit, skin whiter than ice. My father dug his fingers into the dry sockets and pulled his old eyes free, cutting the tendons with a knife. Real tough muscles. I was supposed to turn away but I looked. Please stare at the shade and hold still.' She hunched forward and gently pulled the skin beneath his left eyeball downward. 'Each cornea is different and has its own individual markings. As unique as your fingerprints.'

'That's what you're looking at?'

'First the cornea. To figure out your situation. Then through its iris to the darkness of the retina to understand your future. You must keep still, though.' Sasha's own eyesight didn't seem so hot. One pupil was an odd colour and turned in. She produced a small magnifier and held it to his cheek, studying carefully. 'You're married, but there are no children. Some confusion here.'

Cartland figured fortune-tellers built on the information supplied by their clients and resolved to give as little away as possible. 'What sort of confusion?'

'Well, you've had an argument. Didn't hit her, did you?'

He recoiled slightly. 'No, why would you think that?'

'It was a very big fight. More than a fight, a break. You won't go back, I don't think.'

'I don't know, I haven't decided yet ...'

'It's not really for you to decide. What was this argument about?' Staring into the light was beginning to hurt. She switched the magnifier to his other eye.

'You tell me,' he said. 'You're the fortune-teller.'

'I can't be expected to do everything. Come here.' She yanked at his eye and stared hard into it. 'Jeez, more confusion. Sex, I think. Yeah, definitely sex.'

Cartland coloured. 'What about it?' he asked defensively.

'There's something I think she knows that you don't.' The old woman sat back, considering the matter. 'She tells you that she knows it, but you deny it anyway.'

'No ...'

'Don't lie to me, mister. There's denial in your eyes. You were angry. You left, maybe to change your life.' She paused. 'Why did you stop making love to your wife?'

The suddenness of the question made him falter in surprise. 'I don't ... know.'

'H'm. Perhaps you don't. Now, the future. This is different. I'll show you.' She gestured. 'Come here.'

Cartland sat forward once more, unsettled. He'd give her five more minutes of his time then head for the motel.

'The heart of your eye holds a mirror to your future. The clearer the picture, the nearer the event.'

'Did they really hound you out of Russia?'

'Really. Portents and omens, I could read 'em all. People don't like to know what will happen. Hold very still.' Her eyes narrowed. 'Strange. I think I understand your past, but not your future. Perhaps you can help. The picture itself is very clear, the meaning not so much.'

'What do you see?'

'First, a tall tree and a bright light. The most dazzling of colours, brilliant yellow. Blue eyes, the bluest of blue. Now red. Now stars. And there are words. The words are . . . love. Friend. So very clear.'

She sat back and studied his face, comprehension filling her old eyes. 'It's to be a new path for you,' she said finally. 'I need to double-check, see the same picture from a slightly different angle. Show me your other eye.' She raised the magnifying glass again. 'Yes, it's love alright . . . wait a minute, this isn't right . . .' She sat upright suddenly. 'Odd . . .' Her tanned forehead crumpled in a frown.

'What is it?' asked Cartland, alarmed.

'I don't s'pose you'd believe me if I told you,' she said, half to herself. 'Rational types never do. It's all there in the eyes if you just care to look.' Her voice had a faraway tone. 'There are those in the old country who think that the last thing a man sees before he dies stays on in his eyes. Leastways, in them that die violently . . .' After a moment of silence she reached across and seized his hand. 'But you, why you're alive. Alive! So maybe it ain't just a superstition after all, maybe it's a warning. And you must go very quickly.' She jumped down from the chair. 'Get as far away from here as possible. It's tough for me to interpret all the signs. I ain't always right. For your own safety, you understand. Go right now.'

Virtually pulling him from the seat, she led him back to the door. 'Don't stop, don't talk to anyone. Run, run!'

The door was opened and slammed in his face. Cartland was left standing alone on the porch with the flickering night bugs. The old woman was obviously crazed. How could she earn a living out here if she gave such half-assed advice to her customers? Shaking his head in amazement, he returned to the car. The desert air had chilled the interior. His breath condensed on the windshield as he keyed into the ignition and revved the engine to an angry roar.

Back on the freeway there were fewer cars than before. The dashboard clock read 11.50 pm. Eight miles to the motel. What had the old woman seen inside his eyes? Love, friendship, colours and a tree. Real specific stuff. Dead men's eyes. She'd been right about Amy, though. How the hell did she do that? Had he really looked that guilty to her? A new path, she said. Maybe he was about to find Jesus. That was all he'd been able to get on the local radio stations. He thumbed a cigarette into his mouth and depressed the dash lighter. Looking up, he found a familiar truck drawing alongside, the one driven by the young cowboy from the diner. He remembered the logo, Glover Truck Company, Arizona. The cowboy looked down from his cab as he passed, recognised his fellow traveller and slowly smiled. There was no one else on the road now, no lights in the hills beyond, just an illuminated ribbon of freeway cutting through the landscape toward the San Andreas faultline. Cartland felt an exhilarated sense of freedom, a bond with the young driver who raced beside him through the night. For several minutes they drove like this, truck and car edging ahead in turn, engines thrumming smoothly across the plains, then the cowboy accelerated and the rig sped ahead into the night, crimson taillights vanishing around a curve.

The sign said Exit 15 and sure enough, there was the motel, a low spotlit building with a tar-paper roof and a wooden boardwalk. He was almost reluctant to leave the deserted freeway, but as he followed the ramp around he saw the truck parked at the rear of the motel and felt a tightening in his chest.

It took less than five minutes to check in. The gloomy reception area was filled with faded photographs of the desert taken during freak weather conditions, flood, hail, brush fires.

'I'll give you a discount on the room 'cause you may find the bed a mite damp,' said the old man behind the desk. 'We don't air the cabins every day at this time of the year, there's not enough custom. I said the same to the other fella.' He removed a key from the hook and passed it across the counter. 'Number 27, at the end of the terrace. If you check out before I'm awake, leave your key in the door.'

Cartland returned to the car and collected his travel bag. A single tall date palm stood in the centre of the car park, two spotlights shining through a cloud of bugs at its base. The sound of crickets filled the night air. The riding lights on the cowboy's parked truck still glowed in the dark. Cartland swung the bag to his shoulder and headed for room 27.

The door was already unlocked. He crossed the room and turned on the bedside lamp, waiting for the roaches to scuttle from view. The ubiquitous desert views graced the walls, and a pair of hard, dry towels lay folded on top of the comforter. He unzipped the bag, removing a toothbrush and face cloth. Past the boardwalk, the truck's sidelights winked through the window like friendly red eyes. Cartland wondered if the cowboy had forgotten to switch them off. He turned back to the half-opened front door, unable to prevent his pulse from picking up.

Outside, something dark flew across the porch, batted against the glass and vanished, some kind of flying insect. He turned back to the business of unpacking. Toothpaste. Soap. Shaving foam. No razor. He'd packed in a fury, anxious to be gone. Amy hadn't cried. She'd stayed to watch, calm and resigned, as if his moment of departure had long been anticipated. As he had pulled out of the drive she had stared from the window, an expressionless face behind sunlit glass.

Slow boot steps on the boardwalk. The cowboy passed before his doorway, paused and moved on in the direction of his truck. Cartland remained at the bedside, waiting for the sound of the door slamming and the engine turning over, but no other sound disturbed the night. He moved to the window and peered out, but all was darkness beyond the porch light. Flicking on the radiator beside the bed and setting the thermostat, he sat down, listening. Nothing.

Just then the cabinet lamp flickered and buzzed in time with the porch light, pulsing with fluctuating voltage before they both popped out. He rose in total darkness, swearing beneath his breath. He'd forgotten that this kind of thing happened regularly in the desert. Reaching his arms wide before him, Cartland walked slowly ahead until he came to the doorway. Gradually his eyes adjusted to the moonlight, and he could discern the shapes of his car and the truck, parallel parked in the sandy lot beyond the bedrooms, their engines ticking in the cool air.

The cowboy was leaning against the side of the rig with his hands in his pockets, his angelic face half lost in shadow. It was almost as if he'd been waiting there for

Cartland's arrival. He removed one hand from his jeans and scratched a match across a wheel arch, lighting the Camel which slanted from his lips. Cartland stepped down from the boardwalk, his heart pounding in his chest. He could barely catch his breath. A cloud cleared, the moonlight slowly detailing the man and the truck.

'Lights're always goin' out in this joint.' The glow of the cigarette end cast a red tattoo across Cowboy's cheek. 'Jacob never remembers to check the generators.'

Cartland found his voice. 'You've stayed here before?'

'I'm here all the time. But this is a whole new territory for you, ain't it? Stand closer, I can't see you clear enough. Where you from?'

'I just came out of Phoenix,' replied Cartland, taking a step closer.

'Rose up from the ashes, huh?' Cowboy slowly smiled. 'Guess I knew you was gonna stop here.'

'How did you know that?'

'I heard Myra tellin' you directions in the diner. So.' He pulled on his cigarette, firing up the tip. 'What did you think you'd find here?'

Sweat beaded Cartland's forehead. 'What do you mean?'

'It's way past bedtime. Night's real cold. What was you looking for?'

'I wasn't looking for anything . . .'

'You know damn well what I mean.' He stretched out his hand and brushed the front of Cartland's shirt with his fingertips. 'You gotta know when to make choices, pal. I knew what you wanted the moment I saw you. Way you looked at me in the diner, like I was a hot meal and you was starvin'.'

He enclosed Cartland's wrist in a fist and slowly drew

it toward him, forcing open his fingers, sliding them beneath his trucker's coat, inside his shirt, across his hairless chest. It was as if an electric shock passed through Cartland, but he was unable to move.

'If you don't like it,' Cowboy said, 'you can always take your hand away.'

In the grip of personal revelation, Cartland remained immobile. He saw now that every recent event in his life had been building to this moment. He understood the Russian woman's reference to his fight with Amy. Both women had seen his own blindness. But now that the scales had fallen from his eyes, he was terrified, unable to budge a single inch. This was the moment that Sasha had predicted – the tall spotlit tree, the love, the changing of his path. Once more he experienced the feeling of elation that had swept over him on the freeway. He felt like a child again, about to discover the world beyond the walls.

The look on Cowboy's face cooled as he released Cartland's sweating hand and brushed the ash from his yellow jacket. 'I've seen this so many times before,' he said. 'Regular married guy on the outside, but underneath you're just another desperate guy who don't know which direction he's s'posed to be headed.'

Cartland was starting to shake. 'Now wait a minute,' he began defensively, 'you grabbed me, what does that make you?'

'Well, I'll tell you.' Cowboy ground the Camel stub into the sand and looked him in the eye. 'It makes me the Way and the Truth and the Light. I help to keep this area clean. The old lady – Sasha – she raised me. She says I ain't entirely right in the head, but she looks after me, keeps me from harm. She protects me from guys like you.' He stepped forward, filling Cartland's vision. 'And she protects guys like you from me.'

Cowboy drew the pearl-handled cutthroat razor from his back pocket and carefully unfolded it. The desert night closed in around the two motionless men, separated from each other by a strip of shining steel.

Cartland looked at the scene before him and suddenly understood what the old woman had seen in his eyes. When she had spoken of the picture within, she had meant it literally. Here it was, as if a camera had frozen the moment forever.

The tall illuminated palm, thrusting into the night sky.

Cowboy standing in front of the rig, obscuring the first letter of the 'Glover Trucking' symbol. Desert dust staining the rest so that only four letters were visible.

The folds of Cowboy's jacket reducing 'Friendlier Freighters' to 'Friend'.

The yellow of his jacket.

The blue of his eyes.

But where was the red?

Finally he saw it, reflected in the razor's mirrored blade as it completed the path across his throat and soared into a sparkling sky.

The darkest of angels filled his vision, framed in a universe of stars, a final sight that seared its way into his eyes to stay forever in each ganglion and receptor, imprinted across each thickening lens, engraved upon each retinal wall in a daguerreotype of his death.

What the eye doesn't see, remembered Cartland, *the heart doesn't grieve about.*

The thought failed to comfort him as he fell.

Brian Foot's Blaze Of Glory

Poor old Brian. Most of us know somebody like him, a magnet to misfortune, a hopeless loser upon whom we cannot wish better fortune for the simple reason that he doesn't really deserve any better. I was thinking about hitting the ceiling of one's station in life; Salieri recognised his inability to create the music of the spheres, but what if you fail to realise the miserable truth; that what you get is the most you deserve?

HE HATED his name. *Brian* sounded like something from the fifties, which he was, and *Foot* was, well, feet, as in other people's feet.

He hated his age, which was forty-two. He had stopped enjoying life at thirty, not that he'd enjoyed it much up until then, and now he *really* didn't enjoy it. He could count the things he still enjoyed on one hand; he enjoyed 'Brookside' and something else, he forgot what.

He hated his appearance, which was short and thin and half bald with a large pink head and rimless glasses and hairy hands with spatulate fingers that women seemed to find unpleasant.

He hated just about everything else with the exception of Häagen-Dazs Double Chocolate Chip ice cream, which he couldn't afford anyway. In recent months he'd come to think of himself as an exhausted old bus that had finished its route and was gently coasting back into the shadows of the terminal. The worst part was, he hadn't even realised that it was happening until now.

As a child, he was mercilessly teased at the grubby South London state school he attended; about his name, about his looks, about his inability to catch a ball and about his way of walking like a duck. His mother fretted, his father threatened. 'Be a man and learn to fight your own battles,' he'd say, towering over the frightened boy like a thundercloud. 'Don't let those bullies get away with it.'

'I don't know what you expect him to do,' his mother would counter, 'he's only small.' An argument would start, and pretty soon the cause of it would be forgotten as his parents moved on to problems of their own.

There was a kid the exact same age as Brian at school, but age was all that the two boys had in common. Maximillian had a cool name, a cool dad who drove a silver Mercedes 350SL, a cool mum who wore sexy shorts to Parents' Day and lots of cool friends. Brian always wanted to be like Maximillian, but of course, it was impossible. The whole set of parameters was wrong. Maximillian didn't have to try; he was good at everything. Making new friends, hitting the ball, scoring good test marks. Brian was always the last to be picked for the lunch-time football game. He would overhear a clever remark and hopefully repeat it, only to get beaten up. Kids didn't like him because he was so damned nice that there had to be something wrong, something not normal. Maximillian had the attitude of a midnight iceberg and was surrounded by people who wanted to play Titanic.

Brian couldn't understand it. He tried to stay out of the way and to do what he was told, but the more he behaved himself, the more he was beaten up. He longed to befriend Maximillian, but the social apparatus of the times didn't allow for such a situation; kids like Maximillian came and talked to you, not vice versa. Brian stayed home and read *Spiderman* comics, watched 'Thunderbirds', made elaborate models from plasticine, wrote himself stories, talked to the cat.

He left school with terrible grades because he always got nervous in exams and when that happened his mind went blank. His mother cried for days, and his father stopped addressing him directly.

The awful thing was, school days turned out to be the best days of Brian's life. At least he'd enjoyed reading the *Spiderman* comics. Now he was expected to be an adult, while having no prospects and no idea of what he might be able to offer an employer in the way of job skills.

Two days before his nineteenth birthday Brian was hit in the small of the back by a passing car, and the accident seriously injured his spine. The car didn't stop, and nobody managed to get the licence plate number. He could never stand quite upright or walk in a straight line after that.

He was forced to take a succession of dull jobs in dull parts of the city, nursed his mother for years before she died, and paid the bills for his now-senile father, who had a habit of walking into shops and taking things without paying for them.

But he did manage to find romance. He should have realised that his future wife was trouble when the boy-friend she'd walked out on attacked him in a pub before he'd even had a chance to speak to her. Brian was married for just over three years, between the ages of twenty-nine and thirty-two. Cheryl gave him genital herpes, emptied their joint account and left him for the young man who had previously been convicted for stealing his car.

On the eve of his forty-third birthday, Brian seated himself at his father's old dressing table, studied his reflection and gave careful consideration to his future.

There certainly didn't seem to be much to look forward to.

Brian thought hard; there had to be something.

But he realised with a sinking pit-of-the-stomach shock that there was *nothing* to look forward to, *nothing at all*. How could his life have passed so fast? People always talked about living for seventy or eighty years, but nobody pointed out that only the first three decades were any fun.

He recognised the growing symptoms of depression in himself and realised that although it sometimes seemed as if there was nothing left to live for, there were still little pleasures to be taken. He often thought of Maximillian, whom he hadn't seen since his eighteenth birthday, and created scenarios in which Maximillian, now reduced to begging for spare change beneath bridges, caught tuberculosis and slowly wasted away. Little things like that made him happy.

Until he actually bumped into Maximillian, of course. Maximillian, the creator of the biggest retail fashion chain in South London, the proud owner of houses in Belgravia, Hampstead and Provence, the tanned god who looked like a million dollars and drove a Maclaren F1, which cost about that.

Brian knew that his old classmate had failed to recognise him. Nobody ever remembered him, not even the milkman or the paperboy. His weight fluctuated and his face had the sandy vagueness of a regional newsreader.

'I thought it was you,' he said, having first watched from the corner of the bar until he was sure. 'Brian Foot.' He held out his hand. 'I was in your class at school.'

Brian was ready for a rebuff. He felt sure that Maximillian would peer down his nose and hastily dismiss the notion of their acquaintance. But no, the tycoon was as charming as could be and, after modestly recounting highlights of the intervening years, even invited Brian back to meet the wife, a former top model turned successful actress who was waiting at their charming Belgravia pied-à-terre in a pose reminiscent of the couple's recent spread in *Hello!* magazine.

Brian pulled his jacket sleeves over his frayed cuffs, cast surreptitious glances at Maximillian's tailored Armani suit and thought of his own damp, dark, smelly apartment above Clapham Common tube station. There was something he had to ask, something that had bothered him for years. How did people like Maximillian manage it? What special thing did they have that he could never have?

Brian swallowed his remaining vestiges of pride and asked.

Maximillian smiled secretly when he heard the question.

He leaned forward, until his face was just inches from Brian's.

'It's simple,' he replied. 'I'm ruthless in business, ruthless in friendship.' He smiled again. 'And people love it.'

Brian made his apologies and explained that he had to be going, that he was late enough already.

'Any time you're passing,' said Maximillian with a smile as big as the borough of Bromley, 'please drop in and see us. You must come to dinner one evening. We really would love to have you.' He passed over a calling card of satisfying creamy thickness, and Brian graciously took his leave.

Brian trudged home in the rain, filled with bitter humours. *It's so easy to be nice when you're rich*, he thought. *Showing off about his wife like that.* But beneath this he recognised the dire truth, that he had actually liked the man, and it made Brian hate him even more. *That's how guys like Maximillian work*, he thought. *They tell you they're bastards, and you still like them.*

But he wished to God he didn't.

Weeks passed, and the card sat on Brian's mantelpiece like an accusing finger. One day he started to tear it in half, but the supreme fibre quality of the damned thing resisted easy destruction. Finally he set fire to it in the wastebin, watching the pale green flame with grim satisfaction. What galled him most was the fact that, no matter what happened from now on, he would never, ever achieve a greater moment of glory than his former schoolmate. Maximillian would always be ahead of him. Brian wanted to die.

And then it hit him.

If he was going to kill himself, he'd go out in a blaze of glory. Die in a manner so spectacular, so shocking that the newspapers would talk of nothing else for weeks. History would remember him. He'd make a mark bigger than any chain of shops. What could he do? Throw himself from the roof of the House of Lords during the reading of a particularly controversial bill? Leap under the Grand National favourite? Stab himself to death on national television? Put a gun in his mouth in front of Prince Charles?

Brian knew he could perform none of these acts. If he hadn't been able to organise a single element of his life in forty-two years, how could he hope to lay his hands on a gun or bluff his way into a TV studio? It was pointless even to try.

But a knife, anyone could use a knife. He went to a kitchen shop and bought a small sharp one, £6.99, guaranteed for life and destined to be the instrument of his death. Then he set about choosing a high-profile location for this final, immortalising act.

Several weeks passed, and nothing suitable presented itself.

One morning Brian opened his newspaper to read that Her Majesty the Queen would be performing one of her meet-the-public walkabouts in the East End the following Saturday. If he could just get close enough to her before cutting his throat, why he might even manage to get his death on camera. He could picture the scene: the Queen, horrified, leaping back, blood spattering her blue woollen Hardy Amies coat, and Brian, gore soaked, collapsing across her path as thousands screamed.

It was worth the front page of every national newspaper.

Feverishly, Brian set about arranging his triumphant blaze of glory. He sewed a special leather pocket into his jacket from which the knife could be swiftly withdrawn. Then he visited shops in the Hackney area and slowly pieced together details of the royal route. The Queen was to open a new burns unit for children. After this she would walk along the High Street shaking hands, be presented with bouquets by local schoolkids and chat lightly with a handful of carefully selected shopkeepers. The road was to be closed to regular traffic and waist-high steel barriers were to be placed between the blue-blood and her public to avoid the dangers of intimacy and overcrowding. Brian didn't fancy doing the deed on the other side of a barrier. For one thing, he would have to vault over it if he wanted to land at her feet, a daunting task when your throat was cut. He considered slashing his trachea after confronting the Queen, but the chance of having the knife wrested away from him by security officers was too great.

There were, however, two points along the route where Her Majesty would be more vulnerable; alighting and embarking from her limousine. The arrival spot afforded little opportunity as it would be the most guarded area, with a high police presence and a variety of local dignitaries lined up to press the royal flesh. The end of the walkabout looked more promising. The excitement of seeing the Queen would be wearing off a bit by then. People would be lowering their plastic Union Jacks, saying to each other, 'She's much smaller than I thought,' and heading back to their cars.

Thanks to the early erection of the barriers, Brian was able to locate the exact spot where he would cut his throat at precisely 3.45 pm on Saturday afternoon. The rest would be history.

Suddenly Brian's days were filled with purpose. There were so many things to take care of, standing orders to be stopped, accounts to be closed, letters to be written, milk to be cancelled, an enthralling suicide note to be constructed – something that would look good published in facsimile by the *Sunday Times* – rent to be paid up to the end of the month and clothes to be donated to the Salvation Army.

By 10.30 pm on Friday he had finished. The flat was empty, neat and tidy. It felt as if he was going on holiday, and in a sense he was. To celebrate, he allowed himself a small Guinness, then washed up the glass and set it on the draining board.

Saturday dawned wet and grey. Brian had made allowances for the weather, having already removed two buttons from a raincoat that would allow him to extricate the knife smoothly and speedily. Although he had burned Maximillian's card he still remembered the number and rang it to tell him to watch the evening news, but the line sounded disconnected.

Brian stood in the doorway of his flat looking back, then gently closed his life shut. He felt strangely at peace as he sat on the Hackney-bound tube train, as if his worries had been abandoned along with his belongings. He had thrown away what little cash he still possessed. Money would never trouble him again. His suicide note, a moving masterpiece that recounted a lifetime of thwarted ambition, was carefully folded in his trouser pocket. The knife nestled in its leather pouch, awaiting its one and only occasion of use. Brian's moment of glory had begun.

He had trouble making his way through the churning high-street crowds. There were far more people about than he had anticipated. By the time he reached the royal departure spot, Her Majesty was already inside the burns unit a quarter of a mile away.

Here, onlookers were being held back at the end of the barrier by a young policeman. Television cameras were trained on the crested door of the waiting Bentley. He cursed himself for not arriving earlier. How would he ever get close enough to be seen?

Just then, the weather gave a helping hand. It began to rain, the downpour growing heavier with each passing second. The crowd thinned a little as mothers pulled their children back to the sheltering shop fronts. Brian slithered through a departing family, making his way to the front of the barrier. Soon the rain eased to a drizzle and several people tried to make their way back, but Brian was established in his position; his hands gripped the barrier rail as if he was about to ride a roller coaster.

Suddenly the electricity of anticipation filled the air. She was coming, she was coming – Brian could sense the words buzzing above the sea of peering heads. He drank in these final scenes of his life, the colours, sights and smells. Glory approached.

There she was, a small figure in blue slowly making her way back to the car, her attention being drawn to various interesting sights by a tiresomely talkative councillor.

Brian slipped his hand into his overcoat and allowed his fingers to close around the handle of the knife. She was closer now and the cameras were recording her, the measured gait, the semblance of attention, the oddly appropriate hat. He shifted his right foot to the bottom rung of the barrier and tensed himself. Next to him a small girl was complaining to her father, something about not being able to see.

The entourage was no more than five yards away. Brian withdrew the knife and, hiding the razor-sharp blade within his palm, raised it to his throat, steeling himself for the pain of pierced flesh, the searing streak of fire, the hot gush of his departing life as he prepared to spring across the path of the approaching party . . .

Beside him, the father hitched his complaining daughter onto his shoulder so that she could see. Her suddenly rising leg caught Brian's elbow hard, and he stuck the knife into his ear. The agonising burst of neuralgic pain caused him to lose consciousness for a few moments, and he slipped silent and unnoticed between the bodies of the cheering crowd.

The nurses were huddled together discussing something in hushed tones, as if the topic was too awful to be mentioned aloud in front of sick people. One of them noticed his eyes were open and came to his bedside.

'Wakey, wakey,' she cried jovially. 'How's your head?'

'Hurts,' he managed. There was a bandage covering his right ear.

'Not surprised,' countered the nurse. 'Passed out with the excitement, did you? Can't see why folk get worked up about the royals meself.' Realising that he was having trouble hearing, she started speaking to him as if a sheet of glass separated them. 'You fell on something sharp. Cut your ear. Burst your eardrum.'

'Am I going to die?' he asked weakly.

'No,' she mouthed. 'You're gonna be deaf on your right side.'

The other nurses had regrouped around a television suspended from the wall. The 'Six O'Clock News' logo appeared. This was replaced by a shaky overhead view of a crowded street. He tried to sit up. Had he made the news after all?

'Awful, isn't it?' the nurse was telling her friend. The newsreader was explaining something, but Brian couldn't distinguish his words. People were fleeing in every direction. A clock tower erupted in flames.

'What's happened?' he asked the nurse.

'This bloke's run amuck,' she said, turning to him. 'Kitted himself out with all kinds of rifles and grenades, machine-gunned nearly seventy people before blowing himself sky high.'

'Where was this?' he asked, studying the blurred footage for clues. 'Texas?'

'No. Basildon. He'd been depressed, business had gone bust, wife had left him, usual thing.'

Maximillian's face filled the screen, and Brian jumped back with a yelp.

'Just think,' said the nurse, 'he's one of the biggest mass murderers in history. And he's British. That's one for the record books. Well, we'd better get your dressing changed, hadn't we?' She studied Brian's uncomprehending face. 'Then you can go home.'

She gave him a playful punch on the arm and laughed. 'Might need your bed for somebody more important.'

Mother Of The City

I was commissioned to write this London-based tale by *Time Out* and used it to crystallise a feeling I'd long had about the city; that as an entity it could be benign or unforgiving, and that your reaction toward the ancient guardians tending its interests decides the city's reaction to you. I also fancied writing the nightclub scene, something I've seen happen thousands of times in night-time London.

IF MY uncle Stanley hadn't passed out pornographic Polaroids of his second wife for the amusement of his football mates in the bar of the Skinner's Arms, I might have moved to London. But he did and I didn't, because his wife heard about it and threw him out on the street, and she offered the other half of her house to me.

My parents were in the throes of an ugly divorce and I was desperate to leave home. Aunt Sheila's house was just a few roads away. She wasn't asking much rent and she was good company, so I accepted her offer and never got around to moving further into town, and that's why I'll be dead by the time morning comes.

Fucking London, I hate it.

Here's a depressing thing to do. Grow up in the suburbs, watch your school friends leave one by one for new lives in the city, then bump into them eleven years later in your local pub, on an evening when you're feeling miserable and you're wearing your oldest, most disgusting jumper. Listen to their tales of financial derring-do in the public sector. Admire their smart clothes and the photos of exotic love partners they keep in their bulging wallets, photos beside which your uncle Stan's Polaroids pale into prudery. Try to make your own life sound interesting when they ask what *you've* been doing all this time, even though you know that the real answer is nothing. Don't tell them the truth. Don't say you've been marking time, you're working in the neighbourhood advice bureau, you drive a rusting Fiat Pipsqueak and there's a woman in Safeway you sometimes sleep with but you've no plans to marry.

Because they'll just look around at the pub's dingy flock wallpaper and the drunk kids in tracksuits and say, 'How can you stay here, Douglas? Don't you know what you've been missing in London all these years?'

I know what I've been missing all right. And while I'm thinking about that, my old school chums, my pals for life, my mates, my blood brothers will check their watches and drink up and shake my hand and leave me for the second time, unable to get away fast enough. And once again I stay behind.

You'll have to take my word for it when I say I didn't envy them. I really didn't. I'd been to London plenty of times, and I loathed the place. The streets were crowded and filthy and ripe with menace, the people self-obsessed and unfriendly. People are unfriendly around here as well, only you never see them except on Sunday mornings, when some kind of car-washing decathlon is staged throughout the estate. The rest of the time they're in their houses between the kettle and the TV set, keeping a sidelong watch on the street through spotless net curtains. You could have a massive coronary in the middle of the road and the curtains would twitch all around you, but no one would come out. They'll watch but they won't help. They'll say, 'We thought we shouldn't interfere.'

Fuck, I'm bleeding again.

Seeing as I'm about to die, it's important that you understand; where you live shapes your life. I'm told that the city makes you focus your ambitions. Suburbia drains them off. Move here and you'll soon pack your dreams away, stick them in a box with the Christmas decorations, meaning to return to them some day. You don't, of course. And you slowly become invisible, like the neighbours, numb and relaxed. It's a painless process. Eventually you perform all the functions of life without them meaning anything, and it's quite nice, like floating lightly in warm water. At least, that's what I used to think.

Around here the people have become unnaturally attached to the concept of shopping. They spend every weekend with their families scouring vast warehouses full of tat, looking for useless objects to acquire, shell-suited magpies feathering their nests with bright plastic objects. I shouldn't complain. I've always preferred things to people. Gadgets, landscapes, buildings. Especially buildings. As a child, I found my first visit to the British Museum more memorable than anything I'd seen before, not that I'd seen anything. I loved those infinite halls of waxed tiles, each sepulchral room with its own uniformed attendant. Smooth panes of light and dense silence, the exact opposite of my home life. My parents always spoke to me loudly and simultaneously. They complained about everything and fought all the time. I loved them, of course; you do. But they let us down too often, my sister and me, and after a while we didn't trust them any more.

I trusted the British Museum. Some of the exhibits frightened me; the glass box containing the leathery brown body of a cowering Pompeiian, the gilt-encased figures of vigilant guards protecting an Egyptian princess. Within its walls nothing ever changed, and I was safe and secure. I never had that feeling with my parents. Once my father drove us up from Meadowfields (that's the name of the estate; suitably meaningless, as there isn't a meadow in sight and never was) to the West End to see some crummy Christmas lights and to visit my mum's hated relatives in Bayswater. When he told the story later, he managed to make it sound as if we had travelled from the steppes of Russia. He and my mother sat opposite my uncle Ernie and auntie Doreen on their red leather settee, teacups balanced on locked knees, reliving the high point of our trip, which was a near collision with a banana lorry bound for Covent Garden. I'd been given a sticky mug of fluorescent orange squash and sent to a corner to be seen and not heard. I was nine years old, and I understood a lot more than they realised. My uncle Ernie started talking about a woman who was strangled in the next street because she played the wireless too loudly, but my auntie Doreen gave him a warning look and he quickly shut up.

On the way home, as if to verify his words, we saw two Arab men having a fight at the entrance to Notting Hill tube station. Being impressionable and imaginative, from this moment on I assumed that London was entirely populated by murderers. A psychiatrist would say that's why I never left Meadowfields. In fact I longed to leave my parents' little house, where each room was filled with swirling floral wallpaper and the sound of Radio One filtered through the kitchen wall all day. All I had to do was get up and go, but I didn't. Inaction was easier. When I moved to Aunt Sheila's I finally saw how far my lead would reach; three roads away. I suppose I was scared of the city, and I felt protected in the suburbs. I've always settled for the safest option.

Look, I've taken a long time getting to the point and you've been very patient, so let me explain what happened last night. I just wanted you to understand me a little so you won't think I'm crazy when I explain the insane fix I'm in. It's hard to think clearly. I must put everything in order.

It began with a woman I met two months ago.

Her name is Michelle Davies and she works for an advertising agency in Soho. She's tall and slim, with deep-set brown eyes and masses of glossy dark hair the colour of a freshly creosoted fence. She always wears crimson lipstick, black jeans and a black furry coat. She looks like a page ripped from *Vanity Fair*. She's not like the women around here.

I met her because I was helping with a community project that's tied to a national children's charity, and the charity planned to mention our project in its local press ads, and Michelle was the account executive appointed to help me with the wording. The first time we met I was nearly an hour late for our appointment because I got lost on the underground. Michelle was sitting at the end of a conference table, long legs crossed to one side, writing pages of notes, and never once caught my eye when she spoke. The second time, a week later, she seemed to notice me and was much friendlier. At the end of the meeting she caught my arm at the door and asked me to buy her a drink in the bar next to the agency and, utterly astonished, I agreed.

I'll spare you a description of the media types sandwiched between the blue slate walls of the brasserie. The tables were littered with *Time Out*s and transparencies, and everyone was talking loudly about their next production and how they all hated each other.

Listen, I have no illusions about myself. I'm twenty-eight, I don't dress fashionably and I'm already losing my hair. London doesn't suit me. I don't understand it, and I don't fit in. Michelle was seven years younger, and every inch of her matched the life that surrounded us. During a bottle of wine she told me about her father, a successful artist, her mother, a writer of romances, and her ex-boyfriend, some kind of experimental musician. I had no idea why I had been picked to hear these revelations. Her parents were divorced but still lived near each other in apartments just off Marylebone Road. She had grown up in a flat in Wigmore Street and lived in Praed Street. Her whole family had been raised in the centre of the city, generation upon generation. She was probably the last true Londoner. She was rooted right down into the place, and even though I hated being there, I had to admit it made her very urbane and glamorous, sophisticated far beyond her years. As she drained her glass she wondered if I would like to have dinner with her that night. Did I have to get up early in the morning?

I know what you're thinking – isn't this all a bit sudden? What could she see in me? Would the evening have some kind of humiliating resolution? Did she simply prefer plain men? Well, drinks turned to dinner and dinner turned to bed, and everything turned out to be great. I went back to her apartment and we spent the whole night gently making love, something I hadn't done since I was nineteen, and later she told me that she was attracted to me because I was clearly an honest man. She said all women are looking for honest men.

In the morning, we braved the rain-doused streets to visit a breakfast bar with steamy windows and tall chrome stools, and she ate honey-filled croissants and told me how much she loved the city, how private and protective it was, how she could never live anywhere else and didn't I feel the same way – and I had to tell her the truth. I said I fucking hated the place.

Yes, that was dumb. But it was honest. She was cooler after that. Not much, but I noticed a definite change in her attitude. I tried to explain but I think I made everything worse. Finally she smiled and finished her coffee and slipped from her stool. She left with barely another word, her broad black coat swinging back and forth as she ran away through the drizzle. Kicking myself, I paid the bill and took the first of three trains home. At the station, a taxi nearly ran me down and a tramp became abusive when I wouldn't give him money.

On my way out of London I tried to understand what she loved so much about the litter-strewn streets, but the city's charms remained elusive. To me the place looked like a half-demolished fairground.

I couldn't get Michelle out of my mind.

Everything about her was attractive and exciting. It wasn't just that she had chosen me when she could have had any man she wanted. I called her at the agency and we talked about work. After the next meeting we went to dinner, and I stayed over again. We saw each other on three more occasions. She was always easy-going, relaxed. I was in knots. Each time she talked about the city she loved so much, I managed to keep my fat mouth shut. Then, on our last meeting, I did something really stupid.

I have a stubborn streak a mile wide and I know it, but knowing your faults doesn't make it any easier to control them. Each time we'd met, I had come up to town and we'd gone somewhere, for dinner, for drinks –it was fine, but Michelle always brought her friends from the agency along, and I would have preferred to see her alone. They sat on either side of her watching me, like bodyguards, ready to pounce at the first sign of an improper advance.

On this particular evening we were drinking in a small club in Beak Street with her usual crowd. She began talking about some new bar, and I asked her if she ever got tired of living right here, in the middle of so much noise and violence. In reply, she told me London was the safest place in the world. I pointed out that it was now considered to be the most crime-riddled city in Europe. She just stared at me blankly for a moment and turned to talk to someone else.

Her attitude pissed me off. She was living in a dream state, ignoring anything bad or even remotely realistic in life. I wouldn't let the subject go and tackled her again. She quoted Samuel Johnson, her friends nodded in agreement, I threw in some crime statistics and moments later we were having a heated, pointless row. What impressed me was the way in which she took everything to heart, as if by insulting London I was causing her personal injury. Finally she called me smug and small-minded and stormed out of the club.

One of her friends, an absurd young man with a ponytail, pushed me down in my seat as I rose to leave. 'You shouldn't have argued with her,' he said, shaking his head in admonishment. 'She loves this city, and she won't hear anyone criticising it.'

'You can't go on treating her like a child forever,' I complained. 'Someone has to tell her the truth.'

'That's what her last boyfriend did.'

'And what happened to him?'

'He got knocked off his bike by a bus.' Ponytail shrugged. 'He's never going to walk again.' He stared out of the window at the teeming night streets. 'This city. You're either its friend, or you're an enemy.'

After waiting for hours outside her darkened apartment, I returned home to Meadowfields in low spirits. I felt as though I had failed some kind of test. A few days later, Michelle reluctantly agreed to see me for dinner. This time there would be just the two of us. We arranged to meet in Dell' Ugo in Frith Street at 9 pm the next Friday evening.

I didn't get there until 10.30 pm.

It wasn't my fault. I allowed plenty of time for my rail connections, but one train wasn't running and the passengers were off-loaded onto buses that took the most circuitous route imaginable. By the time I reached the restaurant she had gone. The maître d' told me she had waited for forty minutes.

After that Michelle refused to take my calls, either at the agency or at her flat. I must have spoken to her answering machine a hundred times.

A week passed, the worst week of my life. At work, everything went wrong. The money for the charity ads fell through and the campaign was cancelled, so I had no reason to visit the agency again. Then Aunt Sheila asked me to help her sell the house because she had decided to move to Spain. I would have to find a new place to live. And all the time, Michelle's face was before me. I felt like following her ex-boyfriend under a bus.

It was Friday night, around 7 pm. I was standing in the front garden, breathing cool evening air scented with burning leaves and looking out at the lights of the estate, fifty-eight miles from the city and the woman. That's when it happened. Personal epiphany, collapse of inner belief system, whatever you want to call it. I suddenly saw how cocooned I'd been here in Legoland. I'd never had a chance to understand a woman like Michelle. She unnerved me, so I was backing away from the one thing I really wanted, which was to be with her. Now I could see that she was a lifeline, one final chance for me to escape. Okay, it may have been obvious to you but it came as a complete revelation to me.

I ran back into the house, past my Aunt Sheila who was in the kitchen doing something visceral in a pudding basin, and rang Michelle's apartment. And – there *was* a God – she answered the call. I told her exactly how I felt, begged absolution for my behaviour, explained how desperate I was to see her. For a few moments the line went silent as she thought things through. Once more, my honesty won the day.

'Tomorrow night,' she said. 'I've already made arrangements with friends, but come along.'

'I'll be there,' I replied, elated. 'When and where?'

She said she would be in a restaurant called the Palais du Jardin in Long Acre until 10.30 pm, then at a new club in Soho. She gave me the addresses. 'I warn you, Douglas,' she added. 'This is absolutely your last chance. If you don't show up, you can throw away my number because I'll never speak to you again.'

I swore to myself that nothing would go wrong. Nothing.

Saturday morning.

It feels like a lifetime has passed, but peering at the cracked glass of my watch I realise that it was just twenty hours ago.

I planned everything down to the last detail. I consulted the weather bureau, then rang all three stations and checked that the trains would be running. 'Only connect,' wrote E M Forster, but he obviously hadn't seen a British Rail timetable.

To be safe I left half-hour gaps between each train, so there would be no possibility of missing one of them. I bought a new suit, my first since wide lapels went out. I got a decent haircut from a new barber, one without faded photographs of people who looked like Val Doonican taped to his window. The day dragged past at a snail's pace, each minute lasting an hour. Finally it was time to leave Rosemount Crescent.

I made all my connections. Nothing went wrong until I reached Waterloo, where the Northern Line had been closed because of a bomb scare. It had begun to rain, a fine soaking drizzle. There were no cabs to be seen so I waited for a bus, safe in the knowledge that Michelle would be dining for a while yet. I felt that she had deliberately kept the arrangement casual to help me. She knew I had to make an awkward journey into town.

The first two buses were full, and the driver of the third wouldn't take Scottish pound notes, which for some reason I'd been given at the cash point. I was fine on the fourth, until I realised that it veered away from Covent Garden at precisely the moment when I needed it to turn left into the area. I walked back along the Strand with my jacket collar turned up against the rain. I hadn't thought to wear an overcoat. I was late, and it felt as if the city was deliberately keeping me away from her. I imagined Michelle at the restaurant table, lowering her wineglass and laughing with friends as she paused to check her watch. I examined my A–Z and turned up towards Long Acre, just in time for a cab to plough through a trough of kerbside water and soak my legs. Then I discovered that I'd lost the piece of paper bearing the name of the restaurant. It had been in the same pocket as the A–Z but must have fallen out. I had been so determined to memorise the name of the place, and now it completely eluded me. The harder I searched my mind, the less chance I had of remembering it. I had to explore every single restaurant in the damned street, and there were dozens of them.

I was just another guy on a date (admittedly the most

important date I'd ever had) and it was turning into the quest for the Holy Grail. It took me over half an hour to cover the whole of Long Acre, only to find that the Palais du Jardin was the very last restaurant in the street, and that I had missed Michelle Davies's party by five minutes.

At least I remembered the name of the club and strode on to it, tense and determined. The bare grey building before me had an industrial steel door, above which hung a banner reading 'blUeTOPIA'. The bricks themselves were bleeding techno beat. In front of the door stood a large man in a tight black suit, white shirt, narrow black tie and sunglasses, a Cro-Magnon Blues Brother.

'Get back behind the rope.' He sounded bored. He kept his arms folded and stared straight ahead.

'How much is it to get in?' I asked.

'Depends which part you're going into.'

I tried to peer through the door's porthole, but he blocked my view. 'What's the difference?'

'You're not dressed for downstairs. Downstairs is rubber.'

'Ah. How much upstairs?' I felt for my wallet. The rain had begun to fall more heavily, coloured needles passing through neon.

'Fifteen pounds.'

'That's a lot.'

'Makes no difference. You can't come in.'

'Why not?'

'It's full up. Fire regulations.'

'But I have to meet someone.'

Just then two shaven-headed girls in stacked boots walked past me, and the bouncer held the door open for them. A wave of boiling air and scrambled music swept over us.

'Why did you let them in?' I asked as he resealed the door.

'They're members.'

'How much is it to be a member?'

'Membership's closed.'

'You told me the club was full.'

'Only to guests.'

'Could I come in if I was with a member?'

The doorman approximated an attitude of deep thought for a moment. 'Not without a guest pass.'

'What must I give you to get one of those?'

'Twenty-four hours' notice.'

'Look.' I spoke through gritted teeth. 'I can see we have to reach some kind of agreement here, because the rest of my life is dependent on me getting inside this club tonight.'

'You could try bribing me.' He spoke as if he was telling a child something very obvious. I shuffled some notes from my wallet and held them out. He glanced down briefly, then resumed his Easter Island pose. I added another ten. He palmed the stack without checking it.

'Now can I come in?'

'No.'

'You took a bribe. I'll call the police.'

'Suit yourself. Who are they going to believe?'

That was a good point. He probably knew all the officers in the area. I was just a hick hustling to gain entry to his club. 'I could make trouble for you,' I said unconvincingly.

'Oh, that's good.' He glanced down at me. 'Bouncers love trouble. Every night we pray for a good punch-up. When there's a fight we call each other from all the other clubs,' he indicated the doorways along the street, 'and have a big bundle.'

It was hopeless. My street etiquette was nonexistent. I simply didn't know what to do, so I asked him. 'This is incredibly important to me,' I explained. 'Just tell me how I can get in.'

I'd already guessed the reply. 'You can't.'

'Why not?'

'Because you had to ask.' He removed his glasses and studied me with tiny deep-set eyes. 'You're up from the sticks for your Big Night Out, but it's not in here, not for you. You don't fit.'

At least he was honest. I knew then that it wasn't just the club. I'd never be able to make the jump, even for a woman like her. Despondent, I walked to the side of the building and pressed my back against the wet brickwork, studying the sky. And I waited. I thought there might be a side exit I could slip through, but there wasn't. Everyone came and went through the front door. Soon my shirt was sticking to my skin and my shoes were filled with water, but I no longer cared. See Suburban Man attempt to leave his natural habitat! Watch as he enters the kingdom of Urbia and battles the mocking resident tribe! Well, this was one Suburban Man who wasn't going down without a fight.

But two hours later I was still there, shivering in the shadowed lea of the building, studying the lengthy queue of clubbers waiting to enter. When the steel door opened and she appeared with Ponytail and some black guy on her arm, I stepped forward into the light. One look at her face told me everything. I was sure now that she'd known I wouldn't get in and was having a laugh at my expense.

I'm not a violent man, but I found myself moving toward her with my arm raised and I think my hand connected, just a glancing blow. Then people from the queue were on me, someone's hand across my face,

another pushing me backwards. There was some shouting, and I recall hearing Michelle call my name, something
about not hurting me.

I remember being thrown into the alley and hitting the
ground hard. In movies they always land on a neat pile of
cardboard boxes. No such luck here, just piss-drenched
concrete and drains. My face was hurting, and I could
taste blood in my mouth. I unscrewed my eyes and saw
Ponytail standing over me. The black guy was holding
Michelle by the arm, talking fast. She looked really sorry
and I think she wanted to help, but he wasn't about to
allow her near me. I could barely hear what he was saying
through the noise in my head.

'I told you this would happen. He got no roots, no
family. He don't belong here. You know that.' He was
talking too fast. I didn't understand. Then Ponytail was
crouching low beside me.

'Big fucking mistake, man. You can't be near her. Don't
you get it?' He was waving his hands at me, frustrated by
his efforts to explain. 'She's part of this city. Do you see?
I mean *really* part of it. You hurt her, you hurt – all of
this.' He raised his arm at the buildings surrounding us.

I tried to talk but my tongue seemed to block my
speech. Ponytail moved closer.

'Listen to me, you're cut but this is nothing. You must
get up and run. It watches over her and now it'll fight you.
Run back to your own world and you may be able to save
yourself. That's all the advice I can give you, man.'

Then they were gone, the men on either side protecting
her, swiftly bearing her away from harm, slaves guarding
their queen. She stole a final glance back at me, regret
filling her eyes.

For a few minutes I lay there. No one came forward to

help. Eventually I found the strength to pull myself to my feet. It felt as if someone had stuck a penknife into my ribcage. The first time I tried to leave the alley, the indignant crowd pushed me back. When I eventually managed to break through, the buildings ahead dazzled my eyes and I slipped on the wet kerb, falling heavily onto my shins. I knew that no one would ever come forward to help me now. The city had changed its face. As I stumbled on, blurs of angry people gesticulated and screeched, Hogarthian grotesques marauding across town and time. I milled through them in a maze of streets that turned me back toward the centre where I would be consumed and forgotten, another threat disposed of.

I feel dizzy, but I daren't risk lying down. There's a thick rope of blood running down my left leg, from an artery I think. I'm so vulnerable, just a sack of flesh and bone encircled by concrete and steel and iron railings and brittle panes. A few minutes ago I leaned against a shop window, trying to clear my stinging head, and the glass shattered, vitreous blades shafting deep into my back.

I can't last much longer without her protection.

The first car that hit me drove over my wrist and didn't stop. A fucking Fiat Panda. I think the second one broke a bone in my knee. Something is grinding and mashing when I bend the joint. He didn't stop, either. Perhaps I'm no longer visible. I can't tell if I'm walking in the road, because it keeps shifting beneath my feet. The buildings, too, trundle noisily back and forth, diverting and directing. I feel light-headed. All I know is, I won't survive until daybreak. No chance of reaching safety now. London has shut me out and trapped me in.

It's unfair; I don't think I should have to die. I suppose it's traditional when you screw around with the queen. As the pavement beneath my feet is heading slightly downhill, I think I'm being led toward the embankment. It will be a short drop to the sluggish river below, and merciful sleep beyond.

I wonder what her real age is, and if she even has a name. Or what would have happened had I learned to love her city and stay within the custody of her benevolent gaze. Does she look down with a tremor of compassion for those who fail to survive her kingdom, or does she stare in pitiless fascination at the mortals tumbling through her ancient, coiling streets, while far away suburbia sleeps on?

A Century And A Second

This was the result of a commission from the *Big Issue*, an excellent magazine whose vendors (especially those in Soho) excel in finding imaginative new reasons for you to purchase a copy. I wanted to show how little human nature changes from one era to the next. Anyone enjoying this gently fantastic tale will like Alan Garner's *Red Shift*.

THE MINUTE hand of the illuminated clock was three feet long, made of iron, painted with black lead and scrolled with an elaborate curlicue that resembled the astronomical symbol for the planet Mercury. It hovered before the midnight hour undecided, waiting for the rising ratchet in the mechanism behind its vast cream glass face to propel it into a new day.

One minute to midnight, on a bone-damp November night in 1895.

Nora cast another glance up at the clock, then back along the platform at the arriving train. She stamped her feet, trying to restore the flow of blood. Above, the vast glass steeple of the station roof was lost in a haze of brown smoke, the Midland Railway engine wheezing its last as it reached the buffers at platform two.

Nora tucked the shawl in about herself, staring ahead through smoke and steam. Gone mad tonight, she had, got herself a cab from Charing Cross at the cost of a shilling when a threepenny bus ride would have done, and it was too sodding cold to be standing about waiting for a silly little snit of a girl from the shires. But someone had to do it, and his nibs was too settled beside the kitchen fire to be disturbed for the task. Besides, there was an air about her husband that sparked suspicion in even the most trusting country lass. No, better that Nora should collect her, kindly Nora, plump and motherly in her best grey dress, ready to take the girl off to hot soup and a hearth, and the dream of future comforts; but if you checked the palms of Nora's gloves, you soon saw the threadbare darns, knew that the dream came with cruel demands.

It would have to be a cab back, too, for the last omnibus had already departed. *Bugger London*, thought Nora, huffing out her lower lip as she straightened her hat. *Bugger his nibs and bugger the train for being so late.* Up and down the carriages doors had started slamming open and Nora peered ahead, trying to remember how Little-Miss-Country-Mouse had looked in her photograph. Annie was her name, just turned fifteen, and thought she was coming to the smoke to be a ladies' maid, so of course she would protest at first; they all did, but they all succumbed after meeting the fine gentlemen. Soon Annie would have her britches around her ankles and her legs in the air with the best of 'em. The first time would earn the most; city gentlemen were prepared to pay a high price for a virgin. And there was little danger of Annie being otherwise. No concealed bag of pigeon blood would be necessary for her deflowering. After that, the lassie's country brogue and awkward ways would be enough to prove that she was fresh, not like those rouged old tarts down the Haymarket, and after all, didn't Nora and her husband try to run the cleanest private house in the Strand?

She peered again at the disembarking passengers. From waiting on ladies to pleasuring gentlemen in the space of a few nights, three at the most, for what was the girl's alternative? Nora knew she would have spent her last coin on train fare. Where else was she to sleep? Above her, there was a loud metallic chunk as the minute hand jarred over into midnight.

Annie had tried to open the third class carriage window as the station approached, but a blast of freezing sooty air drove her back. The hour was late, but she had never felt less like sleeping. To while away the journey she had imagined herself in a starched black uniform, curtseying before the lady of the house; she had been fortunate in finding a friend like Nora, for even though they had only written to each other, she felt that a great closeness already existed between them. Annie had confided in her completely, explaining how terrible her home life had become, how desperately she needed to escape. How kind of Nora to take such trouble, offering a job and lodgings to a girl she had not even met!

As the train began to slow she checked her clothes. The dress, taken without permission, belonged to her eldest sister and was too long in the sleeve. She looked through the smoke to the end of the platform and the great moon of a clock, its hands juddering at the midnight hour, as if time itself was imparting electric energy. She studied the greeting crowd and tried to separate from it the woman who would change her life.

'If you come near me with that skateboard again, the doctors'll have to dig it out of your arse, sonny.'

Ronnie pulled what he felt was a menacing sneer and turned his back on the little bastard. Probably get back to the motor and find his quarter light smashed, radio nicked. Sodding kids were all the same these days, with their baggy trousers and backward caps and swaggering attitude, all on the make, all searching for the easy money. Except they didn't want to earn it. What they wanted, what they *wanted* was to sit and watch the footie with a pizza on their laps while some other poor git did every-thing for them. He flicked his cigarette onto the rails and looked back at the clock.

One minute to midnight, on a bollock-tightening November night in 1995. The train was nearly forty minutes late, which meant that they wouldn't get back to the club until half twelve, assuming that Mr Shit-For-Brains had managed to board the right train in the first place.

Ronnie regarded himself as a decent sort. It was nice of him to come and meet the train. Normally he told the boys to make their own way over to Earl's Court. He flicked ash from the sleeve of his grey leather jacket and eyed the coffee stand. He fancied a cuppa, but knowing his luck the kid would get off the train and walk right past him.

He checked the photograph again, one of those passport-booth jobs that made you look like a murderer, but even in that he was still gorgeous, a sexy little pout, nice eyes, said he liked swimming in the letter so he probably had a slim body. He'd also said he was eighteen, but that was unlikely. Sixteen, perhaps, and he could pass for younger. There were men who'd pay much more for a boyish shape and an innocent smile. Boys could hold a look of virginity longer than girls of the same age. He didn't touch the lads himself, of course, it wasn't his cup of tea at all. But he made a small fortune from the men who did . . .

Ronnie watched as the train pulled into the station and the doors began to open. Adam somebody, he couldn't remember the surname. He supposed the boy would want a mobile phone. There wasn't a piece of rent in London that didn't ask for one these days; they'd seen it on the telly. Ronnie assumed that Big Al had already cleared up this sort of detail. After all, the boy had phoned them, said he'd seen the ad in *Guyz* and was leaving home to come to London; didn't mind working long hours, so presumably he knew the score. Imagined himself sitting in a coffee bar in Old Compton Street, no doubt, booking three punters a night on the mobile at sixty quid a throw on a 40/60 split with the club. Dream on, sonny.

Ronnie studied the arriving passengers, the back-packed students and knackered businessmen, and looked up at the clock as the minute hand clicked into tomorrow.

Adam had slept through most of the journey. As the train began to slow he rubbed his eyes and rose, pulling the cheap nylon sack down from the overhead rack. Not much in there; couple of pairs of socks, T-shirt, pants, toothbrush. He hadn't risked emptying the wardrobe in case his dad had sensed something amiss. It had been hard enough getting out of the house without stepping on every squeaky floorboard in the hall.

As he pushed the window down, Adam tried to imagine what would happen when his old man sussed the disappearing act; not a lot, probably. After all, he hadn't made much of a fuss about mum walking out, never mentioned it when he was sober, and never noticed what time his son came home.

The platform was pretty deserted. There was one sleazy-looking bloke in a grey leather jacket and white shoes, sweaty faced despite the cold. Knowing Adam's luck, that was his contact. He wasn't daft; he figured they'd try and get him to have sex with their 'clients', but he'd already made up his mind about that. He'd tell them he wouldn't, couldn't. The ad said 'young escort' and that was what he'd be, going to dinners with tired businessmen. If he was going to have sex with anybody, it would be with a boy of his own age.

He shouldered the bag and opened the carriage door, stepping down onto the platform. Leather Jacket was checking something in his hand, probably the photo he'd requested, and was staring back at him, appraising the merchandise. A chill wind swept the concourse, curling sheets of newspaper up into the night air, and for the first time Adam began to wonder if he'd done the right thing. But to have stayed behind in his father's house for even another day would have been unbearable. Without his mother, he could not find a reason to remain. As the station clock thumped over into midnight, he quickened his pace and aimed for Mr Creepy. Now there was nowhere else to go but forward.

The great illuminated station clock had a thin red second hand, but it had become stuck at midnight ten decades ago, the immobile tin arm warped in its place, unmoved through the passing years. Now something happened within the dirt and oil of the gear shaft. The arm shifted. Freed itself and advanced a single second, exactly one century after it had become stuck. A chill wind swept the clock face. The red metal hand had stopped once more. A century and a second after it had last moved.

Mr Creepy had disappeared. And so had half the lights in the station. The walls were suddenly darker, the roof lost in smoky gloom. The train was – how could it be possible? – a steam-driven locomotive, for Christ's sake, with a soot-rimmed funnel and a driver's cabin and a coal truck. And the clothes of the alighting passengers – they were dressed like characters from some Sherlock Holmes TV play. Yet they were staring at him oddly, as if *he* was the one in the weird outfit! Outside he could hear horses' hooves and what sounded like a barrel organ playing a tune he recognised; 'Three Little Maids From School Are We'.

It was incredible. The century before! A time before everything got messed up! Now this was what he called a *real* change of fortune. With what he knew about the years ahead, he could become a very rich man. The possibilities were endless . . .

Lost in wonder, he walked on to the station exit, passing the maternal figure of Nora, who was frowning as she searched the faces of the arrivals.

Annie shifted her valise from one hand to the other and searched the platform through sighs of steam. Nora had promised to be here. It was after midnight and she was tired; looking forward to settling in a clean warm bed. But something inside her reacted with alarm when she tried to foresee her future. It was as if she knew that there had been an error in judgement on her behalf, trusting her fate to a complete stranger, but what other choice did she have, alone in a city filled with unknown dangers? Where was her new friend?

She looked up at the clock. The wind raced across the platform and plastered her dress against the backs of her legs. A blast of steam erupted before her, and for a moment it seemed that there was someone in her path, a boy passing by with a bag on his shoulder, someone just like her, but when the air had cleared he had vanished, and everything was different.

The poster plastered to the brickwork on her left, for example, an advertisement for the Alhambra Music Hall,

Leicester Square, had changed into a colour portrait of a youth of fearsome demeanour. He was holding a container of something called Jolt Cola and pronouncing it to be 'wicked'. Another poster showed a blonde woman in a shamelessly brazen state of undress, posed lewdly with her bare legs wide apart, beneath a blasphemous caption: Madonna – The Girlie Tour.

The orange brick walls and dark stone floor of the station had gone too, transformed into shiny surfaces of pale marble. Dazzling white lights illuminated the roof, replacing the dim electric bulbs and gas mantles. And instead of Nora, there to meet her was a puzzled-looking man in a jacket of grey leather. She passed him with the briefest of glances and found others in the corridor beyond, similarly dressed in loose-fitting clothes striped with bright primary colours. Some were sipping from straws affixed to red cardboard containers. Others were devouring buns filled with aromatic meat. The train times were printed on flickering glass screens. The new electric light was everywhere.

Annie felt in her valise for the meagre savings she had managed to amass at home. The coins would not last a minute in the metropolis. How would she ever survive in this strange new place? The shining city she could see beyond the station was doubtless as dangerous as it was enticing. There was only one thing for it – she would have to take each new challenge in her stride, be brave and triumph.

Annie stepped outside and paused on the steps to fill her lungs with cold night air. Then she continued on, out into a world filled with the freshest of fresh possibilities.

Ronnie gave up waiting, flicked his fag onto the rails and

turned to leave. So the kid hadn't made the train; there'd be plenty more who would. For a brief moment he wondered who the weird bird in fancy dress had been. But who knew what kind of nutters hung around the station at night? He pulled his jacket tighter at his throat and set off. He only hoped that the little sod with the skateboard hadn't slashed his tyres.

His nibs would not be pleased. Annie had already been promised to a gentleman anxious for a bit of fresh, sight unseen, and now excuses would have to be made. Nora was surprised by the girl's nonappearance. Perhaps her nerve had failed her at the last moment. It was getting harder and harder to find virgins. A sign of the times we live in, she thought. She'd told his nibs they should have diversified, but given Mr Wilde's trouble with the Marquess of Queensberry at the moment, the bottom had dropped out of the boy market.

Nora reknotted her shawl at the neck and searched for a cab, cynically reflecting on the difficulties of earning an honest wage in a modern city.

'It's about time somebody fixed that bloody clock,' said one of the workmen. 'It wants replacing with a digital.'

'You can't get rid of that,' countered his mate, looking up at the great cream face. 'It's an antique. Besides, it's only the second hand that's stuck, and who needs it?' He pointed out at the mass of commuters churning along the station platform. 'One lousy second ain't going to make a difference to anyone.'

SHARPER KNIVES

Christopher Fowler

Take a trip to the cutting edge of terror and discover:

Why an obsession with sixties British comedy stars can make you a murderer . . .

The mother who dreads the sound of hymns – with good reason

How schooldays can be the weirdest days of your life

A couple who regularly visit the supermarket from Hell . . .

And why people who collect table-mats are dangerous – only when they're dead . . .

'One of the hippest and sharpest horror writers around' *iD*

'An Alan Bennett-like enjoyment of domestic trivia in Fowler's work . . . provides a foil for the horror and an unexpected seam of humour' *Sunday Times*

WARNER BOOKS
0 7515 0766 0

☐	Spanky	Christopher Fowler	£5.99
☐	Red Bride	Christopher Fowler	£4.99
☐	Darkest Day	Christopher Fowler	£5.99
☐	Sharper Knives	Christopher Fowler	£4.99
☐	Psychoville	Christopher Fowler	£7.99

Warner Books now offers an exciting range of quality titles by both established and new authors which can be ordered from the following address:

Little, Brown and Company (UK),
P.O. Box 11,
Falmouth,
Cornwall TR10 9EN.

Fax No: 01326 317444.
Telephone No: 01326 317200
E-mail: books@barni.avel.co.uk

Payments can be made as follows: cheque, postal order (payable to Little, Brown and Company) or by credit cards, Visa/Access. Do not send cash or currency. UK customers and B.F.P.O. please allow £1.00 for postage and packing for the first book, plus 50p for the second book, plus 30p for each additional book up to a maximum charge of £3.00 (7 books plus).

Overseas customers including Ireland, please allow £2.00 for the first book plus £1.00 for the second book, plus 50p for each additional book.

NAME (Block Letters) ....

....

ADDRESS ....

....

....

☐ I enclose my remittance for ....

☐ I wish to pay by Access/Visa Card

Number ☐☐☐☐☐☐☐☐☐☐☐☐☐☐☐☐

Card Expiry Date ☐☐☐☐